FREE STORIES

Pixies, Shades, and tribal Magick—having a baby is hard enough, but having a Magician's baby is in a league all of its own...

Sign up at www.martin-shannon.com to get "Danderous Delivery," the Tales of Weird Florida short story only available to newsletter subscribers.

BEATEN PATH

MARTIN SHANNON

To my sister, whose tenacity is the stuff of legend.

PART I
GOOD INTENTIONS

STEEL-TOE SLUMBER

*W*ater dripped from the dive bar's leaky faucet. It left a dark orange rust stain on the previously white sink before disappearing into the void of an open drain. I gripped that dingy porcelain and stared into a streak-filled mirror.

The locked bathroom door banged again. "Hurry up!"

"Screw you!" I shouted back, pounding my hand against the sink. "I'll be out when I'm out."

Whatever choice words the man on the other side of the door had for me, I wasn't paying attention to them; in fact, I wasn't paying attention to much of anything at that moment.

Even with a dead Imp laying on the dirty tile behind me like a lump of week-old Christmas pudding, my mind couldn't stop replaying the last conversation with my own Minor Demon.

They took her. No, it's not possible. Is it?

I had an iron-clad contract with the House, or that's what I'd been promised. In exchange for ten lifetimes of service, I had its assurances my daughter would be returned to me.

I'd seen it all with my own two eyes. She was Cathy, *my* Cathy. Wasn't she?

Stewart the Annoying couldn't lie to me, especially now that he'd been properly named in a fit of frustration and bound to servitude. He was as tied to me as stink on a dead rabbit, and he said they took her.

Who took her? Why do you care? You let her go. You condemned your own daughter to the fires of everlasting damnation.

I closed my eyes and was instantly greeted by the same nightmare that was my every night—the swirling Hellgate from all those months ago, my daughter clinging to the fiery edge, her screams echoing in my ears.

You weren't alone... The Defiler...

In my mind's eye, the many-tentacled Asaroth was there too. His corrupting arms reached for Cathy, and then beyond her, into our world. The inky monster was a primordial force of unchecked destruction and untold evil. On that night he'd been like a kid at Christmas, tentacles a flutter and ready to shuck our skin like discarded gift-wrap.

Not on my watch.

It was the impossible dilemma: stop the monster, or save the daughter.

I let her go. No, I commanded Stewart to protect her.

My eyes drifted to the dead Imp slowly decaying on the floor behind me.

Not exactly sending in the marines...

Stewart the Annoying, like the Imp whose body rotted on the floor, wasn't physically imposing. He was no Gillyfinkus Demon, or monstrous Thrull—frankly I'd seen raccoons around the trash cans more imposing than my Minor Demon. What could Stewart's rubbery little bat-winged body have done to keep her safe in the horrifying depths of the netherworld?

I turned the faucet on and let the water splash into the sink in broken bursts.

He was an Imp, which should have been exactly what she'd needed. They were the Jeopardy masters of the supernatural world. Monsters like Stewart knew the places, the players, and all their games. Those little rubbery bastards moved like rats in the underworld, always knowing exactly how to slip in and out unseen. He'd have found a way to hide her—I was sure of it.

But would she have let him?

I splashed the near-scalding water on my face, wiping at the dirt that had built up between unshaven bristles.

Cathy was as headstrong as her mother. Would she have fought him? Would she have tried to escape herself?

I shuddered. With Ariadne's Thread cut like a parade ribbon, Cathy would have been a lost balloon, drifting on the whims of the evil that prowled the shadows.

Please, for the love of God, please don't be like your mother just this once.

But Cathy was safe at home, I'd seen it myself. Those last two weeks after she'd been restored to us had been nigh Magickal in their own right. We'd done so many things together as a family: theme parks, restaurants, movies, the beach. But it wasn't one of those moments that stuck out, it was something simple.

'What ice cream do you want, Dad?'

'You know what I like.'

'Don't make me guess.'

The memory of Cathy's words hit me like a sucker punch to the gut. I had to catch my breath as the now scalding water sent a cloud of steam up to cover the mirror.

Don't make me guess.

She didn't know—why didn't she know?

Don't make me guess.

How had I missed that?

There was only one answer, and Stewart had told me just as much only moments ago—she wasn't Cathy.

'Not your daughter.'

How did you let this happen? What evil is living in Cathy's

skin? What is making its bed in the house your wife and son sleep in?

I turned off the water and wiped a hand across the dirty glass.

"It's time to get some answers."

My voice echoed in the empty bathroom and mixed with the live music worming its way through the thin walls.

"I can't leave your corpse here for someone to find. That's all I need, another urban legend springing up in the Strange Shine State."

The dive bar I'd tracked this Minor Demon to wasn't far outside Dade City, a tiny town in the center of the state and home to more than a few reclusive Bridge Trolls. Most of the time it was wise to steer clear of Bridge Trolls—I'd made that my mantra for many years—but the hunt had brought me here.

Sal's Bar.

You could practically smell the Bridge Troll in the air at Sal's. This made perfect sense given how close their territory was to the seedy watering hole. Still, I'd done my best to keep some distance between myself and those wrecking-ball-sized week-ruiners and had slipped into Sal's under the cover of darkness.

Window maybe?

I sized up the dead Imp versus the tight confines of the side window.

Working for the House had been a challenge to say the least. It took more than a little creativity to find a way to merge its directives with the other driving goal in my life—finding Tristan. It'd been tricky at first, but after a few weeks I'd gotten the hang of it.

I'm going on a Tristan hunt... I'm not afraid, but that bastard should be.

Tristan, Cathy's last boyfriend, the kid that had broken her heart, had snapped her Thread, and stolen the single most powerful book in my meager library. That teenager was a grade-A jerk as far as I was concerned, but he was also something else: damn tough to find.

I looped my fingers around the edge of the side windowsill and pulled my less-than-athletic body up far enough to see outside. It was dark, which limited my view, but the cross-breeze told me two things.

First, that side window was right over top a dumpster.

I'll take it.

And second, there was a little Bridge Troll scent in the air.

That's fine. I'm not hanging around.

I scooped up the gelatinous Imp carcass and maneuvered it under the window. Black and sticky Demon blood oozed down my hands and over my shirt.

Great.

One final heave got it up to the ledge and then over.

Splat!

The dead Imp's body landed in the dumpster with a sickening wet thump and effectively re-affirmed my desire to leave through the main door.

Honestly, I was somewhat surprised I'd heard the impact over the crowd of people drinking their troubles away at Sal's tonight. The converted bungalow served as a favorite watering hole for a unique cross-section of Florida.

Ladies night...

The band kicked it up a notch, and I wiped what I could of the Demon blood off on the last unused patches of paper towel scattered around the tiny bathroom.

Knock! Knock! Knock!

Someone banged against the door three times in rapid-fire succession. They weren't the petite raps of a gentleman keen to use the facilities, these impacts made the door rattle on its hinges.

"Yeah, listen. I said I'd be out when I was out and I'm wrapping up, so you just need to—"

I didn't get to finish my retort before the door to Sal's men's room blast inward right off its hinges. Two barrel-chested men that could have given Popeye a run for his money, and a young skinny kid not far into his twenties, poured into the tight confines of the tiny bathroom.

I raised my hands. "Right, so I'm all done. It's all yours—"

The fists came before I was ready for them. The first rammed into my gut with the force of a jackhammer, while the next caught the side of my skull.

Someone works with their hands...

For the second time that night I got to experience the unique displeasure of having all the air ejected from my lungs. Falling forward, I realized just how hard it was to use Magick without air.

Laying on the dingy tile, I didn't get much time to contemplate that challenge before a steel-toed boot ushered me into a deep and dreamless sleep.

2

BOILED OR ROASTED

I opened my eyes to the fuzzy outline of black boots and a face full of wet concrete.

We aren't in the bathroom.

My hands were tied, which made it difficult to do much more than mentally dog paddle my way back toward consciousness.

"Mrrrmph..." My word production wasn't quite up to par yet, but it was enough to get the attention of at least one of the boot owners.

"He's waking up."

Nothing gets past this guy.

I twisted my head and took a deep breath.

Peanuts?

"So, what do we do next?"

That question came from the gentleman whose fists had gotten the jump on me earlier. An oversized, meaty hand squeezed at the modest fat that had built up around the back of my waistline. There was a little more now than there'd been a year ago, but life on the road will do that to a guy. "Hmm, are you guys sure he's the Demon?"

What?! No, let me answer that for you, he's not.

"I'm nert," I said, my mouth still struggling to form words, the concrete making it far more difficult than it should have been.

"Listen, he's trying to say something." Strong hands grabbed my jacket and pulled me up.

"Don't turn him over, Donnie—"

"Huh?" Clearly confused, Donnie dropped me back on the hard floor.

Whump!

"Mr. Ed said you can't talk to Demons. They're bad hombres, and if you listen to what they say they'll pervert your thinking."

I blinked my eyes a few times and twisted my head, hoping they hadn't broken my nose.

One, I'm not a Demon, two there are not enough brain cells between the three of you to qualify as thinking.

"I'm nrrt a Dermmon," I cried, my mouth finally forming partial words, even though hitting the floor a second time made that all the more difficult.

"I think he's saying he's not a Demon…"

"What would you expect a Demon to say? Good Lord, Donnie, there are days I can't believe we're even related."

I can.

Donnie didn't appear convinced. "But didn't Mr. Ed say he would be all purple and rubbery?"

The Imp? They're after the Imp I killed for the House… These three knuckleheads couldn't catch an Imp if they'd filled their underpants with warm bourbon.

"He did…"

It was the third voice's opportunity to respond, and for a moment I had hope that this unseen individual would realize I was *not* an Imp.

"Yeah, listen, I think Donnie's right. I don't think this is the demon—"

Oh thank goodness. Now, if you'll just untie me, we can—

Donnie's mouth-breathing voice trampled my hopes. "Then he's in league with the Demon. Mr. Ed left the Viewmaster. We should try those."

Viewmaster? What have these swamp people found?

"No guys," the younger voice of reason said, a hint of concern coloring his words. "We can't use those on him. We don't know what he is, and we don't know what they'll do to him."

Listen to this one, he's got some smarts.

"But what if he and the Demon are buddies, you thought of that?" Donnie asked, his voice clearly finding this entire conversation difficult to follow.

Let him up so you can talk to him would be a great plan.

"No..."

"What about you, Maurice? Any ideas?"

"We banish it, that's what we do."

Like hell you do. I've got a daughter to save and a House to confront. I don't have time for this.

I struggled against the zip tie holding my wrists tight behind my back.

"He's moving again—" Maurice said, his feet shuffling on the dusty concrete.

"Hit him with the Holy Water."

I'm a Magician guys, I'm not a Demon. Holy Water isn't going to do anything.

Lukewarm water splashed on my face and arms. It stung like bleach and I squirmed against the ground trying to wipe it away.

Holy crap that hurts! What the... The deal with 69 Mallory Lane. Am I tainted?

"He's squirming, Maurice."

"Yep."

I imagined those two knuckle-draggers sharing a knowing nod while staring down at me with arms crossed.

Clang.

Maurice set down what sounded like an empty bucket. "Uh, huh. Well, I've texted Mr. Ed, so he should be here shortly. He'll know what to do."

I wasn't about to lie around on holy concrete any longer than I had to, nor was I going to wait for Mr. Ed—even if a small part of me was keen to see if he was actually a talking horse. I was getting out of here, now.

Focus.

I closed my eyes and reached for my Magick. That swirling cosmic energy flowing like a turbulent sea beneath my skin. It was there, just like it had always been, but now it was different. Ever since my deal with the House, the churning Magick trapped inside me floated beneath an oily sheen. Dark shapes squirmed within that layer of mental grime, angry and violent visuals I'd have to push through to reach my Magick. I'd done it before—many times, in fact—but in each instance I knew a little more of the House's tainted Magick left its mark on my soul.

Somewhere a phone chirped. It wasn't mine. Like a fool, I'd left mine in the car.

Maurice's gruff voice read off the text message. "Mr. Ed's a few minutes out and he said to rotate the peanuts."

"I got it," Donnie said, his heavy boots shuffling on the dusty concrete. "We never should have switched to roasted from boiled. It's way too much work, and everyone prefers them boiled."

Boiled Peanuts? Shit, these really are *Demon Hunters.*

The side-roads and byways of rural Florida were littered with boiled peanut vendors, and at least half of them moonlighted as Demon Hunters. It was an old tradition, one that I didn't know too much about, but they had a reputation for zeal —it was legendary even in Magickal circles.

Now's the time you get your butt out of here. Pronto!

I pushed aside my worries and reached for my Magick again. The darkness was still there, waiting and hungry. This time it brought terrible visuals, vicious and destructive visions of pain and suffering I couldn't unsee. Thanks to the power of 69 Mallory Lane, these Demon Hunters wouldn't know what hit them.

No!

I closed my eyes and focused on the room, painting a mental picture as best as I could. There had been three of them when the evening started, so I had to assume that was still the case. It was critical that I get this part right—the better the visual, the better the Magick.

A boiling peanut cauldron filled my mind's eye, and inside I found my own head floating in the brownish water.

Stop it, Gene. You've got to focus. Think about the zip tie.

I shifted my attention to the tight string of plastic wrapping my hands. It was easier to imagine and had far less chance of turning me into a boiled Magician head. All I had to do was coax it off. It was plastic, so there was a good chance it'd stretch with a little heat. The key was to bring the burn gently.

The burn!

Last year when I'd closed the Hellgate and left my only daughter in the hands of a fast-talking Imp, I'd burned my wrist on the ring of fire that encircled that gate. The burn had healed, but only partially, and the skin there never stopped being hot. I supposed that was part of the sacrifice, but tonight it might serve an even higher purpose—saving my bacon.

I concentrated on that singed skin: its waxy pink color, the complete lack of hair, and finally the heat.

Oh, the heat.

I let my Magick gently rise, the House's taint bubbling up with it. It started small, like the Dad Wagon's hood after a long drive, but then it got hotter.

"Hey, Donnie, you smell that?"

"I only ever smell peanuts, man."

Maurice sniffed the stuffy air like a bloodhound. "Burning plastic…"

"I smell it too," the younger of the three voices said. "Did one of you leave something against the burner?"

"I don't think so. I'll check." The squeaky hinge of the screen door echoed in the tiny room.

I kept up the pressure, fighting back against the darker inspirations the House had given me. It was a losing battle. I'd gone up against 69 Mallory Lane countless times since I'd left home, and in each instance it had succeeded in pushing me just that much closer to becoming someone, or something else, entirely.

Magick snaked between my wrists, and the tight plastic stretched ever so slightly against them.

Bang.

The screen door swung shut and Donnie spoke again. "Nope, nothing there… I smell it too, though."

The phone chirped again. "Hey, Mr. Ed says he's getting something from that chicken place off Main. Do you want anything, Donnie?" Maurice asked.

"Twelve piece, extra crispy."

That's what I'll be if I'm not careful.

"Man, you are making me hungry. I can smell the fried chicken."

Maurice wasn't imagining anything. I could smell it too, because my Magick had gone off the rails, and I was now frying my arm like chicken, extra-crispy chicken to be exact.

Snap!

The zip tie popped in two and I scrambled into action. Sadly, my body had little interest in the panther-like moves I was imagining. All those late nights watching kung-fu movies and eating Chinese food hadn't done me any favors. I stumbled to my feet and turned to face the three stooges of Demon Hunting. The twisted sheen of the House's tainted Magick churned above my own.

"Don't move," Donnie cried, a cheap plastic Viewmaster in his fingers. Shaped like a futuristic set of cheesy binoculars, the toy shone in the stark fluorescent lights. The Demon Hunter jammed a white paper wheel with little black squares into the front and held it up to his eyes.

What the...

"Listen, guys," I said, my hands raised. "I don't want trouble."

"Do it, Donnie!" Maurice slammed a hand down on the large man's shoulder. "Do it before he does something to us."

I shrugged my frustrated shoulders. "But, I'm not doing anything."

The younger man reached for Donnie. "Wait, don't do it. We don't know what he is or if—"

"I've seen enough." Donnie shrugged off the younger man and pushed the orange lever down.

Click!

An eruption of Deep Magick rocked the shed like a crashing wave. Cosmic power tore through me, peeling my soul apart like an overripe banana.

I screamed—with an immediate echo.

There were two Gene Laws in the room now. One with a little extra road fat, and the other: trim, dark, and terrifying.

Ah, hell.

3

SOUL-SPLITTING GOOD

*S*oul-Splitter.

    How on earth did Larry, Moe, and Curly get their hands on Deep Magick like that?

A puff of smoke drifted from the Viewmaster. It twisted in the air above an equally tiny flame that peeked out from the slot that held the paper wheel.

"Crap," Donnie cried, yanking the burning circle out and tossing it on the floor. He licked his singed fingers. "You guys ever seen that happen before?"

Maurice frowned and stomped on the paper wheel, putting out the fire. "No. You broke it."

"I didn't break it."

Donnie's brother reached for the plastic toy. "Yeah, you sure did. You broke it and Mr. Ed's gonna be pissed."

Donnie pulled the toy back from his brother. "You were the one that told me to do it!"

The younger man, whose name I'd yet to discern, picked up the burnt paper wheel. "You used the Spanish one?"

"Well, we didn't have a whole a lot left. Beggars can't be—"

"Hola, me llamo Gene..." the dark half of my nature grumbled. Not unlike a house of mirrors, the Soul-Split version of Eugene Law was a twisted copy of the original. Evil Gene's hair might have been slicked-back, and his five o'clock shadow looked a little closer to seven-thirty, but the rest of him was a spitting image of me—if I spoke Spanish and enjoyed glaring.

Maurice grabbed the toy. "What the hell, Donnie."

"It was all I could find. It's the one with that girl and her talking backpack, I don't know—"

"Hola! Mi llamo Gene!" my shadow yelled, this time with a lot more gusto.

Soul-Splitting was an old-school Demon Hunter's go-to Magick when dealing with the possessed. The reason it was old-school was that, more often than not, it backfired in epic proportions. It wasn't hard to see why—splitting off the Demon from its possessed and trying to capture the monster without getting your face chewed off was no small task. All of this was often made a lot easier by having an actual trap ready and waiting for when the evil made its curtain call.

The peanut brothers didn't appear to have thought that far ahead, and worse, they didn't know they'd violated a cardinal rule of Soul-Splitting, one that had been in circulation for as long as there'd been Demon Hunters crazy enough to try working that sort of Magick.

Never Soul-Split a Magician.

I'd learned that lesson the hard way a lot of years ago. While in the end it had worked out for me, it had been sheer luck more than anything remotely bordering on solid planning. The point remained, the number one rule among those combing the Sunshine State for Demonic entities was never, under any circumstances, Soul-Split a Magician.

"Hola! Me llamo Gene!" the split-half of my Magickal essence yelled in terrible Spanish. Sure, he was evil, and more than a little linguistically confused, but neither of those problems were the real concern. My real concern was that he had gotten all my Magick—every last drop.

Dark and twisted Gene placed his hands together, and the sudden surge of cosmic power was enough to set the hairs on my arms at attention.

"What's it doing?" Donnie asked, leaning forward to get a closer look, a small black kazoo dangling from a chain around his neck.

Honk!

The kazoo went off like an ambulance siren, ramping up to holy-hell loud in an instant.

"It's Magick," Donnie cried, backing up from Evil Gene.

No shit, guys. This is what happens when you Soul-Split a Magician: near limitless access to Magick in the darkest half of his being. Great plan.

"Duck!" I threw myself into the trio of backwater Demon Hunters, knocking them to the ground just before a very powerful blast of soul-searing Magick roared over them. The plastic toy bounced out of Maurice's hands and skidded across the concrete.

Once a soul is split, there were only a couple ways to get put back together. The hardest one was the reconciled merger. Basically, with the help of a lot of Magick and more than a little luck, one of the two halves got to take control of the newly rejoined soul. Seeing as I was the one without any Magick, it wasn't hard to imagine who would get the top bunk in that merger. My best plan was to get a member of the peanut posse to use the Viewmaster on me and my evil twin, and quickly.

"What do we do?" Donnie scrambled to his feet.

"We don't do that." I yanked on his peanut-oil-stained flannel and pulled him back down. "It should take him a few seconds to—"

Boom!

Another blast of Magick hit the steel wall behind us, melting Donnie's early warning kazoo to his chest, and scorching the arms of his heavy shirt. "Argh!"

"Hola! Me llamo Eugene!" the Shadow shouted. Magick dripped from his outstretched fingers.

Maurice rubbed his head. "What is he saying?"

Donnie pushed the other Demon Hunter away and grabbed a shotgun near the screen door. "I don't give a shit what he's saying—" he gave it a pump, enthusiastically chambering a round—"I'm going to put a hole in him a mile wide."

This really was their first Magician Soul-Split, and based on what I was seeing this might be their last.

"Stop!" I yelled, scrambling to my feet to grab the gun. "Don't shoot it!"

"Get him out of my way, Maurice." Donnie's brother and the still unnamed Demon Hunter pulled me back, giving the big man a clear shot.

"Eat silver, you son of a bitch!"

Boom!

If you've never been in a small steel shed when a shotgun goes off you should count your blessings and revel in the fact your eardrums are still intact and relatively happy.

A swarm of angry silver shot blew through my dark half. It ripped apart skin, flesh, and bone, spraying the back wall with all the above and leaving my shadow soul collapsed against the dirty ground.

Well, that's just surreal.

Donnie chambered another round and took a step toward the shadowy Eugene. "Keep a hold on the other one, I don't want him getting away."

Maurice and company held me tight.

I struggled to free myself. "Guys, you don't want to do that. You need to get your Viewmaster before—"

"Shut up before I put a round in you," the melted-kazoo-

wearing Demon Hunter said, reaching out with his gun barrel
to poke at the shadow soul.

"Is it dead?"

*It's not living, so no, technically, it's not dead. It lives on dark and
violent energy—and you knuckleheads just blasted it with a shotgun.*

The gun barrel pushed into my shadow soul's cheek. "Sure
looks like it."

"Nice work, Don—"

Dark Eugene's eyes burst open, and he grabbed the gun
barrel. "Hola! Me llamo Eugene!" My shadow self yanked the
hot steel forward, tossing the muscle-bound Donnie aside like a
rag-doll, and slamming his body into the steel wall. Fire raced
down Evil Gene's flesh and closed the holes left by the silver
shot, and if it was possible, gave him an even better chance of
taking top billing in all my future nightmares.

"What the hell?" Donnie cried, trying to right himself.

Maurice and the remaining Demon Hunter let go of my
hands and scrambled behind me, Donnie's larger brother inad-
vertently kicking the Soul-Splitting Viewmaster to my feet.

"Where's the trap?" I scooped up the Soul-Splitter.

The meatheads gave me varying looks of sheer confusion.
"Trap?"

Dark Eugene got to his feet.

"Yeah, the trap. You guys Soul-Split a Magician without
having a trap ready to suck up the high-voltage Darkling hellbent on teaching us Intro to Spanish?"

Two perfectly blank looks greeted me.

Splendid.

"Okay, typically there's a sigil-bound object to hold the
Darkling."

Maurice scratched at this head, while the smaller un-named
individual shuffled his feet.

Oh, come on, do I have to do everything...

"Hola! Mi llamo—"

"Stop. Enough already. I get it," I placed a foot on the singed photo wheel. "Your name is Gene Law. But I've got news for you, muchacho. It's not."

The shadow tilted its head.

"That's *my* damn name, and I'm not letting you have it without a fight."

Evil Gene smiled, and somewhere in the corner Donnie's melted kazoo honked like it was attached to a three-year-old high on pixie-sticks.

This is brilliant. You do realize you have no Magick, right?

I shoved the picture disc into the Viewmaster backwards and tossed it to Maurice. "When I hit him, you need to pull the lever."

"Uh, I…"

"One… two… three," I cried, launching myself at the Darkling. If Maurice came through I'd be re-united with the shadow-side of my nature, but also with my Magick. The scary part was that this entire exercise was dependent on a backwater Demon Hunter who for all the world looked like a deer caught in the high beams.

Don't panic.

I had the Darkling in my sights and extended my arms for a full on tackle.

Come on, Maurice, where's that click?

Twisted Magick crackled around Evil Gene like a cloud of angry bees.

This is going to hurt like hell.

The door to the shed swung open and my hands grasped at empty air. The Darkling had lunged to the side and avoided me, before whooshing past the latest person to join our party.

I was not that fast, and couldn't defy the laws of gravity. Instead of catching my amigo, Evil Gene, and restoring my

Magick, I crashed headlong into the shed's corrugated steel wall with brain-jarring force.

And this day had been going oh so well...

4

MR. ED

A shadow crossed my face and I opened my eyes. Individual features were hard to make out in the newly wrecked staging shed, but one thing stuck out clear as day. I now had a finely honed machete blade pressed against my neck, wielded by a chicken-bucket-carrying gentleman who carried that weapon like he knew exactly what do to with it.

"Which of you morons used the Viewmaster on him?"

"That was Donnie," Maurice said, throwing the other Demon Hunter under the bus with practiced grace.

"Never Soul-Split a Magician, Donnie, holy crap. How many times do I have to—" The man paused mid-sentence and leaned forward, his face blocking out the overhead light. "Eugene?"

Where do I know that voice from?

"Yeah…" I said, trying to make out the figure's face.

"Eugene Law?"

Mr. Ed? Oh, you've got to be kidding me.

"Ed Lovely?"

My old college roommate's infectious grin emerged.

Ed and I'd lived together the first few semesters in college. To say Lovely was a unique guy was a gross understatement. He possessed an encyclopedic knowledge of Magick, which—when coupled with the fact that he lacked any Magickal ability what-soever—made for a very interesting pairing. When I'd known him, Ed had been equal parts Demon Hunter and devilishly good-looking lady killer. The girls had swooned for those long blond locks—locks that appeared to have moved on for greener pastures.

My old roommate shoved the bucket of chicken into Donnie's hands and lowered his machete. "Holy heck, Gene. How long has it been? And what the hell are you doing in Dade City?" He extended a hand out of the harsh light to help me up.

"It's a long story—"

"Whoa!" My old roommate jumped back as soon as our hands touched and immediately dropped me on the floor. A small plastic spider ring twitched violently on his finger. Ed frowned and brought the machete back front and center.

"Yeah, listen, I can explain—"

"Sal's Spidery Sense—I don't know who you are, but there's no way you're Eugene Law. Donnie, get the Philips cap."

I slid back slowly, my body still smarting from its introduction to the shed's steel wall. "Ed, it's me, Eugene Law. Damn it, man, we lived together. We did the Demon Hunting together for a few years, before I got busy with... other things."

"Stop," the bandana-wearing man said, his machete danger-ously close to my neck. "Get him up."

Maurice pulled me to my feet, but Ed's razor-sharp blade never wavered. My old roommate held up the plastic ring, the tiny spider's legs still twitching. "The Eugene Law I knew would *never* have made a deal with whatever the heck it is you made a deal with."

Donnie returned with a dingy trucker hat. He held it with the same reverence a normal person would reserve for religious artifacts.

Ed kept me at the pointy end of the blade. "Last hole..."

Donnie hesitated. "Are you sure? No one's ever done the last hole…"

"He's a Magician, he can take it. Last hole, Donnie."

"Correction, he *was* a Magician. Larry and Moe here ripped my Magick from me, and you let it slip out the door."

The junior Demon Hunter adjusted the sizing strap, and it gave off an audible pop as he clicked the plastic into place.

Ed pointed to the dirt-smeared hat. "This is a—"

"It's a Truth Cap. Damn it, Ed. I know a Truth Cap when I see one. Sure, you know what, give me the damn hat and I'll tell you the same thing I would have told you before. It's me, I made a terrible mistake and now I'm going to put things right."

"We'll see, Mr. Magician." Ed tossed the cap at my feet. "Put it on. I've got questions."

The sharp smell of burnt peanuts filled the small shed.

"Damn it, Maurice. Toss those out and start over before you ruin the roaster."

Donnie's brother hurried out the screen door.

I picked up the hat and felt the Magick immediately. This was different from the Viewmaster. It had a soft, almost feminine touch to it. Ed wasn't a Magician, but this clearly had the trappings of a deft hand.

I placed the hat on my head, or at least I tried to. Donnie hadn't been kidding—the hat was about as tight as humanly possible. I pulled it past my hair and down to my ears. The undersized band squeezed the blood vessels of my temples like a pair of vise-grips. It reminded me of that time in High School I'd tried out for the football team and blacked out from the undersized helmet.

Ah, the days before lawyers and safety waivers.

I blinked back the pain. "Okay, Edwin Lovely, ask away."

Donnie tilted his head. "Lovely? Your last name is Lovely?"

The machete swung around. "Sure is—you got a problem with that?"

"Nope."

Ed brought the pointy end of his blade back to me. "Good. Okay, Eugene-Law-looking-thing—who are you, really?"

"I am Eugene Law, now former Magician, and all-around idiot," I said, the words falling out of my mouth without the slightest hesitation.

Yep, this hat was made by a woman.

"Just as I thought, you—" Ed started to press in with the machete, then paused. "Wait, what did you say?"

"I'm Eugene Law, now former Magician and—"

My old college roommate lowered his blade slightly, then ran his hand over his head. The brightly colored bandana fell away to reveal a shiny bald head.

"Holy shit, is it really you?"

"Yup. What happened to your hair, Ed?"

The Demon Hunter ignored me. "It's been years—"

"More than twenty, to be exact."

"But, if you really are Eugene, then tell me, why you set off Sal's Spidery Sense?"

"I made a deal with the House."

Donnie scrunched up his face. "Does he mean the Seminole Casino? Oh crap, are we not supposed to make deals with the casino? I'm asking for a friend…"

Ed shook his head slowly. "He's not talking about the casino."

"He's not?"

"No," I said, the hat band digging into my scalp like an overzealous boa constrictor. "I'm not. I'm talking about the—"

"Stop." Ed cut me off. "The less they know about 69 Mallory Lane the better. Why did you do it, Gene? Why did you sell yourself to… to that?"

"My daughter."

Ed's hard exterior softened. He stepped into the light just long enough for me to watch his sunburned face droop. I'd known that swamp-dwelling cypress rat since our early days in Gainesville. He was a good bit smarter than he looked, but then again he also was quite adept at wrestling alligators, so some of those smarts could be called into question.

"You have a daughter?"

"I did… I do… I honestly don't know anymore."

Ed rubbed a hand over his gray stubble. "Wait, you didn't get back together with Morgan, right?"

"God no. Wait, how did you know she's back?"

The Demon Hunter let his machete droop a little more. "Yeah, I didn't, but I had a feeling. She's too cunning to stay trapped inside that place forever."

"Well, thanks for the warning."

Ed waved me off and gave me one of his signature grins, even if it was far more wrinkled than I remembered. "Nah, you'd just have worried."

"And for good measure," I said, equal parts happy to see my old roommate, and ready to choke him to death—Ed had that effect on people.

The Demon Hunter shrugged his shoulders. "Just so long as you didn't end up with her. She was a bad girl, Gene, and not the kind I'd have wanted you to be with."

"You're telling me. If I recall, weren't you the one that directed me toward her in the first place?"

"I didn't know that at the time. I mean, she puts on quite an act, and I know how you are with… you know."

"Boobs? Yeah. Thanks for airing my weaknesses, and for having Larry, Moe, and Curly here Soul-Split me. Now I am right and properly screwed. May I take this off?"

Ed nodded, and Maurice popped the suction-cup Truth Cap from my sore noggin.

"Eugene Law." Ed shook his head. "It's been a long time."

"Too long," I said, hoping time and tides had washed away the last things I'd said to my old roommate.

I extended a hand, but Ed ignored it. He threw his arms around me and pulled me into a warm embrace. The peanut vendor's arms felt like steel tongs, but it had been so long since anyone had touched me I wasn't quite sure how to respond. "Uh... it's good to see you too, Ed."

The Demon Hunter patted me on the back with a bit more vigor than I might have preferred—still smarting from hitting the wall and all—then let go to get a good look at me. "You have a daughter?"

"And a son," I replied, the heady smell of peanuts and fried chicken lingering on my clothes.

"No shit?"

"None."

Ed handed the machete to Donnie, then clapped his hands together. "You ended up with Porter didn't you?"

I dusted the broken peanut shells and dirt from my jacket. "How'd you guess?"

A hint of disappointment appeared in Ed's eyes, but it vanished just as quickly as it came. "Because you two were good together, really good. She's a special one, Gene. Don't screw that up."

"Too late."

Ed's face got serious. "What do you mean? Is Porter okay?"

"I don't know anymore, Ed. I lost her. I lost all of them." Bile bubbled up in the back of my throat, the painful memories of the Hellgate flooding my empty stomach with an acid-wash reminder of that fate-filled evening.

Don't let me go, Dad!

"That's what I'm here for, Gene," Ed said, placing a hand on my shoulder. "Tell me what happened."

"I CAN'T BELIEVE IT," Ed said, shaking his head slowly as I rolled my sleeve over the Hellfire scar. "You did all that and still lost Catherine?"

"Well, I didn't know that until now."

"I can't say I approve of the Imp binding. You could always have called me. You know I've been doing this a couple of years and would have given you a decent rate."

"Yeah, well, now I'm screwed. The House has double-crossed me, or found some loop-hole I didn't know about. Cathy's lost in Hell and I've got to get her back. Then, to make an already terrible situation a thousand times worse, my Magick just walked out that door."

Ed nodded, his face processing my words. "Yep, you are right screwed, my friend. Now let's get you unscrewed, eh?"

For a moment I hesitated, and not from the truth-telling hat that had all but cut off the flow of blood to my higher brain functions. It wasn't that overly tight band that kept my mouth from working, it was the mild shock of having someone call me friend.

I hadn't heard those words since I'd all but dropped off the face of the earth, and I was surprised at how they made me feel —wanted—and not in the 'kill him now' way I was used to.

"You aren't going near the House, Ed. It's stronger now, and I don't care how many relatives or kids you've got in the swamp around here, you'd need an army to take on that place."

"Who said anything about the House—"

"Ed, the Darkling could be anywhere by now."

The peanut vendor ran a hand over his shiny bald head. "And it would appear that one's on us. I think it'd only be right to get you and your Darkling back together, but I've got to ask, are you sure you want to?"

"What do you mean?"

Ed wiped his face with the bandana. "I mean, you're free now. You can just be Eugene Law, fastidious man of the people. You could start a new life, walk out that door and be a new man.

The House won't care about you, it'll find new victims. You can live a normal life."

I grabbed my old roommate's shoulder. "Damn it, man, I don't *want* a normal life. I want my daughter and my family back. I want to fix my mistakes."

Ed smiled, that mischievous grin returning from a past I'd tried to bury, then tied the bandana back on his head. "And that's what I wanted to hear. Now, let's go find your Darkling and get that daughter back."

"Did you not hear me? I've lost my Magick. I'm about as useful as man-nipples."

Ed shook his head. "I'm no Magician and I do just fine. Guys, load up the gear. We're on the clock."

5

MIDNIGHT RIDERS

A rust-stained, ruby red pickup roared over the jagged ribbon of country road outside of Dade City. Behind that truck, swinging dangerously and bobbing along with the poorly maintained pavement, was a trailer filled to the brim with the tools of the trade—Demon Hunting and peanut vending both.

"It's a calling, really," my old roommate said, adjusting the rear-view mirror.

I gestured to the bouncing trailer. "A calling, eh?"

"Yup. I get a great deal on salt."

Ed wasn't the only peanut-vending Demon Hunter in the Sunshine State, but he must have been one of the more successful ones. The red rust-bucket did have a nice extended cab, yet even with that extra leg room, two muscly Demon Hunters, a skinny kid, and one Magickless Magician made for tight ride.

Ed rolled the windows down and let the cool night air wash over us. "Eugene Law," he said, shaking his head. "Didn't think I'd ever see you again."

"Why not?"

"Have you forgotten our last conversation?"

I hadn't, but I'd sure hoped he had; it wasn't a conversation I was particularly proud of. "What conversation?"

"Exactly," Ed said before checking the rear-view mirror. The road behind us remained dark. "That's how I feel about it as well. Besides, you're here now, and that's what matters, isn't it?"

My fingers absently traced the window edge. "No. I'm sorry. I've been saying that a lot recently, but still, I'm sorry for how all that went down."

"Gene, you don't apologize to me again. I mean it. I was a piece of work back then anyway, and you were right to push back. You were going places, and I was standing in the way of that."

"No you weren't. You were just trying to get me to see the bigger picture."

Ed leaned back in his seat. "Well, I'm guessing you did... eventually."

"Yeah, you can thank Porter for that."

My old roommate chuckled. "Why does that not surprise me?"

Headlights flashed in the side-mirror—close enough to be concerning, yet far enough away that I couldn't tell exactly what was behind them. "Ed, should there be anyone else on this road?"

The Demon Hunter adjusted his rear-view mirror. "No..."

The lights separated perfectly and slipped into outside lanes; those weren't car headlights.

"Ed?"

The Demon Hunter flipped open the center console and removed a silvery six-shooter. Ornate Scrollwork covered the gun's dingy metal. He checked the cylinder before tossing it in my lap. "One-shot Willie's Pistol. It's dinged up, but I loaded it with Dead Sea salt rounds. It's not much, but it's better than nothing."

Each side-view mirror now held a single light, and they were gaining on us.

"What are they?"

Ed didn't answer me; instead, he directed his attention to Donnie and the boys in the back seat. "Look alive, boys. We've got incoming."

Donnie turned around to get a look out the back window. "I don't get it. We had a truce. We stay out of their business, they stay out of ours."

Ed tugged the wheel. "Damn it, they're Demons, they don't follow logic. We should have banished Viten the Curdler when we had the chance."

"A truce? I thought you never dealt with Demons?"

Ed fished a machete out from the gap between the seats and handed it back to Donnie. "By policy I don't, but this was a special occasion—one I will not repeat. Banish *first*, ask questions later. Donnie…"

The back window slid open and the meathead hunter pulled his considerable bulk through it and onto the truck bed. "I got it. Come on, Maurice."

"Don't either of you fall off. I'm not going to explain to your mother why their sons aren't coming home for Christmas, you understand me?"

The roaring wind mixed with the rumble of motorcycle engines made it all the more difficult to hear the elder Demon Hunter.

Ed turned his attention to the youngest member of the peanut crew. "Little Ed, you—"

"I know, Dad, I'll keep my head down."

Dad?

"He's your son?"

Ed nodded. "Yeah, but now's not the time, Gene. I'll fill you in later."

The first rider's howl split the air and sent my now non-Magickal fingers racing for the six-shooter.

"Viten the Curdler wouldn't happen to be the Imp also known as Sear Spit, would he?"

"Yeah, why?"

I checked the cylinder of Ed's salt cannon, letting the rounds spin before flicking it closed—I'd watched a few westerns in my day. "And you had a deal with him?"

"No... Well, it's complicated. I'll explain later, what are you getting at?" Ed said, his eyes switching rapidly between the road and the truck's various mirrors.

"What I'm not telling you is I killed Sear Spit roughly," I glanced at my watch, "three hours ago."

"Killed?" The truck jerked under my roommate's surprised fingers. "You killed an immortal Demon?"

I shrugged. "It comes with the job. What do you think I do for the House, cut the grass?"

Ed got the truck back under control and gunned the pick-up's engine. "Seat belts on!" The peanut hauler roared down the dark pavement, but the lights still gained on us. "Wait, that's been you?" He pushed the accelerator to the floor. "You're the idiot killing off Demons and turning the whole state sideways?"

"Uh, yeah..."

"Damn it, Gene! There's an order here: good and evil, up and down, left and right, Yin and Yang."

"Throw an 'A, B, Start' on the end of that and you almost have the Contra cheat codes," I said, unhooking my seat belt.

"Damn it, I miss our gaming nights," my old roommate said, a hint of sadness coloring his words. "Still, I'm serious."

"So am I. I do what the House says and my family stays safe. I'm not risking Porter, Kris, or Cathy for some outdated notion of cosmic balance."

The Demon Hunter frowned. "But the balance is all we have."

I cocked One-shot Willie's Pistol and used the overhead bar to pull myself partially out the window. "It might be all *you* have, but I have this nifty salt gun and nothing left to lose. So, if you don't mind, I'm going to put it to good use and deal with Sear Spit's posse."

"You're not getting out of it that easy. We're going to continue this conversation later."

"Sure thing!" I shouted over the roaring wind and motorcycle engines. "Let's just wait until after I send the Riders to summary judgement."

Midnight Riders.

It wasn't technically midnight, but I wasn't going to waste my breath asking the screaming undead roaring up alongside the trailer if they could tell time—that answer was likely a resounding no, anyway.

Riders were revenants, a word that had made its way into Webster's Dictionary a few years ago. The official definition was spirits of the wartime fallen that had come back to haunt the battlefield. The Rider's shrieks cut what remained of my soul to the core.

Thanks, Webster, but I'll take it from here.

Sear Spit had been a nasty Imp, but a well-connected one. He'd made a few enemies, mortal and otherwise. His revenants had been necessary muscle to try and keep the little purple Demon safe from people like me.

It hadn't worked before, and it wasn't going to work now.

Last time you escaped them you had access to a nigh-infinite source of Magickal power...

I took aim with the revolver, but it bounced around like crazy as the truck roared across the broken road.

These particular revenants had been Civil War deserters. To them they were still living out those last few semi-heroic charges and hadn't fled to the swamps of Florida to make a deal with one very nasty Imp.

Another yell split the air, and the chopper roared up alongside me. The bike, as well as its rider, was black as pitch, because that's what they were covered in. The black tar of the Eternal Shame smothered them and what had once been horses. The viscous fluid almost sparkled in the edge of the peanut truck's headlights.

"Don't get it on you!" I shouted to Donnie and Maurice, who were already in the truck bed and retrieving blades from the tool chest behind the cab.

"What is it?" Donnie yelled.

"It's deserter's pitch, and it's the last thing you boys need —trust me."

The truck hit a bump and almost sent me tumbling onto the pavement, but instead I swung face-to-face with one of Sear Spit's undead soldiers. The featureless and tar-covered visage let out another scream; this one was delivered at close range and rattled me more than I cared to admit. A saber cut the air above my head with the practiced effort of hundreds of midnight rides.

"Ed, how far are we from the Croom Wildlife Sanctuary?" I ducked the blade and pulling myself back into the cab.

The Demon Hunter swerved the truck hard to avoid another stretch of broken road. "Not far."

Another scream split the air, but this time my head was far enough back in the cab to avoid the spectral sword.

"Florida National Cemetery's still on the edge, right?"

My old roommate nodded. "Unless they moved it."

Skreech!

Ed and I did a double take when a saber tip tore through the peanut truck door like tissue paper.

"Let's hope not. Punch it, Ed!"

"Way ahead of you," the Demon Hunter shouted, his hands clutching the wheel. "Hold on everybody."

Tar-covered fingers grabbed the edge of Ed's door.

"Full recline, Lovely!"

My roommate pulled the seat release and flopped backward into his son's lap just as I unloaded a round from One-shot's Pistol.

Boom!

The Dead Sea round peeled the black tar rider off the window.

"Get me to consecrated ground, Lovely."

Ed snapped his seat back. "Damnation, nice work. You ever thought about Demon Hunting?"

"What, and take all your business?" I shouted over the screaming undead. "Just get us there in one piece. Oh, and Ed?"

"Yeah."

"It's good to see you again. Hell, it's good to see *anyone* again."

The Demon Hunter's bandana flapped in the wind, giving him a distinct World War I aviator vibe. "Next time stop at one of my peanut stands before you go making deals with the v—"

A black tar saber cut through the driver's door, stopping just short of my old roommate's spleen.

"Less talk." I ripped off a few more rounds through the open window. "More driving."

6

TRAILER TOSS

*T*he tar-covered undead vanished from the window, but his scream told me the salty ammunition had only served to piss him off further.

"Damn it, Gene," Ed swerved in the gathering mist. "That was almost my nose—I've got a look to maintain."

"Anything to distract from the hair, right?" I climbed into the back seat. "Little Ed?"

"Yeah?"

"I'm Eugene Law."

"Pleased to meet—"

"Save it for later. I'm practically your uncle. Here, take this." I dropped the revolver into Ed Lovely junior's lap. "I think there's still a few rounds, make them count and keep your old man alive, you got it?"

The young man nodded, his hands shaking around the hot steel.

"What are you doing, Gene?" Ed asked, fighting to keep the trailer from fish-tailing.

"I'm going to help the rest of Jersey Shore and keep Dumbo's snack wagon from coming apart at the seams. You get us to the

National Cemetery—"

Another Midnight Rider's scream, along with the sound of shearing metal, cut over my words.

"—and try to do it quickly, I don't know how much longer the nutty buddy here'll hold up."

"It better hold up. I just got done paying it off," my old room-mate said, his hands tight on the wheel.

I climbed over Little Ed while the truck's engine rumbled like a thundering herd, and squeezed my way out the rear window. If Donnie and Maurice could do it, there was little reason to believe I'd have problems, yet it took a push from Ed's son to get my belt buckle over the sill.

"Thanks." I hit the truck bed and realized it might have been a lot smarter to just stay in the cab.

Clang!

Donnie and Maurice were doing their best to keep the black tar sabers from slicing through the tires, but the machetes they carried weren't really built for the task. A Midnight Rider's sword sliced along the lip of the bed and sent sparks raining down. I pulled Donnie back moments before he received ACL surgery at the edge of that wicked blade.

"Thanks," the big man said as he tried to regain his balance.

Chopper engines roared alongside us, rider swords cleaving deep grooves in the truck metal like it was aluminum foil.

Well, at least it's not a lease.

"You guys salt the peanuts, right?"

Maurice deflected a saber swing, then pointed to the back of the truck. "Yeah, but we keep it on the trailer."

Of course you do.

The steel trailer bounced like a kid's toy behind the truck bed. There had to be at least a dozen razor-sharp-looking tools rattling around on that metal death-trap.

You've got to be kidding me.

"Think you guys can draw their attention?"

A black blade pierced the truck bed between Donnie's legs. "Uh, sure..." he said, raising his foot to stomp it down.

"Stop," I cried, pulling him back. "Do *not* get the tar on you!"

"Why?" both men asked, suddenly acutely aware of the black liquid staining their machetes.

"Just don't, okay?" I pushed up my sleeves and placed both hands on the rear gate.

I didn't get a response, but there were too many screams and too much tearing metal to have heard it anyway.

One of these times they'll cut the tires, then we're really screwed. Come on, Ed, get me to that cemetery.

The truck hitch rattled beneath the rear gate, bucking like a wild bull as it whipped the trailer side to side. I swung my foot over and onto the rattling steel knob.

See? Not so bad. Your backup career in rodeo arts is a viable option...

"Hold on," Ed shouted from somewhere in the main cab.

"Wait, Ed, don't—"

My old roommate's truck swung hard into a narrow turn, taking us off the main highway and into the Croom Wildlife Refuge. I knew this because had I not caught the edge of a large peanut roaster and hung on for dear life, I'd have ended up plastered to the steel sign welcoming us to said refuge.

"Damn it, Lovely. Some of us are doing terribly dangerous things back here. More warning!"

Cypress trees whipped by at a frenetic pace. Long branches from the dense swampland smacked the sides of the trailer. Salt bags skidded across the wooden floor while I clung to the sharp metal sides of an oversized roaster that did nothing but want to topple over. Ed clearly had better things to do than listen to me, as the truck continued to bounce over the rough road. I white-knuckled that roaster in the vain hope I'd avoid ending up a pavement stain for future generations to admire.

The road that encircled the Croom was narrow, which

meant the choppers had to fall back to keep up with us. This was exactly what I didn't want, as it put me face to face with the tar of the Eternal Shame.

"You better leave now before I open up a tall boy of Magickal beatdown," I cried, trying to find a better place to put my feet. The floor of the trailer had become a minefield of salt and peanut bags, all of which I tumbled over when Ed hit a massive pothole.

Damn it, Lovely.

The sudden lunge sent me stumbling to the back edge of the trailer. I caught the rear gate with my hands, but that left my head expertly positioned against the railing like a backwater guillotine.

Crap.

Ed ramped up the speed and squeezed me against the railing. Just above my exposed head, the pitch-black blade of a Midnight Rider appeared ready to give me a quick shave, French Revolution style—so much for being deterred by my bravado.

So this is how I end? Beheaded by a walking ink spot whilst clinging to the back end of the nutty buddy wagon? That's a lot to put on a grave marker.

I waited for the final blow, but it never came.

Cling!

Donnie's machete stopped the saber inches before it could make contact with my soft pink and squishy skin. Donnie himself had leaned over the trailer bed door and was doing his damndest to keep me from ending up a footnote in Sunshine State history.

"We're even!" he shouted.

I slipped below the blade and scrambled into the middle of the swinging trailer. "Hardly. You split my soul in half."

"Just get the damn salt bag," the muscle-bound Demon Hunter said, deflecting another saber slash.

The truck swerved and cracked the trailer like a whip. Donnie fought his way back to the truck bed, while I went face first into a rucksack of sea salt.

Bingo.

The road opened up after the last turn and it was easy to see why—the cypress swamp was giving way to manicured grass and well-maintained easements. We were closing in on the Florida National Cemetery.

Just a few more minutes...

Midnight Riders weren't the smartest muscle in the supernatural world, but getting them to drive onto consecrated ground was a big ask. That was where the salt came in.

If I could just piss them off enough...

I shoved my hand into the bag and shoved handfuls of crystalline sea salt into my jacket pocket. It was right about that point when I started to get the feeling we might make it out of this relatively unscathed.

Boom!

A tire blew, and the truck lurched to the side, sending the trailer bouncing into the swale. The massive pickup had four back tires, but losing one was still a problem.

"Son of a bitch. Ed, can you keep it on the—"

I didn't get to finish my sentence, as what words I had left caught in my throat when the Riders sliced the trailer hitch free from the back of the truck.

Oh, crap.

Traditional trailers weren't designed for autonomous navigation—what with no front wheel and all. Ed's peanut hauler suffered from the same design flaw.

The front edge dropped, digging into the dirt and tossing me, along with the various sharp implements of road-side peanut vending, like a drunken bull-rider and his rodeo clowns into the tall grass at the entrance of the cemetery.

I did my best to roll with it, but that's hard to do when you hit the unforgiving ground with the force of a thunderclap. I looked up just in time to see Ed's truck roar past like a space coast rocket now that the trailer hitch was a distant memory. My old roommate might have wanted to stop, but the truck had other ideas.

The Riders!

The choppers' throaty roar pushed me to my feet and got those feet moving.

Just get to consecrated ground...

I would love to say I outran those spectral motorcycles and their damned riders, but I'd just been tossed from a peanut trailer at high-speed, so my running was more or less a highly motivated limp.

Just a few more yards...

The gate was closed.

Crap.

I stopped my limping and turned to face the undead monsters, still backing up toward the closed gate. "You guys remember what happened the last time you faced a Magician, right? You sure you're ready for a second beat down?"

I was lying—the only one beat down here was me. This was going to be a long and painful death. The black tar of the Eternal Shame would see to that.

With an unholy yell, and its blade held high, the lead Rider charged on his bike. In my haste I fell backward, my foot catching on something along the roadside.

What the?

It was a cross—a simple, painted reminder of the poor person who'd died along this road an untold time ago.

The chopper closed in and I raised my hands in a final act of defiance. Well, that's how I want to remember it, but I'm sure it looked more like sheer terror—thankfully there was no one there to see it.

Clang!

For the second time that night someone stopped me from taking a deserter's saber to the face, but this time the one who did it wasn't even living. Silver saber, strong in the translucent hands of my spectral savior, turned aside its tar-covered equal.

The Rider shot past before angrily coming about.

"Hooah," the young soldier yelled, his weapon keeping my head attached to my body. "Stay behind me, sir."

Not to be the person that looks a gift of death avoidance in the mouth, I did what any sane Magickless Magician would have done: I got behind that skinny spirit and his sword. "You got it, kid."

7

COLLAR POPPING EVIL

*B*lack pitch oozed from the Rider's rumbling exhaust pipes. Grass wilted beneath the bike's vile touch. The Midnight Rider circled back around, his tar-covered chopper roaring in defiance.

"Nice job," I said, huddled behind the translucent young man.

Baby-faced and clean shaven, my savior wore a set of poor-fitting fatigues, and had a black beret clamped down on his short-cropped hair. "Who are these guys?"

The Riders' rebel yells set my hairs on end. "Don't worry about them. We've just got to get to the cemetery and we'll be safe. That's consecrated ground." I pointed to the rows of markers just past the darkened gates. "Just need to get them in there… somehow."

The soldier shook his head, but kept that saber and his eyes trained on the Riders. "I can't go in there, sir."

"Well, crap. That's a problem."

The Midnight Riders revved their engines, the heavy choppers spewing more black tar.

"Get down," the soldier cried as the twin bikes exploded off their marks and roared toward us at high speed.

"Holy—"

"I said get down," the kid knocked me back, then twirled around and spun that sword like a young man possessed. He parried tar-black blades and separated the Riders from their steeds with an expert precision. Pitch-covered bodies tumbled into the tall grass.

"Are you okay, sir?" The young man turned to help me up.

"Yeah," I said, accepting his ghostly hand. "I'm... look out!"

The Midnight Riders' broken bodies got to their feet, injuries healing beneath the shifting tar of the Eternal Shame. The spectral soldier yanked me behind him again and kept that silver blade between us and the advancing undead.

"I don't suppose you have a weapon, sir? It would be very helpful right about now if you did."

"No, I don't. We can't all carry swords around."

Black blades dripped with inky tar.

"I see. Then we appear to be FUBAR."

Glistening in the hazy moonlight, the deserters circled slowly, looking for an opening. The acrid smell of the Eternal Shame's tar was nigh overpowering.

"Don't get it on you." I crouched behind the young man and pointed at the oily pitch.

"Don't get what on me, sir?"

"The tar."

"Why?"

"It's soul-binding stuff," I said, doing my best to move in tandem with the young swordsman. "There isn't a Stain-Stick in the world that can get that evil out."

The young soldier tilted his head. "Good to—"

"Look out!"

One of the Riders sensed an opening and lunged. His tar-covered saber slashed with a wild fury at my savior's midsection, but the young man was faster. He parried the blade and cut back with a strategic and well-timed strike of his own.

"Nice work! Where did you learn to do that?" I asked, limping behind the young fighter.

"North West Florida Saber Champion of nineteen ninety-nine, sir."

"Ninety-nine?"

The soldier parried two more strikes from the advancing Riders, but had to turn in the process. They were herding him away from the cemetery gates and back toward the small white roadside cross.

"Did you die?" I asked, my eyes on the weather-beaten cross.

"I am a ghost."

Clang! Pling!

Silver and black flashed beneath the moonlight.

I pointed to the roadside marker. "No, I mean did you die right over there? Where that broken cross is?"

"Yes, sir!"

Crap.

"They're pushing you back to your Death Spot," I said, trying unsuccessfully to adjust the young man's trajectory. "You can't let them do that. Do you understand?"

The young soldier held his ground, but the fury of those twin black blades was rapidly becoming too much even for him to defend.

"No?"

I slipped around him, just as a black-tar blade cut the air where I'd been. "That's your *Death Spot*. If they push you back onto it, they might be able to trigger your ride."

"My what?"

"Damn it, kid." I ducked under another whirling blade. "Your ride. You know, your ticket to the afterlife? Paradise, Valhalla, the Happy Hunting Grounds, or whatever it is that you believe in."

"My family is Southern Methodist, sir."

"Heaven it is," I said, twisting to the other side to avoid another killing lunge. "Haven't you seen your ride before?"

Pling! Clang!

"I am having a very hard time managing two blades at once. Would you mind not talking quite so much?"

"Right, sorry," I said, my eyes on the quickly approaching Death Spot. "Listen, uh..."

"Private Petty."

Clang!

"Are you serious? Like Tom Petty?"

"Sir, the talking..."

"Right," I said, keeping the young private between me and the Midnight Riders. "Okay, Private Petty—I can't believe that's your real name—I'm going to destroy your marker. That means we won't trigger your ride, which could keep you here for a lot longer than you should be. It's kind of a jerk move, but I promise I'll find a way to make it up to you, okay?"

"Sir, yes, sir!"

The kid had no idea what he was agreeing to, and I certainly felt terrible doing it to him, but the Riders were a lot smarter than they looked, and I wouldn't last five seconds without him.

"I'm sorry, kid," I said, pulling up his tiny roadside cross and smashing it across my knee. "We'll find you another way to the good place."

Oh yeah, how you are going to do that?

I kicked aside the faded plastic flowers and shoved a splintered piece of the white cross wood into my pocket. In doing so, I remembered what else I'd shoved in my pocket just a few minutes ago.

There's just enough left—I hope.

I looked up just in time to find one of the Riders had broken away from Private Petty and had me in his sights.

"Hey, nice blade," I said, backing away with my hands up. "Stupid Yankees, right?"

I wasn't sure which side of the war the Rider had been on, but I figured either way I had a shot at buying a second to dig into my pocket.

The Rider hesitated, giving me all the time I needed.

"Baseball needs a salary cap!" I shouted, throwing a fist full of sea salt at his face before making a break for the gate.

The sizzle of the salt didn't last long, but it bought me a few seconds, and I used each one of them to run like hell.

The gate was close, only a few yards away, yet the wild yell behind me told me I really needed to lay off the cheese fries. "Can't have a decent conversation about baseball without it becoming violent anymore."

The black metal bars of the gate filled my vision, just a few more feet and I'd be safe on consecrated ground. I reached for cold metal, but my foot caught on an errant tree root and sent me sprawling like a circus clown.

Son of a...

I rolled over to find the Rider standing over me, his blade high. The sound of Private Petty's fencing prowess was on full display back at what had been his Death Spot, and not here, where I desperately needed it.

I closed my eyes and covered my face, bracing myself for the end.

I'm sorry, Catherine.

The end didn't come.

I opened my eyes to find the Midnight Rider standing over me, now the proud owner of a shadowy fist through the chest. Vile black tar poured into that fist as my Darkling absorbed the deserter like a shammy. Evil Gene didn't stop until everything that had been the Rider was gone.

"Hola! Me llamo—" the Darkling coughed, clearing his throat—"oh, that's much better. I felt like a broken record."

Well that's a terrible turn of events...

Deserter tar filled in his gaps like child's putty, leveling the empty spots before turning them a fleshy pink. Evil Gene was not the blackened Spanish-speaking shadow he had been—he now resembled me in every way but one.

He looked cool—damnably cool—and I hated him all the more.

"Son of a gun, that feels so much better. Do you have any idea how annoying that was? Look at me talking to you about annoying when all you've ever done is annoyed the hell out of me," Evil Gene said, flipping up the collar of his jacket.

The bastard even pops his collar.

I shuffled backward toward the gate, my fingers catching the cool metal.

"All that crap about not enjoying the new job: guilt, frustration, shame. What a pain in the neck." My Darkling took a deep breath. "You smell that?"

"Uh…"

"Of course you don't. You wouldn't know freedom if it crawled up your backside and laid an egg, but that's not what I'm talking about. Can't you feel it in the air? Something is going down—something big. It's like the last few minutes before the ball drops on New Year's Eve, seven minutes to midnight, and the Cuban Missile Crisis, all rolled into one."

Clang! Pling! Clang! Pling!

Beyond my Darkling, Private Petty was still locked in a dual of epic proportions, but something else appeared on the road behind him—the peanut wagon had come back.

Please remember what to do, Maurice...

I turned my attention to the Darkling, hoping to buy us a little time. "What are you talking about?"

Evil Gene scoffed and pushed up his sleeves. "You always miss the details, Gene, always. There's a static in the air, I can feel it. We're nearing the main event, but don't worry, I'll make sure we come out on the winning side."

"But what about the—"

"House? Gene, I am you," the Darkling poked a finger at my chest, "but I'm also something far greater. Unlike you, I've put it all together, and that means I know what's coming."

You haven't put everything together, buddy.

Ed's truck crept up behind my shadow-self, with Maurice and the Viewmaster standing in the truck bed.

It's time to end this stupidity. I've got a daughter to save.

I grabbed hold of the Darkling's wrist and pulled him toward me. "Now, Maurice!"

8

PRUSSIAN PAUSE

*M*aurice held the toy to his face and reached for the handle. It all happened so fast. Before that Demon Hunter could pull down the lever, Evil Gene pushed me aside and spun around to face the peanut posse.

"Irritum Facit!" my Darkling shouted, unleashing a shockwave of Magick at the rusty pickup.

An unmaking!

The Viewmaster shattered in Maurice's hands, sending him reeling and costing me my best chance of reassembly. To make matters worse, the leading edge of that Magickal wrecking ball ripped through Private Petty and the remaining Midnight Rider, snuffing out the young soldier like a match on a windy day. The combined cosmic power hit me like a boot between the eyes.

I crashed into the tall grass, my hands trying desperately to squeeze the pain from my head, but the Darkling didn't waste a second. He drove a knee into my chest and pinned me to the ground.

"What... did you... do," I choked out, my lungs squeezed

beneath his bulk. "That was our best chance of reassembly. You... needed that as... much as I did."

"Still missing the details, Gene," he said, fishing car keys out of my pocket. "We don't need Team Legume's toys. Have you forgotten what's sitting in storage?"

"Storage?"

With Private Petty up in smoke the remaining Midnight Rider had his opening. He let loose a wild yell and charged the two of us—that horrifying scream would be his last.

Evil Gene took his knee off me and caught the tar-covered monster by the throat, not flinching when the black blade pierced his side. "Not bad. Not bright, but not bad."

The Darkling absorbed the Midnight Rider just like the one before him, leaving nothing but a dried husk that vanished in the evening air.

Evil Gene pulled me up by my shirt, while I struggled to get air back in my lungs. That jerk slapped my face a few times. "Come on. Keep it together, little brother. You did all this to Delia, or don't you remember?"

"I didn't—"

My Darkling cut me off. "Oh yes, you did. You can't lie to me. I was there. You split the Sangre Reina in two like you were cutting open an apple. Sucks to be the apple doesn't it?"

My mind reeled. I hadn't thought of Delia since Miami, but the dark half of me was right, I *had* done this before.

"The Skeeter..."

The Darkling nodded. "Yeah, see, you remember. Now, do you remember what we have in storage?"

"The mirror..."

"Look at you." Evil Gene cranked a hand down on my already sore shoulder. "Now you're getting it. It's time for us to get that mirror and put an end to this."

"But if you're holding the mirror..." My mind reeled.

My Darkling only smiled.

The truck's door creaked in the misty evening air.

"No one is going anywhere," Ed Lovely said, dropping out of the pickup, machete in hand.

"Don't, Ed. He's too powerful. He's absorbed both the Riders."

Evil Gene dropped me on the ground and rolled his eyes before turning to face the Demon Hunter. "Good grief, how many of you Demon Hunting peanut people are there?"

My old roommate pushed off his bandana and let it fall on the ground behind him. "It's just you and me now."

Evil Gene took a few steps toward Ed, then stopped to sniff the air. "Nice try, Lovely, but you can't cheat a cheater. Facite!"

There was a surge of Magick followed by the explosive crack of gunfire.

"Donnie," Ed cried, turning back to the truck.

"I fixed your math. *Now*, it's just you and me."

"What have you done to him?"

Evil Gene shrugged his shoulders. "I haven't *done* anything to him. He really should consider taking a class on firearm safety. Never point a gun at something you don't intend to shoot."

My old roommate hesitated. My Darkling had Ed exactly where he wanted him—unsure.

"Listen, Lovely, you do your thing and I'll do mine. I'm going to get on that bike," Evil Gene pointed at the tar-covered chopper laying on the side of the road, "then I'm going to get my car and take this Gene with me. I need him around until our reconciliation is final."

Ed held his machete out and advanced toward the Darkling. "I can't let you do that."

My black-souled doppelgänger slapped his forehead. "You can, it's easy. You get back in your car before Donnie there bleeds out in your front seat, and you take him to the hospital.

I'm thinking he has about twenty minutes before he's pushing up daisies—nearest hospital is at least that far away. You better hurry."

"Donnie?"

No response.

"Go, Ed! Just go," I cried, finding my voice again. "You can't beat him."

My old roommate tried to keep his eyes on the Darkling, but risked a glance back at the truck. "Donnie, are you okay?"

The complete lack of response from inside the truck told me he wasn't.

Evil Gene seized the opportunity, closing the distance in a flash and slashing hard with an oily black saber that appeared in his hand.

"Look out!"

The Demon Hunter whirled around just in time to parry a killing blow from my evil half.

Clang!

Not deterred, Evil Gene swung again, this time aiming for Ed's jean-covered legs. The wiry old salt jumped backwards and cut down with his own blade, narrowly missing the Darkling's over-extended arm.

I was too busy watching the sword fight to notice my old roommate's son sneaking up behind me in the tall grass. I didn't see him until he was practically on top of me.

"Gene," Little Ed whispered. "We've got a plan. Give me your hand."

"Huh?"

Ed's son produced a porcelain bowl, ornate and painted with a wreath of expertly designed flowers. Magick pulsed inside that bowl, a deep and earthy power from a forgotten age that frankly scared the hell out of me. "That's a Prussian Wedding Bowl. How the hell did you get your hands on one of those?"

"I don't have time for the whole story," the youngest Demon Hunter said as he poured a clear liquid into the ornate bowl. "Just give me your hand."

I hesitated. Prussian Wedding Bowls had a history. There were only so many of them left, and pretty much all of them were cursed in one way or another. The exact nature of the curses were different, but the end results were roughly the same: uniformly bad. Still, there were a few bowls that remained that didn't carry a terrible power, but even then they were more than terrifying enough to give me the willies, and that was when I *had* my Magick.

"What are you going to do?"

The sounds of steel on steel played out behind me, and I turned back to find the older Ed rapidly running out of steam.

"Do you trust us?" Little Ed asked, his voice calm and controlled.

"Do I have a choice?"

The younger version of my oldest friend shook his head. "Not really."

I pushed my hand into the bowl and the icy cold water inside it. "Didn't think so."

Magick surged through me. It was like the time I'd tried to re-wire the kitchen and woke up twitching on the tile floor—except this time no one was going to call 911. My gut instinct was to yank my hand out, but it wouldn't budge—in fact no part of my body was willing to move. I was frozen stiff, along with my doppelgänger.

Even with his back to me I could tell Evil Gene was fighting the Prussian Wedding Bowl, and I would have loved to have told that to the Eds, but my lips weren't having anything to do with moving.

"Nice work, son." The elder peanut vendor tried to catch his breath. "Hold him still while I check on Donnie."

"I'm trying, Dad, but he's strong."

"Just keep the other one's hand in it."

Evil Gene's Magick trickled through me like that oily sheen on the surface of a dirty pool. He was probing at the bowl, trying to find a weakness. He should have known better. Prussian Wedding Bowls were Deep Magick, and their long-dead creator had known what they were doing, meaning it was going to be tough to find a flaw in that expert design.

Unless it has a crack.

The moment I thought those words, Evil Gene's Magick shifted. We were connected, him and I, and like an idiot I'd just reminded him what to look for.

Damn it.

The older Ed reappeared with a bloody Donnie. The younger Demon Hunter sported a bandana tightly wrapped around his leg.

"He's bleeding bad. That evil thing wasn't lying. We've got to go."

"Dad…"

A hairline crack spread under my submerged fingers.

"What?"

"The bowl is dripping."

I couldn't see it, but the patter of droplets on the ground below was a dead giveaway.

"You know what you have to do," Ed said, pointing Donnie back to the truck.

"Dad, you can't be serious! He's your friend."

"He *was* my friend, but now I don't know what he is. That isn't Eugene Law, at least not the Eugene Law I remember."

Like hell I'm not. Damn it, Ed. I'm still me!

The cool night air brushed the back of my hand. The water was receding, and as it did, my muscles stirred.

"I don't… I don't know if I can," the younger Ed said, his hand retrieving a ruby red bottle from his jacket pocket.

Hold on a second now, guys. It's me, it's Eugene. I'm sure we can find a way to make all of this work.

"Damn it, son. Donnie's not going to make it if we don't get moving now. I don't like it any more than you do, but it has to be done. Pour the vinegar in and stop his heart."

Wait, what?!

9

BLACK HEARTS AND RED BLOOD

*L*ittle Ed held the dark bottle above the Prussian Wedding Bowl. Below that basin, a much wider crack dumped freezing-cold water on the tall grass at an alarming rate.

I could turn my head, but wasn't expecting what greeted me.

Black tar crawled its way up my old roommate's arm, dripping from his hand and onto Donnie's make-shift bandana tourniquet.

I struggled to speak, my mouth still fighting the bowl's power. "He's not…"

"Don't listen to him, son. He's evil, and he needs to be killed. It's what we do."

Little Ed hesitated, his baby-face hovering above mine. "That's not what we do."

"Stop arguing with me, damn it. Donnie's not going to survive much longer if we don't do something. Pour the vinegar before it escapes!"

"Don't… do… it… tar…" I moved my eyes like a bouncing ball trying to get Little Ed's attention. He uncorked the bottle and hit me with the scent of soured balsamic vinegar.

"Do it now, son. The Darkling is starting to stir!"

The tar-stained peanut vendor was right. Evil Gene twitched once, then again. His body was beginning to break free of the Prussian Wedding Bowl—in seconds that monster would regain control.

The first drops of vinegar hit the water and a wave of terrible cold washed over me.

"Do it. Pour the whole thing in, damn it. You're wasting time. He's got to die!"

It was hard to see my friend anymore, but that's what the tar of the Eternal Shame did—it compromised its victims. It took their darkest instincts and amplified them. Sure, Ed would have wanted the Darkling gone, but the Ed Lovely I knew would never willingly sacrifice another human being. It would have gone against everything he stood for. The real question was whether his son would figure that out in time.

Little Ed pulled back on the bottle. "No."

"What do you mean no?"

"I mean this is wrong and you know it. We don't kill people. We don't do this."

The senior Ed fumed, his face turning red and the black tar on his arm expanding like the swelling tide. "I'll show you what we do."

"Let me go..." I said, my voice barely able to rise above a whisper.

"What?"

"He's got the tar on him, and so does Donnie. They aren't your family now—you've got to let me go."

"What about the Darkling?"

I turned my face toward the cemetery gates. "We just need to get under that gate."

"But what about my dad?"

"What about me?" the senior Lovely said, wrestling the vinegar from his son's hand.

"Dad, don't!"

The Eternal Shame swirled along the elder man's arm. It moved fast, consuming my friend like an oily plague. "You'll understand one day." Ed held the bottle above the ornate basin and turned it over.

"No," his son cried, yanking the bowl away before the deluge of heart-stopping vinegar could reach the surface. He slammed that cursed bucket against his father's knee. Ed buckled, and the fragile Prussian Wedding Bowl shattered.

Crap!

A surge of Wild Magick erupted like a well-placed firecracker. That shockwave of unpredictable cosmic power rolled out over the tall grass, curling blades and knocking Ed and Donnie to the turf. True to form, my Darkling absorbed the majority of it, which gave me an opportunity to grab the younger Ed's wrist and make a run for the gate.

"What about my dad?" he cried, looking back at the scene unfolding.

"We'll figure something out, I promise, but first we have to keep from getting killed ourselves. Do you trust me?"

"Do I have a choice?"

I pointed back to my recovering darker half. "Sure, you can stay with him."

"No thanks."

We reached the gate and hit the deck. Together we scrambled under the black steel bars, while behind us all hell broke loose. We could only watch helplessly as Donnie melted away into black tar, his body consumed in the slow-moving wave of liquid evil.

"Donnie!"

Ed was next. Realization flooded his face, but it was too late. The Demon Hunter stumbled forward, grabbing at his arm. For a moment, I thought he had the upper hand, but it didn't last. The Eternal Shame was too strong. It knew his weaknesses, and exactly how to manipulate him. Twisting strands like black licorice snaked around my old roommate's shoulder, wrapping his neck and trapping his chin.

"Dad," Little Ed cried, scrambling to get back under the gate.

I grabbed his arm and wrestled him back. "No, you can't leave the cemetery."

Ed Lovely, my oldest friend, faded beneath the tar until only his eyes remained, hatred burning in their fiery depth.

The Darkling now had his own Midnight Riders.

"No, Dad!" Little Ed broke my grasp and scrambled for the gate. "No!"

"He's not your dad anymore." I caught the younger man's collar. "At least not right now."

The Darkling stretched out his arms then turned to face us. "Weak-willed me is right, as much as I hate to admit it. It's just not worth the hassle right now. First, I get the mirror, then I'll come find you."

"Maurice!" Little Ed tried to get the attention of the last member of the peanut posse. Somehow I'd forgotten about the senior roasting assistant now coming to his senses in the back of the pickup.

"Hey guys," Maurice said, rubbing at two black eyes. "Wow, that packed a wallop."

Little Ed grabbed at the black steel bars. "Run, Maurice!"

The last member of their merry band shook the sense back into his head, then caught sight of the new Midnight Riders and took a step back. "Donnie? Ed? What the heck is going on?"

Evil Gene brushed off his sleeves and popped his collar back up. "Well this is just perfect. Gentlemen, if you would save me the trouble."

The Midnight Riders' unholy screams echoed in the misty air.

Little Ed banged on the heavy gate. "Dad!"

"Fight it, Ed," I cried, joining the young man.

The pitch-covered Demon Hunter approached the pickup, a black-as-night saber solidly in hand.

Maurice hesitated. "Ed?"

His old boss didn't respond.

Maurice scrambled off the pickup, only to find Donnie on the ground waiting for him.

"Run, Maurice." Little Ed banged on the metal bars.

My Darkling nodded. "Yes, please run. It's so much more fun when the prey gives a little chase, right?"

I pointed to the truck. "Salt, Maurice! There's got to be some salt in the truck bed, if you can get a circle going you might be able to stop them."

The Demon Hunter pulled down on the rear gate and reached for a bag of peanut salt, but his hand didn't stay attached. Donnie's blade cleanly separated it from his body, leaving Maurice's blood to splatter atop the snow-white salt.

Maurice screamed and clutched his arm to his chest, making a futile attempt to stem the blood.

Little Ed tried to squeeze his body through the bars, but I held him back. "Damn it, kid. I'm not losing another one of you today."

Evil Gene brushed at his hair and checked his nails, giving the dying Demon Hunter no more attention than an injured cockroach. "Come on, gentlemen. We have a long ride ahead of us."

Two new heavy choppers rolled into view from behind the pickup, called up by the Darkling's power.

Donnie climbed aboard one and made room for Evil Gene.

My Darkling swung his leg over the seat before pointing to the struggling Maurice. "Finish it."

Little Ed slammed his fists against the iron. "Don't do it, Dad! This isn't you. Listen to me it's not you. You've got to snap out of it."

The eldest Demon Hunter hesitated with his black blade perched against Maurice's throat.

Can he do it? Can Ed Lovely beat the Eternal Shame?

The black pitch oozed along his face and arms, covering all that remained of the man's skin and clothes.

Evil Gene shook his head. "He can't hear you anymore, all he hears now is me."

"Dad!"

Ed rammed the saber home, ending Maurice's life at the edge of that black-blade. In that moment, I had my answer. Maurice dropped like a stone, his blood soaking the ground and his gurgling voice fading beneath rumbling choppers. Ed joined Evil Gene, and together they kicked up gravel and disappeared into the misty night.

Little Ed hung against the darkened gate, his shoulders slumped.

"That's not your dad, kid. Trust me."

The Demon Hunter's son white-knuckled the bars. "I didn't do anything... I'm a coward."

"Kid, there are moments where it makes more sense to retreat and live to fight another day. This is one of those moments. Trust me. Discretion is the better part of valor, or however the quote goes. We'll figure this one out."

The wind picked up, blowing across my back and carrying with it the faint moaning of the dearly departed.

Little Ed turned around. "Gene?" he said, pulling on my jacket.

I turned to find a full regiment of spectral warriors in perfect alignment behind us. These weren't New Dead, with their scorched and blackened souls, nor were these the chaotic and unpredictable Old Dead, which was too bad, since I had experience with both of them.

This was something all together different, but just as terrifying.

"You see them?"

Little Ed nodded. "What do we do?"

Seven soldiers stepped forward with rifles raised.

"I don't know."

PART II
THE ROAD TO HELL

WING-HALLA AWAITS

I slumped back against the steel bars. The small white piece of Private Petty's cross tumbled out of my jacket and landed just outside the gate.

"Now that's a send off," said a familiar young voice.

"Private Petty!"

The spectral soldier I'd thought the unmaking had destroyed stood next to the piece of road-side cross outside the gate.

"Who's that?" Little Ed asked, his head on a swivel between the advancing firing squad and the saber-carrying spectral private.

"That's Private Petty, he saved my—hey, wait a second, how are you seeing all this?"

Little Ed turned back toward the regiment and ignored my question.

"Ready," a deep, ghostly voice cried from the firing line.

Little Ed dropped to the ground and crawled under the gate. "They're going to shoot us."

"I don't think so…"

"Aim!"

"Aw, hell," I said, crawling out behind the junior Demon Hunter. "I'm not going to stay here and find out. Wait for me."

"Fire!"

The air shook with the force of seven rifle shots. I scrambled to my feet on the other side of the steel bars and pat down my body. "Were you hit?"

Little Ed brushed the dirt off his chest. "No. You?"

"Nope."

Private Petty sighed and removed his beret. A single tear glinted in his eye

"Maurice," Ed's son cried, racing to the body of his fallen friend. He fell to his knees at the bloody mess of what had been the assistant roaster. "I'm sorry, I..."

"Dang," came the smooth drawl of a ghostly Maurice, standing over his mutilated corpse. "Well, that just sucks."

The regiment commander barked out another command. "Ready."

"Maurice? Is that you?" Little Ed asked, still kneeling next to the corpse.

"I think. Damnation, I took it right in the neck, eh?"

"Aim."

"He didn't mean it, Maurice. I know he didn't. That wasn't my dad, that was something else. He didn't mean to..."

The spectral peanut vendor rubbed his neck. "Yeah, I hope not. That looks pretty gruesome."

Private Petty approached the spectral Demon Hunter. "Pardon me for asking, but did you serve in active duty?"

"Afghanistan, yeah."

"Fire!"

Seven more shots rang out in the misty night.

Private Petty saluted Maurice and stepped aside. "Godspeed."

"Maurice," I said, helping Little Ed to his feet. "You are going to get a ride any second. I need you to take that ride. You understand?"

The thin mist that clung to the tall grass like snarls in the shag carpet shifted, floating closer to the Demon Hunter.

"Eh? I think. What sort of ride are we talking about?"

"It doesn't matter. You just take it. You got it? How many Demons did you banish?"

Maurice bent down to fiddle with the bloody gash on his corpse's neck. "Um, by myself or with Ed? I'd say we did at least fifty, wouldn't you agree, Eddie? Yeah, fifty."

The mist swirled, sliding between the Demon Hunter's legs like a hungry python.

"That's exactly what I was afraid of. Until your ride gets here you're fair game, and I don't have anything in the way of Magick to protect you."

"Ready," the regime commander barked again.

"Hah! Hey, that tickles," Maurice said, pulling his spectral foot up out of the mist.

"Don't leave your Death Spot," I said, trying to keep the newly deceased from stepping too far from his corpse.

"Well you should tell that to whatever is tickling my—" the Demon Hunter vanished, pulled under in the rising mist.

Little Ed lunged for the spot his friend had been. "Maurice!"

"Aim."

The Demon Hunter's spectral hand appeared briefly in the frothing white before being dragged under again.

"Crap. Okay, Petty, can you grab him?" I asked, but the ghost was gone.

Gah!

"What do we do?!" Little Ed shouted, pawing through the mist for his friend.

Maurice's hand appeared again and frantically waved in the air like he was caught in a fast-moving river. The mist had dragged him a good distance from his Death Spot.

"Get one of those bags of salt from what's left of the trailer."

Little Ed jumped to his feet. "What are you going to do with it?"

I chased after Maurice's hand. "I'm going to keep him from missing his ride. You worry about the salt."

"Fire!"

The final volley exploded into the night air, and that meant his ride would be here shortly.

The Demon Hunter's hand vanished into the mist again.

"Damn it, you peanut-roasting bastard," I shouted, digging through the mist. "Your ride is coming."

A clarion blast rung across the empty road.

Mist swirled around my legs. "Oh man, you may not know this, but you don't get a lot of chances at this. Do not miss your ride, trust me. I don't know what you're doing down there, but whatever it is you'd best man the heck up and punch it in the nose—your ride is almost here!"

"I've got the salt!" Little Ed ran back toward Maurice's Death Spot with the heavy rucksack clutched to his chest.

"Good work…"

"Where's Maurice?"

I ran a hand through my hair. "Damn it, kid. I'm working on that. Just give me a—" The Demon Hunter's hand appeared in the swirling mist and I lunged for it. "I got you."

Maurice's face appeared above the mist, his eyes wide in terror. "Gators!"

"Did you banish a Sobek?" The hunter's face slipped below the mist again and I caught the flash of dark scales. "I'm going to take that as a yes. Crap."

A Sobek, named after the Egyptian god of the Nile, was the patron spirit of the race of Alligator Men that lived along the spine of the state. I'd tangled with Alligator Men once, down in the Everglades, and once had been more than enough for me.

I caught the edge of Maurice's fingers and yanked his head above the mist. "How's my salt coming, Eddie?"

Ed's son gave me a confused look. "What do you want me to do with it?"

More dark scales, like the mountainous ridges of a bull gator's back, surfaced in the hazy mist. "Hold on, Maurice," I cried, dragging the oversized, ghostly Demon Hunter through the clinging white like I were trolling bait. "Circle the wagons!"

Little Ed set the bag down. "Huh?"

"Make a salt circle around his body. Don't get any on him and make sure the ring is big enough for us to stand in."

"Oh, got it," the young man said, tearing open the industrial-sized bag of salt and pouring it heavy on the sandy earth.

An alligator tail slapped against my leg, and I thought for sure I was going to fall smack into the Sobek's snare. "Damn it, Maurice. Can you kick or something?"

"I'm trying." The recently departed's head dipping below the mist again.

"Try harder!"

I dragged the peanut vendor to the edge of the circle. "Wait, kid, you have to leave a spot for him to get in. Don't close it."

Little Ed stopped, then kicked aside a pile of salt on the far side of the circle. "Shoot, sorry."

"The other side, really?!"

The sound of horse hooves on the hard pavement grabbed our attention.

A chariot? Maurice dies, and he gets a damn chariot.

It wasn't just any chariot. The ornate, gold-plated Roman taxi rumbled down the black asphalt toward us. An honest-to-goodness Centurion stood tall on the back of that ride to the hereafter, the reins in one meaty hand, and a long spear in the other.

I dragged the Demon Hunter out of the mist just long

enough for him to see his ride. "That guy looks like my great-uncle Steve."

"Move." I pushed Little Ed aside and tossed Maurice onto his Death Spot. "Close it!"

Little Ed dumped the last of his salt bag across the ground, closing the Demon Hunter up on salt island.

"Gene?"

"Yeah," I said, trying to catch my breath.

"Since we closed him up in the salt circle how will he catch his ride?"

"He'll... Damn it, kid."

Little Ed pointed at the approaching chariot. "I don't mean to be rude or anything, but I figured you had a plan for that."

"I... I'm working on it."

The chariot rolled along the pavement, the war horse's powerful hooves scoring the asphalt.

Little Ed smiled. "Great! What is it?"

"Give me a minute."

Thick black gator scales brushed against the edge of the salt circle. The Sobek might not have been here for me, but he appeared ready to claim a prize and wasn't going to let something like a Magickless Magician stand in his way. "You ever wrestled an alligator?"

"What?" Little Ed cried, dropping the empty bag. "Just cause I grew up in the Green Swamp doesn't mean I wrestle alligators."

"Can you?"

"That was one time," Little Ed held up a single finger, "I was a kid, and it was a baby gator..."

"Works for me. On the count of three."

"Wait," Little Ed cried, fumbling with his shirt.

The chariot tore over the black pavement. "Running out of time..."

The junior Demon Hunter gave up on his buttons and instead just pushed up his sleeves. "Let me at least—"

"Three!" I shouted, kicking the salt circle apart.

The monster gator's head erupted from the mist, jaws wide and reaching for Maurice. True to his word Little Ed pounced on that demonic reptile like he was going to ride it into the sunset and clamped its mouth shut with his scrawny arms.

The chariot rolled to a stop outside of our circle, and then the Roman soldier leaned down and extended a hand to Maurice.

"Take it!" I shouted.

The Demon Hunter didn't have to be told twice, he grabbed onto the soldier's strong arm and was quickly hauled into the golden chariot.

"No shit. Is that you, Uncle Steve?"

"Heck yeah it's me," the rider said, completely breaking my mental image of what a golden-armored chariot driver should sound like.

"What's Heaven like?"

The Centurion smiled and cracked the reins. "It's like a never-ending order of hot wings and cold beer."

"No foolin'?"

The gold chariot raced down that empty highway, Maurice and his Uncle Steve at the controls. The Demon Hunter's last words echoed in the misty gloom. "Are there wing girls too?"

"It's Heaven, ain't it?"

11

HOME WRECKER

*L*ittle Ed and I tossed the last of the peanut bags on to the truck bed, along with anything else that had the Lovely name on it.

"What about…" The junior Demon Hunter gestured to Maurice's body.

The sky was quickly lightening. What had been velvety darkness was now a deep purple—dawn was coming fast.

"Viking funeral," I said, pointing to the torn-up and largely empty trailer.

It took ten minutes to get the Winghalla-bound Maurice's mortal coil onto the trailer, and another twenty to get the stupid trailer to the swamp's edge.

"One more push, ready?"

"Go!" Little Ed shouted, throwing his shoulder into it, as together we set the trailer in motion toward a dark and muddy end.

Blub, blub, blub…

The younger peanut man and I collapsed at the water's edge to watch the final voyage of the road-side roaster.

"Hey, I know it might be nothing," the younger Demon

Hunter said, pulling something out of his pocket. "But I found this on the truck bed."

The picture wheel.

The paper disc and its sixteen dark squares shined in the coming dawn.

Little Ed frowned. "I'm really sorry we did that to you."

"Me too, kid." I held up the wheel to get a better look at the images. Half of them were completely black, but the eight images remaining appeared to be still frames from my life. There was an image of my son's toy cars from the last day we raced them around the living room, along with a handful of images from my daughter's later years. But there was one image, a single still frame, that stood out among the rest—not because it was special, but because I didn't understand it.

A single still of Cathy's first bike lying on the street.

"Can you do anything with that?" Ed's son asked, watching me spin the disc slowly.

"Without my Magick? No. It looks like in unmaking the Viewmaster, the Darkling left us with a sort of reconciliation wheel."

"A what?"

I gently tucked the paper in my back pocket. "Sixteen images, half of them mine, and half of them lost to the Darkling. Those images keep track of the score."

"Huh?"

"Which soul-half is the one that should take over in a merger. We're even, as long as I can keep my cool he won't get the upper hand—but don't worry about it. I've got something back in Tampa that'll make all this moot."

Little Ed nodded and watched the last of the bubbles reach the muck's surface.

"Nice work wrangling that Sobek," I said, breaking the silence.

"Thanks, but I didn't do anything. As soon as Maurice was on the chariot it just... vanished."

"Yeah, that's pretty much what I expected."

Little Ed frowned. "You did?"

"Well, it was a guess. I figured it was only there because Maurice had banished one in his time."

Little Ed got to his feet. "Right, yeah."

"And since you've never banished anything in your life, it was going to all but ignore you."

The junior Demon Hunter's face turned red. "Huh? No, I have. I totally have—"

I cut Ed's son off before he could dig himself an even deeper hole. "No, you haven't. I can tell. Besides, you really aren't the Demon Hunting type."

Little Ed folded his arms. "What do you mean I'm not the type?"

"I mean you aren't the type. It takes a special breed of crazy to do that job, and you don't have it. I hate to break it to you, but you're a good, smart, and level-headed person. These are traits not frequently ascribed to Ed Lovely, or Demon Hunters in general."

"And how do you know all this? We met only a few hours ago."

I got up, brushed the mud from my slacks, then headed for the truck, patting the young kid on that back as I walked past. "I know this because I saw you with the bowl, and how you inter-acted with the dead. You are no Demon Hunter, you're a Magi-cian—whether you care to admit it or not."

"What? That's crazy."

I climbed into the passenger seat and waited for the junior Magician to get in.

"Believe what you want to believe, but I know what I saw."

Little Ed reached under the dash and fiddled with the wiring. In a few seconds, the truck engine turned over.

"We've got to get to Tampa. I know that's where the Darkling headed, and wherever my evil twin goes, Donnie and your father won't be far behind."

"We can't face that thing again empty handed," Little Ed said, dropping the shifter into drive. "We need to stop at my mom's place first."

"Your mom's?"

"Yeah, she made the hat."

Bingo.

"I assume that was her bowl too?"

Little Ed nodded.

"Good, we can tell her you were the one that broke it. Let's go."

The pickup lurched forward, then stuttered to a halt—a bright orange light on the dash bathing us in its angry light.

Low fuel.

IT HAD BEEN REALLY nice of that family to call us a tow. We'd looked like quite the pair I'm sure—two muddy hobos sitting on the front bumper trying to flag down a passing motorist.

Thank God they'd stopped, as we hadn't seen any others for hours.

The sun had already baked the mud on my jacket and pants a nice muted brown when the tow-truck showed up.

Little Ed lay down in the back seat, no doubt exhausted from the events of the previous night. I on the other hand couldn't do anything but wring my hands in frustration. If those damn Demon Hunters hadn't Soul-Split me I'd be neck deep in the lakes of fire and on my way to finding Cathy—but no, here I was, sitting in the tight confines of a wrecker cab, with a beefy-looking woman at the wheel.

She wore her hair in a tight mass of ringlets, tucked up

under a hat not unlike the one that had Magickally squeezed the truth out of my head a few hours earlier. The rest of her was a mess of oil stains and cigarette burns, but I couldn't complain— I resembled one of my son's finger-paintings.

Is he even still finger painting?

"He sure is, sugar."

The House!

The truck driver smacked the steering wheel. "Bingo, Gene. You're getting so good at this. I haven't met a monkey with that kind of talent since—how long have you been around? It's so easy to lose track."

Anger roared in my blood and I ripped open the glove box— flare gun. I grabbed the bright red plastic pistol and pointed it at the truck-driver-shaped House. "You cheated!"

"Uh, no, sweetheart, I most certainly did not."

"Stewart told me! He said Cathy is still in Hell, you didn't save her! You lied to me. Our whole deal was to get her out. There is no contract."

The House smacked her lips on a piece of gum and chuckled. "You are trusting an Imp to tell you the truth? You know they're basically rubbery, little lying machines right?"

"He is bound to me. He has to tell the truth."

"Wrong," the House said before dropping into another gear. "You have tremendous talent, Eugene Law, but you really don't study much do you?"

"I know about Imps. I dealt with one in college. Stanley Flaterhaus covers them in his—"

"Flaterhaus! Oh, man, well that explains everything. It's amazing you are even still alive. Flaterhaus? Really? That guy was a self-inflated hack. He couldn't conjure up a cold, let alone manage Minor Demons."

"No." I put a finger on the trigger. "I don't believe you."

"You believe what you want to believe. I'm not in the 'believing' game, Gene. You see me out there gathering up worshippers? Do I require fasting on certain days? What about the lighting of special candles or incense? Nope, nada, and a resounding no. You want to shoot me in the head? Go for it."

I started to squeeze, my hand trembling.

"But," the House said, switching on the blinker to change lanes. "I'd hate to think about what happens to Porter and Kris if you do. You know he's growing up so fast. Would you believe he's in first grade now? Kid's far more like your wife—which is great for him. He's a beast on the playground. You should see him run."

The cold plastic bit into my finger.

"Yep," the House ignored the shaking flare gun, "kid sure can run, but can he outrun *me*?"

I lowered the weapon, my hands still shaking.

"Smart," the House said, patting my leg. "I've always said monkeys were great at this sort of thing. All that juicy moral compass stuff. I mean, your whole noggin is one great mess of competing values and confusion. It's like a cauldron of crazy all wrapped in a nice ball of readily manipulated flesh—damn near perfect."

I held up the gun again, but found it wasn't a gun at all—it was an old pen, heavily chewed on one end.

"Didn't think I'd give you a real one, did you?"

The House chuckled, then slammed a meat-hook-sized hand against my chest, pinning me to the seat. "Now, we have a problem you need to solve. You let yourself get split by the three stooges back there. Limitless cosmic power, yet you find a way to lose it to Mr. Peanut and the cashew crew."

Is that concern I hear?

"You're damn straight it's concern. You know how long I've been working on this? Of course you don't, your tiny little primate brain would tear itself apart at the mere hint of that sort of complexity."

"I don't know how you expect me to stop him."

Those truck driver fingers dug into my chest. "He may have taken the Magick, but he didn't get that special bit of Eugene Law that we all know and love. I bet if I dig a little deeper I'll find it."

I tried to push those sausage fingers off my sternum, but the wrecker woman was too strong.

"I…"

"Say it with me, Gene. 'I'll get my shit back together'"

"I'll…"

The hand pressed harder, and I was sure my ribs would crack at any second. "I'll get my shit back together."

"Splendid!" the House said, letting go of my chest and turning the big tow truck onto a dirt road.

The landscape changed quickly. Gone were the rolling fields of north central Florida with their lazy cattle and short barb-wire fences. Now there were only dense trees and hanging vines. We were in swamp country now, Green Swamp country. Cypress, with their long trunks that swelled up in the murky water, lined the road. The noonday sun quickly vanished, lost among the dense canopy, and taking with it the warm light.

Our wrecker pulled into a muddy clearing and slowed to a stop, its tires dipping gently in the soft earth.

"Why are we stopping?"

The truck driver smiled and smacked her gum, her voice no longer the House's. "Far as I can go, otherwise I'd need a tow myself." She looked at the rear seat with Little Ed fast asleep, then turned her attention back to me. "So, who's paying?"

12

TROLLS IN THE MIST

I placed my last few bills into the truck driver's hand. Little Ed and I watched her deposit the pickup, then three-point-turn that exhaust-belching monster back onto the dirt road.

"Eddie, where the hell are we?"

Little Ed opened the back door of the truck and retrieved a small backpack. "Green Swamp."

"You don't say." I swatted at a mosquito setting up on the back of my hand. "Let's try another one. *Why* are we in the Green Swamp?"

"Mom lives here."

Very little wind made its way down to the forest floor, but what breeze there was brought with it the unpleasant smell of rotting vegetation, fetid water, and Bridge Troll.

"Your mom lives *here?*"

Little Ed nodded and shoved his hands through the backpack's straps. "Sure does."

"And why are we seeing your mom again?"

The young Demon Hunter patted me on the arm before

taking a narrow path between a pair of short and spiky saw palmettos. "I saw what that thing did. We need help."

"And we're going to find that help here? Does your mom know this place is thick with Bridge Trolls?"

"Yup, she wouldn't have it any other way," the young man said before slipping out of the clearing.

"Don't tell me this is one of the 'Bridge Trolls in the Mist' sort of things?"

Little Ed didn't respond.

"It is, isn't it?"

I brushed another mosquito away from my neck and flipped my collar up, knowing full well it didn't look half as cool on me as it did on my evil twin.

Jerk.

THE GREEN SWAMP of central Florida took its name from the overabundance of dense vegetation that grew in it. Tall cypress soaked up the shallow water like great straws, while long globs of Spanish moss hung like animal pelts from the lowest branches. Black mud squished under our feet, each step another opportunity to sacrifice a shoe to the swamp gods. Yet, thanks to Little Ed—and I'm guessing his mother—we had a narrow trail to follow through the stifling greenery.

"You grew up here?" I said, my shoe sinking in the muck just enough to make me stumble.

"Sure did."

"Wow, Ed lived here."

"Nope." The junior Demon Hunter pulled back on a springy lower limb and ushered me past. "Dad and Mom didn't see eye to eye. They separated when I was little."

Safely on the other side of the whipping branch I stopped to let the younger man retake the lead. "What's your mom's name?"

"Kaylee."

Nope, doesn't ring any bells.

"And she lives way out here by herself?"

"Yup." The young Demon Hunter shimmied over a moss-covered log.

"Why?"

My guide placed a hand on my chest and another against my mouth the second I came down from the fallen log. Little Ed's eyes directed me to a dense mound of saw palmetto—something was moving on the other side. The young man crouched down behind that bush and turned my attention to a small gap in the fronds.

Bridge Troll.

The Volkswagen-sized beast had his back to us, thick legs standing in murky, hip height water. He wore clothing, or what you could loosely describe as clothing. It was more a patchwork of skins, furs, and discarded tent material. Bridge Trolls were bald by nature, and this Magickal wrecking ball was no exception. A slate-gray head was perched on shoulders that had long ago consumed his neck.

If Bridge Trolls could play football, they'd win the division every year—unless they were arrested for eating the cheerleaders.

"What's he doing?" I whispered.

Little Ed shook his head. "Just wait, she's working."

"That's a 'she'?!"

The Troll tilted its head slightly, and Little Ed gave me a glare not unlike the ones my wife had been so good at doling out.

"No, damn it. Just wait," he whispered.

The black water rippled gently as the beast spoke. Well, it sounded like words, Bridge Trolls weren't known for their fine oratory skills. Most of the communications I'd ever had with a Bridge Troll centered around crushing, grinding, breaking, and a fantastic process for repeating that same general thought in perpetuity.

Now, not all Bridge Trolls were that unintelligible, but the rare ones that weren't were typically cursed souls like the young Tommy Tillerson from my daughter's first Teeball team, or the half-troll I'd worked out a few trades with at the Brooksville Flea Market. Still, a full-on Bridge Troll, in the dim light of the Green Swamp, was more than enough to put my short hairs on edge.

"So we go around?" I asked, my feet slowly sinking in the muck.

"No, just wait, she'll be fine."

"Who'll be fine?"

A few of those hits to the head I'd taken in the last twenty-four hours must have been stronger than I'd thought, as somehow it hadn't occurred to me that if the Bridge Troll was talking, it was most likely talking to someone else. They weren't known for their rousing monologues.

Little Ed shifted his position just enough to point past Troll-mountain. "There. Look."

Jutting out of the swamp like an impromptu pulpit stood the thick stump of a dead Mallaluka tree. The paper-bark invader was not native Floridian flora and appeared to have been cut down years ago. Parchment-like strips of the tree peeled back like the curled pages of a beaten down book. At the top of that stump, nose-to-nose with our Bridge Troll, was one freckle-faced redhead.

She sat cross-legged on the crumpled paperbark. She held a clipboard in her hand, while a ratty ball cap pressed down over her shoulder-length auburn hair.

"That's your mom?" I said, craning my neck to see farther.

"Yeah, that's what she does."

"Risk her life for no good reason?"

Little Ed frowned. "No, she studies the Trolls."

"What's there to study? It's not like they put on Shake-spearean plays or are known for their keen talent at differential equations."

"I assume you do both of those things?"

He had me there. "Well, no, but I'm also not a Bridge Troll."

Little Ed's mother couldn't have been much older than me, but she had a youthful energy about her that was easy to admire. It was clear she loved what she did, even if it did make her just short of bat-shit crazy.

I leaned forward to get a better look.

"Be careful," the young Demon Hunter said, grabbing the back of my muddy collar. "They don't take kindly to strangers."

"Right, right…"

Something bright pink flashed in the Bridge Troll's hand. Pink certainly didn't seem to be a color you found in the Green Swamp, especially not manufactured hot pink.

"What's it got?"

"Huh?" Little Ed leaned around the palmetto with me. "I don't know. Looks like a… flamingo?"

"A plastic flamingo?"

"Yeah," the young Demon Hunter said, leaning against my back. "I think so, why?"

The Bridge Troll's tone shifted into a more animated, almost aggravated one, as he swung the pink plastic flamingo against the palm of his massive hand.

Relax, Gene, it's most likely just some trash.

The pink bird's coal-black eyes stared at me from beneath the shadowy canopy, then blinked.

Or not.

What was the Flock doing here?

I pondered this thought, and others, and was completely engrossed in those worries when Little Ed's weight shifted, sending me, my thoughts, and what remained of my dignity headfirst into the swampy water.

An immediate and healthy fear of alligators sent me gasping for air along the algae-speckled surface. I opened my eyes to find what little sun we'd had blotted out by the sheer enormity of a very displeased Bridge Troll.

"Uh, hey," I said as I wiped the goo from my face. "How's it going?"

The monster's hand slammed into the murky water and grabbed the front of my shirt with all the delicacy of a front-loader. In seconds I was flopping above the filth like a noodled catfish.

"Don't hurt him," Little Ed's mother said, although her tone wasn't really conveying much in the way of non-hurting conviction—to say she appeared displeased was a mild under-statement. "What are you doing in my swamp?"

"I'm really not sure. Your son brought me here after his dad and the rest of Team Peanut cuddled up with the Eternal Shame and got themselves turned into Midnight Riders."

The Troll gave me the same once over I would have used on an insect moments before I introduced it to my shoe.

"Hi there," I said, waving to the Bridge Troll and trying desperately to keep the few peanuts I'd snaked from my old roommate's supply in my stomach. The Bridge Troll's earthy bouquet was making that immensely difficult.

"Mom!" Little Ed popped up from behind the palmetto blind, waving to his mother. "It's true. This is Eugene Law, he's a friend of Dad's."

The ginger women shifted her hips and pursed already displeased lips. "Great, just what I wanted to do today... Meet one of your father's friends."

"Uh..."

"Kaylee," the woman said, frowning at me beneath her ball cap.

"Great. Kaylee, any chance you could direct the shambling mound of unpleasant here to put me down?"

"You got it."

At least that's what I think she said. Hitting the swamp water a second time made it really hard to tell.

13

MODERN MAGICK

I scrambled for the surface, breaking through the muddy water to gasp for breath only to be pulled up into the air.

"What the—"

The Bridge Troll nodded, then dumped me right back into algae-laden sludge.

"Mom!"

Ed's ex-wife said something to the Bridge Troll in a language that sounded like a mixture of grunts, sniffles, and beatbox, and in turn he dumped me onto the muddy bank.

In a show of strength, I wheezed like an old man for a few seconds, then vomited up the peanuts and a fist full of greenish swamp-water.

"Gene, are you okay?" Little Ed asked, sloshing his way through the shallow edge of the Troll pond.

"If he's one of your dad's friends he'll be fine. Every last one of them has a head as hard as Stinkstone here."

"Mom! He saved my life, and he's going to help me save Dad!"

I am?

I finished coughing up The Swamp Thing's younger brother and rolled onto my back, giving myself an excellent view of Stinkstone and his fervent environmental protector.

"I'll try," I said, my words intermixed with coughing fits. "I have my apprentice to look out for too."

"Apprentice? You're a Magician?" Kaylee leaned over to look down on me from her paper-wood tree stump.

"I... it's a long story, but yeah I'm a—"

I didn't get to finish my response, as the junior Demon Hunter's mother said something to Stinkstone and his fiery red eyes cut me off mid-sentence.

The Trolls fist came down with remarkable speed and I'm not ashamed to say I did what any newly non-Magickal middle-aged father of two would do when faced with near-certain annihilation. "Not in the face!"

Boom!

Stinkstone's fist rammed into the ground beside my head, kicking up a minor shockwave of mud and costing me at least two of my remaining lives. The Troll said something to Kaylee in his native tongue then shuffled off into the murky water.

I wiped the muck away to find myself face to beak with a plastic pink flamingo, its sharp metal skewer legs only inches from my cheek.

"He doesn't like strangers in his swamp, nor does he care very much for Magicians."

"I get that." I propped myself up. "I don't care much for them either."

Little Ed pulled me up out of the mud with a very undignified pop. "Sorry about that, Gene."

I brushed at the swamp bits on my pants and jacket, but that only made it worse. "It's fine. Listen, I'm sort of burning daylight here. The Darkling, your dad, and Donnie the peanut hauler are on their way to Tampa, ostensibly to collect what they need to remove me from the circle of life, and if they can knock off my apprentice in the process, they'll consider that a bonus."

"Donnie?" Little Ed's mother asked, her voice abruptly sliding up an octave. "What happened to Donnie?"

"I'll explain, Mom. First, we found Gene here at Sal's and—"

"Sorry, kid," I said, jumping ahead to the bad parts. "Short version. Donnie wears the Eternal Shame like a summer frock. He's become a Midnight Rider under the control of—"

Kaylee jumped down from the stump. "Sear Spit? That goddamn Imp has been a thorn in my side since…"

The ginger woman realized she had both of our attentions and let her words trail off.

Yeah, that's not suspicious at all.

"No, it's not Sear Spit. Gene killed him."

"You did what?!" Kaylee advanced on me like a water moccasin, the whites of her eyes showing like that cotton mouth snake. "You killed an immortal Demon in my backyard?"

"Okay." I held my hands up in defense. "It would appear that is really pissing a lot of people off. I can't say I understand why, as he was a slimy, bat-winged pain in the ass, and I was doing the whole community a favor by taking him—"

Kaylee didn't let me finish; instead, the naturalist put herself a few inches from my face. She wasn't tall, maybe a few inches shorter than Porter, but she had that same passion—plus she carried a long oak staff. That stick was doing a great job getting her point across as it pressed against my chest.

"Doing us a favor? Goddamn city Magicians. They come out here and 'do us a favor,' and end up turning everything sideways. Then they shuffle on out like they were never here. Oh thank you, Mr. Big Time Magician, thank you for coming here, screwing up my swamp, and putting my son's life at risk."

I took a small step back to remove the staff's pressure from my chest. First, it wasn't hard to see Little Ed's mom was on tilt, and I wasn't sure she wouldn't decide to show me the business end of that staff. Second, the amount of Magick rolling through her bang-stick was enough to curl my already wavy chest hair in unpleasant ways.

For a girl who doesn't like Magicians you've got a decent amount of Magick. I wonder...

There'd been rumors of a Witch taking up residence in the center of the state. Somewhere along the way she'd picked up the wildly original and well conceived moniker, 'Swamp Witch.' Could Ed have married then summarily divorced one Kaylee the Swamp Witch?

That did sound suspiciously like Ed Lovely.

"Got it. Like I said, I'm going to head back to Tampa. I have an apprentice to save, and a House to confront. If you'd just point me back to the main road, I'll get a move on."

Little Ed jumped in between us. "Mom, Gene knows how to find Dad and Donnie, plus he kept Maurice's ghost from being eaten by a Sobek Demon before—"

"Maurice is dead?"

Little Ed, we need to work on your communication skills.

"Right, like I said, if you'll just point the way to the main road I'll be out of your swamp and your life ASAP—Magician's honor."

"He is," Little Ed said, letting his shoulders droop. "We used the Viewmaster on Gene."

Kaylee gasped. "You created a Darkling."

Little Ed frowned. "And that thing killed Maurice."

Kaylee staggered a little before coming to rest against the creme-colored trunk, the tree's paper-like bark breaking off in large chunks. "Maurice is gone..."

"I'm really sorry. I didn't plan for any of this to happen." I gave the fiery Kaylee a wide berth. "I'll level with you. I made a deal with... Well, let's just say I made a really stupid deal to save my daughter from the fires of Hell. Now, as it turns out, I may have been duped, and to make matters worse there's a really good chance my daughter is still in Hell. I'd go find her myself, but your husband—"

"Ex-husband."

"Right, your *ex*-husband and his Demon Hunting crew split my soul and took my Magick along with it. So as you can see, I'm about as screwed as humanly possible. I've got no Magick, a supernatural deal in jeopardy, a teenager in Hell, and an apprentice who is most likely going to become target number one for a high-powered Darkling."

"He's not lying, Mom."

Thanks, kid.

Kaylee wiped her eyes with the back of her hand then adjusted her ball cap, brushing her hair back underneath it and trying to keep me from seeing the glint of tears in her eyes. "Goddamn Magicians."

"Right, like I said, I don't want to cause you two any more trouble than I already have. So if you'll just angle me toward civilization, the trail, path, or whatever you call it, I'll hike my non-Magickal butt right out of here. I'll square up my Darkling and in doing so find a way to untar Donnie and Ed. You have my word."

Kaylee reached down and picked up the pink plastic flamingo. She tucked it under her arm and shook her head. "Nope, you aren't going anywhere."

"Uh—"

"It'll be dark soon—evening comes fast in the Green Swamp. In here you're likely to drown, be eaten by an Alligator Man, or worse," she said. "Besides, you smell worse than Stinkstone. I think I've got some of Ed's old clothes that would fit you. You'd be doing me a favor getting rid of them."

"Wait, what about my apprentice? I need some way to contact him. I've got to warn the kid. I can sense the Magick coming off that staff. Do you have anything I could use, maybe a scrying pool?"

"Nope."

"What about some sort of messenger animal? Scrub Jays are chatty, but they'll get the message across."

Kaylee shook her head and walked deeper into the dense palmetto brush. "I don't do birds."

"Okay, okay. Let me think… What about seeing-stones?"

"All we have here is limestone."

"Damn it. I've got to get a message to him."

Kaylee pushed aside a frond with her staff. "Fine. I might have *something* you can use."

The ginger's face faded in the diminishing light making her a difficult read.

Is she smiling?

"Really? What? There's not a lot else I know of, but if you've got something Magickal we can use to get a message to him that would be huge."

"I've got something."

"What is it?"

"They call it 'the internet.'"

14
EMAIL MELTDOWN

*K*aylee and Little Ed led me deep into the Green Swamp, past thick copses of towering cedar, and around the muddy banks of suspiciously dark watering holes. We traveled until the sun slipped below the uneven tree line, Ed's ex-wife directing me to a set of uneven planks rising up out of the muck.

"Ed put them in years ago," she said with more than a hint of frustration in her voice. "God, he's terrible with his hands."

I took a few steps on that rising deck and immediately understood what she meant. Not only were the boards uneven, they were also not well secured, nor particularly balanced. I had to keep my eyes down to avoid falling through and ending up in the watery muck beneath. The deck gave way to stairs, the petite woman taking them with almost dancer-like precision as her slender feet found the strongest spots in the otherwise decaying wood.

I was not nearly as precise, but thankfully I had Little Ed behind me to keep me from falling in the deep water.

"We're here," he said, helping me up the last step.

Their house was small and less-than-inspiring, with a

crooked cedar shingle roof unlikely to hold back the rain. A wide front porch ran the length of the tiny home and slanted terribly to one side. Taking a fall on it was sure to put you in the murky water.

"What do you think?" Little Ed asked, pride in his voice.

"Kid, it beats the pants off sleeping in my car."

Kaylee dumped the plastic flamingo on the front porch alongside a growing pile of identical yard ornaments, then leaned her staff against a narrow cedar bench. I paused, half expecting the entire flock of plastic to slide into the swamp, but it only rustled slightly in the cool evening air.

Maybe they're just yard art?

Kaylee pulled open the weathered screen door and walked inside, holding it open for me.

"You don't lock your door?"

The Demon Hunter's mom shrugged her shoulders. "I don't get a lot of visitors."

The last rays of a setting sun snuck between the gaps in the sheer curtains that lined the tiny house's few windows.

"Give me a second." She fiddled with a glass hurricane lamp on one of the tables. It was one of the old types with a curved top and wide base full of a bright green fluid. She removed the smooth cover and fumbled with a plastic lighter until the filament ignited. The wick burned bright, filling the home with a warm and inviting glow.

"Gah!" She pointed to the muddy prints my shoes had tracked into her house. "Outside, now! Take those nasty things off and try coming back in like a civilized person."

This from the woman that talks to Trolls?

Little Ed's shoes were already outside the door.

Thanks for giving me the heads up, kid.

I returned in socks to find Ed's son sweeping the dried mud into a hole in the floor that led to the murky water below. Once he appeared satisfied with his work, he flipped the cover back down and returned the floor to normal.

"Here." Kaylee shoved jeans and a plaid shirt into my hands. "These should work. Don't worry about the peanut oil stains. It's impossible to find anything of Ed's that doesn't have them."

"Uh, thanks. Where do I…"

"Change? Wherever you want. I've seen it all before."

I rejoined my shoes on the front porch and clawed my way out of the mud-covered clothes. I clenched the photo wheel in my teeth, but not before stealing a glance at the images another time.

Even.

Eight pictures for the Darkling, and eight pictures for me. That meant I hadn't done anything stupid—yet.

I took a deep breath and enjoyed the relief that came from dumping wet threads on the edge of Kaylee's porch, but unlike the flamingos, my wadded-up duds slid down the deck and splashed into the water below.

Great.

That free feeling of standing practically naked in the dusky evening lasted all of ten seconds before the first mosquito found me. Ten seconds after that, one bug had become a few hundred. All of this was perfectly in line with the first law of vampire insects— there was never just one. I swatted at the troublesome mosquitos as I forced my way into Ed's old clothes. Kaylee was right, they 'fit,' but only in the loosest term of the word. Ed was thinner than me in some spots, and thicker in others. The end result left me with jeans that looked suspiciously like capris, and a plaid shirt whose sleeves I must have rolled up a half dozen times before I gave up.

Without waiting to see if I had pants on, Ed's ex-wife burst through the screen door and grabbed the latest plastic flamingo off the pile. She turned it over in her hands a few times before sighing and shoving it under an arm.

"You said you had internet here?" I asked, swatting at a small festival of mosquitos enjoying themselves on my exposed ankles.

"Inside."

Kaylee held up the yard ornament briefly, almost as if she was going to ask me something, but then thought better of it.

I tucked the picture disc in my pocket and headed back inside the tiny house leaving Ed's ex-wife outside. Inside, her son was busy setting up a small grey box that looked suspiciously like a typewriter on the table.

"Eddie?" I asked, eyeing the very non-technical device.

The junior Demon Hunter smiled. "Give me a second, I almost have the Mailstation set up."

"Mailstation?"

"I got this for my mom for her birthday."

"When? In the 1800s?"

"Very funny," Little Ed said, popping a switch on the side of the device and filling the room with a faint hum. "It's a dedicated email machine. You type here and it appears on the screen there."

The Mailstation's screen couldn't have been larger than a hardback's spine. It lit up with a bright green flashing cursor.

"You've got to be kidding me."

Little Ed shook his head. "No, listen, it works. I mean, you'll have to use Mom's email, but you can send a message to your apprentice."

I took a seat at the small table, Ed's Capri pants hugging my calves.

"You don't have a phone, eh?"

"Nope. Mom says they can give you brain cancer."

"I see… but you have the internet?"

Little Ed pointed up. "Satellite."

"I… Never mind. Thanks for getting it set up."

The junior Demon Hunter beamed. "Sure thing. I'm just glad it's getting some use. Mom never sends any emails."

Really? I find that shocking.

"I wonder why?" I said, my fingers over the keys.

"I know, right? I hear it's a great way to keep in touch."

Obviously sarcasm was not something the Lovelys had spent a lot of time teaching their son in between lessons on Demon Hunting and avoiding brain cancer.

To: magickman-adam@...

Subject:

I paused, unsure of what to write that wouldn't end up being discarded or considered spam. My apprentice was certainly tech savvy, but he was also apt to toss out an email from an address he'd never seen before.

In the end, I settled for being direct.

Subject: It's me, Gene Law. Open this damn email ASAP.

Message: I am writing to you from the Green Swamp. I am wearing a boiled peanut vending Demon Hunter's old flannel and have been Soul-Split. The Darkling is coming for you. Ignore all calls from me and get off your butt pronto. Come to...

"Hey, Eddie. Where are we?"

"Green Swamp."

"Damn it, I know that. I mean what's the closest city?"

"Lacoochee."

"Excuse me?"

"The closest city is Lacoochee."

He's never going to believe this. Maybe I should try to track down a Scrub Jay...

After a few attempts I gave up and asked Little Ed to spell it for me.

Come to Lacoochee. Yes it's a real place. I'll find a way to meet you there. Bring the large box in the back of the storage facility. We're going to need it.

I paused again, this time wondering what the right closing

should be. For a second time that night, I settled on direct.

- Gene

PS - Why are you still sitting? Go, now!

I pressed the bright red *send* button on the tiny keyboard and chuckled. The junior Demon Hunter had been right, it really wasn't that hard to use.

ERROR - MESSAGE EXCEEDED MAXIMUM LENGTH.

Fifteen attempts later, both I and the Mailstation keyboard had just about reached our breaking point. As I would later discover, the tiny email box must have been made by the same jerk who had come up with the minuscule character limit for social media posts. In the end my message had more in common with a kidnapper's demands than any well-conceived missive.

Message: No Magick. Stuck in Green Swamp. Bring self and big storage box. Avoid me. Bad Magick. Go to Lacoochee. Not fake place. Y U no leave? Go! -Gene

I held my breath and pressed the send button, waiting for the tiny device to give me the digital middle finger again.

SENDING...

The smell of cooking meat snaked its way past my frustration filters and suddenly reminded me how long it had been since I last ate a real meal.

"Eddie? What are you cooking?"

The junior Demon Hunter's head appeared around the edge of the tiny array of kitchen cabinets. "Gator."

"Of course you are. Where's your mom?" I asked, now acutely aware I hadn't received a snarky comment questioning my actions in quite a while.

"I thought she was with you."

"No. I left her outside…"

The sound of water splashing against the underside of the house caught us both off guard.

"What was that?" I asked, pushing back from the table.

"Probably just a catfish going after something."

Thump, thump, thump.

Something heavy hit the rickety steps outside; in fact, it sounded a lot more like many somethings. Each thump shook the tiny house and sent the ancient Mailstation one step closer to shimmying off the table all together.

Little Ed appeared from the kitchen, a steaming platter of fluffy white meat in hand. "What's that?"

"Damn it, Eddie, it's your house, I don't—"

I froze mid sentence, my words lost to the reflection of unblinking eyes in the inky darkness beyond the screen door. Those Golden globes caught the hurricane lamp's shine and reflected it back with a reptilian sparkle.

The junior Demon Hunter set his platter down. "Gene…"

"I see them."

Alligator Men.

15

FIRE AND FLOWERS

*A*lligator Men were a throwback to an all-but-forgotten era in Florida. Much like their traditional relatives, they held more in common with the dinosaur than the modern supernatural beasts that made the Sunshine State their home. Simply put, Alligator Men had been here first, and they'd probably still be here long after the rest of us were gone.

Possessing the broad snout of a classic American alligator and the scale-covered body of a human being, they were quite a sight to see. In fact, I'd argued in the early days at the University of Florida that our mascot was actually a classic Alligator Man, most likely inspiring the early founders of the state's oldest university.

At the time Morgan thought I was crazy—I was, but I still think I was right about the mascot.

I had plenty of time to contemplate these and other thoughts as I swung from straps tied to a cypress sapling. It wasn't a very dignified way to travel, but Alligator Men weren't known for their illustrious transportation options. Little Ed dangled from a second sapling, his arms and legs also tied up like a Christmas pig, but his head bounced loose—he'd been knocked out cold before we'd left his mom's house. In doing so, he provided a valuable safety tip: do not be serving gator meat when Alligator Men show up to kidnap you.

Tall reeds slapped against my back. Mercifully, the Alligator Men appeared to be avoiding the deep water, which meant while I'd still get wet, I wouldn't drown.

I tried to get a count of how many reptiles we were dealing with, but in the relative dark of the swamp that quickly became impossible; instead, I spent my time ruminating on just how bad things had gotten in such a short period.

Catherine was still in Hell, my Magick was walking around in an infinitely cooler version of myself ready to tear Adam the apprentice a new one, and two members of the Three Musketeers were now Midnight Riders.

Am I missing anything?

"Yes, you are missing the part where you promised you'd help me get to Heaven, Sir."

Private Petty!

The ghostly soldier walked next to me, the soft glow of his spiritual form casting a faint light on my captors.

"Right. Sorry, Private. I did promise you I'd do something."

"Sir, you promised me you would 'make it right.'"

Sigh. I did, didn't I?

"Yes. You did."

"Okay, first things first, Private. You stop listening to my thoughts. You got it?"

"They are very loud."

"Get used to it, Private. Just stop answering them."

"Sir, yes, sir."

The Alligator Men hauled us deeper into the Green Swamp, and before long my back began dragging through shallow water.

"Is his head above water?" I said, directing Private Petty toward the unconscious Little Ed.

"It would appear so… at least most of the time."

Great. Let's hope he's just breathing most of the time too.

"He does appear to be breathing."

"Private!"

"Sir, yes, sir."

"Why don't you make yourself useful and cut us down?"

The young ghost drew his saber and slashed down at the straps holding me aloft—his blade passed through them without making so much as a nick.

"Huh, it would appear—"

"Right, that's what I figured. These guys aren't Magickal. How could they be? They're Alligator Men. Heck, they're more Florida than we are."

The ghost returned his saber to its scabbard and tilted his head. "What do you want me to do, then, aside from not listening to your extraordinarily loud thoughts?"

The reptiles carrying me turned a tight corner and slammed my ribs against the rough bark of a large live oak.

"Ugh. Since I'm stuck here slowly losing all feeling in my fingers, why don't you entertain me with the sure-to-be-fascinating yarn of how you ended up dying outside the Florida National Cemetery and not being buried inside it?"

"It isn't something I prefer to talk about."

"Private, I'm swinging from a cypress sapling suspended above what I can only hope is water, and I'm being buffeted by the smell of two Alligator Men that appear to have been boycotting hygiene since forever. Give me something to take my mind off all this. Also, if I'm going to get you to your final destination, I'm going to need to know how you got stuck."

"I see," the young ghost said, though his tone indicated otherwise.

"Humor me, Private."

The pensive ghost frowned and appeared to be taking a moment to absorb the gravity of my situation before continuing.

"Where would you like me to start, sir?"

"The beginning."

"Right, I was born on—"

"Private?"

"Yes?"

"Let's skip ahead to the part when you died."

"It was a car accident."

I opened my mouth to respond, but the brown hotdog-like ends of a clump of cattails slapped against my face like a chorus line, forcing me to spit out more than a few noxious pollen pods before I could continue. "A little more detail, please?"

The young man positively squirmed in his fatigues. "Sir, I'd prefer not to say."

"Fine," I said, twisting my head to avoid a patch of sharp Sawgrass hellbent on cutting a line through my neck. "If you won't tell me, I'll guess. Let's see... drunk driving? Is that it, Private? You got so plastered one night after celebrating your umpteenth saber trophy that you careened off the road and ran into a ditch at high speed."

"No!"

"I didn't think so."

"I mean, no, I did not get drunk, and there was no careening."

The Alligator Men turned again, this time evening out my bruised ribs by bumping the opposite side against a sap-covered pine trunk.

"Fine, Private Petty. I'll go with door number two. You had some 'special ladies' and were out driving fast to show off. Trying to get them all hot and bothered so you could take them back to the Petty-pad and peel off their painted-on clothes with the majestic splendor of your fencing trophies."

Private Petty's face softened, and he looked away.

Are those tears in his eyes?

"No way," I said, craning my head to get a better look at the young ghost. "Is that really it?"

"Sir, there were two ladies in the car."

"Ha! I knew it. You're a handsome devil I'm not—"

"They were my wife and unborn daughter."

Oh, crap.

My already exhausted stomach churned, and rightfully so.

"I'm... Uh, shoot. I'm sorry."

"It was my fault. I did not see the deer until it was right in front of the car."

"Kid, it was a deer," I said, scrambling to improve the sullen kid's demeanor. "They're like headlight magnets, it could have happened to anyone. You can't blame yourself."

"With all due respect, you don't know the whole story."

"You're right. I'm sorry, please continue."

The orange light of a roaring fire washed over me, complete with the crackle of wet wood and the acrid scent of burning cedar.

"Sir," Private Petty said, his ghostly form fading quickly. "I don't think we have time to go into this right now. You appear to have arrived at your destination."

"Crap. What can you see?"

The stoic ghost squinted in the firelight and shook his head slowly. "That's a really large fire."

"I got that part. What else?"

The Alligator Men carrying me slowed down.

Private Petty craned his neck, even as he faded further into the dark evening air. "There's a very large reptile monster, sir."

"That would be the Bull Gator. What else?"

"Is there something in particular I should be looking for? I would assume the fire is a big enough deal, sir."

"Not necessarily. The Bull Gator, is he wearing any flowers?"

"Flowers?"

"Alligator Men love orchids—they use them in all sorts of ceremonies. Listen, I dealt with these guys in the Everglades a few years ago. Most of the time I could work out a deal with them—granted that was when I had my Magick—but all of that is dependent on whether they are in 'sacrificial mode' or not."

"I see, sir. How would one determine if they were in 'sacrificial mode'?"

The ground underneath my captors rose up gently, telling me we must be getting close to the mound. "The Ghost Orchid, is the Bull Gator wearing a Ghost Orchid?"

"What is a Ghost Orchid?"

"Damn it, Private. Is he wearing a big white flower around his neck?"

There was a long pause, and then the final vestiges of Private Petty faded from view. "There's a…"

And like that, the pain-in-my-ass spirit vanished.

"Petty!"

"Gene!" Little Ed shouted, waking up just in time for both of us to be tossed on the muddy ground. "What's going on?"

An immense Bull Gator loomed over us, his impressive jaws doing little to hide the ferocity behind those golden eyes. Behind that enormous Alligator Man a bonfire roared, outlining him in a hellish orange glow; none of that mattered, however, not even the bright white necklace of woven Ghost Orchids dangling from his thick neck.

My brain blotted all that out, and instead focused on a single image, a tiny piece of the crazy puzzle that was my life. Tucked under a loop of animal hide that functioned as a make-shift belt was the cover of a book I didn't think I'd ever see again.

Ten Spins' Infernal Constructs.

The old volume had been stolen from me by the young Magician responsible for cutting my daughter's silver thread and stranding her in Hell. It also happened to be the same Magician I'd spent the last few months tracking up one side the state and down the other—Tristan Shelldeck.

Son of a bitch...

SINS OF THE FATHER

*S*omewhere fate was laughing at me.

A hush fell over the Alligator Men. My newly prone position gave me an opportunity to count up just how screwed we were.

Twenty-eight, twenty-nine...

By my best guess, we were thirty-plus Alligator Men past completely screwed. That was only a guess, though—it was likely far worse.

"Gene," Little Ed asked, shimmying over to try to get my attention. "You have a plan, right?"

"I'm working on it."

Can't let the kid know I have no idea what to do. If you're listening Private Petty, you need to clamp that mouth shut.

The Bull Gator's gravelly voice rumbled over the assembled tribesmen and women. I figured there must have been Alligator Women in attendance, but I was not about to go checking undercarriages—I was already in more than enough trouble as it was.

"Can you speak Alligator Man?" Little Ed asked, his fingers already tugging at the restraints.

"If I had my Magick, sure, but I never bothered to learn it. I mean, how often do you need something like Alligator Man?"

"Damn," the young Demon Hunter said. "Would've been really useful right about now."

"You're the one that grew up in the Green Swamp. You're telling me you don't understand what he's saying?"

One of the Alligator Men that had been tasked with carrying us noticed Little Ed's attempt at escape and placed a scaly foot on top of his fingers.

Crunch.

"Argh!" Little Ed's cry cut off the Bull Gator's speech and drew the attention of the surrounding tribesmen.

"Hey," I said, directing my attention to the reptilian horde. "Why don't you overgrown yard lizards untie us so we can sort this out like men?"

My only response was the crackling of the bonfire and the occasional cricket.

"… or maybe we could sort this out like Alligator Men? I'm completely open to both. However, before we do I'd like to know what the heck happened to the scrawny little pain-in-my-ass carrying that book?" I said, pointing my head at the grimoire dangling from the Bull Gator's belt.

"Gene," Little Ed said, his voice ragged. "I don't think they understand us."

"I think you're right, kid."

The Bull Gator resumed what I assumed was a cleverly worded and inspiring speech; of course, he could also have been reciting his favorite ways to consume raw chicken, I had no way of telling the difference. Scaly hands grabbed our poles and hoisted the young Demon Hunter and I back up into the air.

"Where do you think they're taking us?" Ed's son asked, concern in his eyes.

For the first time that night I noticed just how young and

scared my companion was. Had my old roommate kept him away from the bulk of this terrifying occupation?

We swung back and forth between the assembled Alligator Men, giving me an opportunity to get a glimpse of where we were headed—I didn't like it.

"Okay, so I have good news," I said, the heat of the fire starting to dry the water from my borrowed flannel.

"You do?"

"Yes. There's very little chance of us coming back as lost spirits."

"Why is that?" the younger man said, swinging side to side behind me as the Alligator Men hauled him toward the fire.

"Because I don't think they'll leave any bones behind."

The humanoid reptiles positioned two makeshift spits across the roaring fire. It wasn't a stretch of the imagination to guess where we were headed.

"You guys realize you're going to cook us unevenly, right? With this set-up you won't be able turn us properly—I grill, I know. You're going to end up with one side blackened, and the other terribly undercooked. This whole thing is borderline unsafe, actually."

The heat from the fire was strong enough to force me to close my eyes and turn away.

Private Petty, get your translucent backside out here on the double. I need some options, kid. That's an order.

Much to my frustration, the junior spirit did not appear.

"Plan," Little Ed cried, tugging on his restraints "What's the plan?"

"Give me a minute... I'm working on it."

"In a minute we'll be roasting."

Damn it, kid. You don't think I know that? Any other time I'd use my Magick.

I knew it wasn't there, but I reached for it just the same. I pushed past the borrowed jeans, chafing underwear, and uncomfortably warm flesh. Typically, there was a reserve of power down there, more than enough to help me bend a little reality, and barring that, at least coax it into something a little more amenable.

That well was dry.

"Gene!"

I tried to blot out the junior Demon Hunter's voice and closed my eyes to scrape at the walls of my reserves. There had to be something, anything, down there. Little Ed and I were ill prepared for dangling over a roaring bonfire—we needed help, and fast.

"Pluvium…" I whispered, desperately hoping whatever vestiges of Magick the Darkling had left me with would be enough.

We need rain.

"Pluvium!" I squeezed at my soul like an old tube of tooth-paste and pushed whatever was left into a final butt-saving act.

Nothing happened.

My arms went limp as the Alligator Men hoisted my pole onto the spit. "Sorry, kid."

Maybe this is for the best.

A large and cold raindrop hit me smack between the eyes.

What the?!

That one was followed by another, then another still, and in seconds the splattering rain had become a typical summer downpour. I don't care how good your fire is, none of them survives a Florida rain.

"You did it, Gene!"

I did? Just go with it.

"Yeah, I did…"

"No, you didn't," Kaylee of the Green Swamp shouted from her perch atop Stinkstone. The Troll-riding Witch appeared at the edge of the Alligator Men village, an old and torn umbrella in her hands. Rain poured through the holes in that umbrella, soaking the ginger-haired woman beneath it. You didn't have to be an expert Magician to feel the Magick coming off that largely ineffective rain gear.

"Mom!"

Kaylee whispered something to Stinkstone before being gently placed down beside the monstrous Troll.

The Alligator Men appeared unsure of what to do, and turned their attention to the Bull Gator. It was difficult to read Alligator Man body language, but I was pretty sure he was pissed—really, super pissed, truth be told.

"Thanks for the help," I said, using my head to gesture to the straps holding my arms. "Any chance you could get these undone too?"

Kaylee ignored me and instead focused all of her attention on the Bull Gator. She said something in what I assumed was her very high-pitched version of the guttural grunts of the Alligator Men.

The Bull Gator hissed, the sound of which set the un-singed hairs on my arms at attention.

That can't be good.

The large reptile then responded to her with a series of grunts and clicks.

"What is he saying?" I asked, shaking the rain from my face.

Kaylee frowned. "He's saying you stole his children."

"I've done some pretty terrible things, but kidnapping baby alligators isn't something I'm known for."

"Was it your Darkling?" Little Ed asked, reminding me of my lesser half.

Kaylee's attention never wavered from the Bull Gator. She took a few steps forward, then changed the tone of her unintelligible words.

"What did you tell him?"

Kaylee closed the umbrella, the rain coming to a gradual

stop. "I told him you could not have kidnapped his children, because you are too weak and spineless."

"Works for me."

The Bull Gator growled and pulled the grimoire from his belt. He held the book in the air for Kaylee and the rest of his tribe to see.

"Is that your book?" Kaylee asked, her words taking on an edge I hadn't noticed before. Her fingers tightened ever so slightly against her staff.

"Yes, but it was stolen from me. Tell him a junior Magician took it and—"

Kaylee cut me off with her hand. "The person who snatched his eggs carried that book, and it smells like you."

I twisted my head around to get a good look at the Bull Gator. "Of course it smells like me. It has been in my house since college. How could it *not* smell like me? I bet it smells like Tristan too. Tell him that's the smell he should be looking for. Once he finds that twerp, though, he needs to get in line, because I have first dibs on the cord-cutting, book-stealing, Defiler-serving weasel."

"Gene," Kaylee said, her voice now certainly far less commanding than it was before. "That's not how Alligator Men work."

"Oh yeah? How do they work?"

I was too busy paying attention to Little Ed's mom to notice my captor slice through my bonds and drop me on the rain-soaked ground. The sudden impact took the air right out of my lungs.

Son of a bitch.

Kaylee waited for me to stand before answering. "If you won't accept responsibility for the thief's actions, then you must fight."

I shook out my sleeves and pushed them up again. "Wait, I must what?"

One of the Alligator Men that had been carrying the pole shoved a rickety spear into my hands.

"I warn you. I have decades of spear experience. Decades!" I shouted, hoping to set my opponent on edge, but, given my undersized capris and oversized flannel that plan had little chance of success.

Angry bubbles broke the surface of the water not far from the now extinguished barbecue pit.

"I don't know how to translate it," Kaylee said, backing up. "I believe they call it Grundel?"

Bright orange eyes broke the surface, big as basketballs and set atop a head that would have no problems swallowing me whole.

Oh, great.

17

DINO DIVE

*W*hat had been a few bubbles quickly turned to a frothing torrent of choppy swamp water, and I was reminded of my wife's take on hot tubs.

'Oh no, Gene. Not gonna happen. God only knows what lives in there, and you want me to get in it knowing the only thing between me and that slime is a thin slip of spandex? Hell no, you'll need a new wife for that.'

I didn't have a new wife, but I didn't have Porter either. What I did have was a slightly annoying spirit eavesdropping on my thoughts, a crude spear, and my winning personality.

Yep, I was clearly ready to face whatever was rising up from the algae-choked depths.

Private Petty? You there? Any chance you know how to use a spear?

Once again the young, dead soldier displayed an exceptional prowess for disappearing at just the right times.

Ah, to be a kid again.

Glowing golden eyes broke the surface of the water, riding high on the head of the largest alligator I'd ever seen. Even without the benefit of a roaring bonfire to light up the water it wasn't hard to guess the sheer enormity of this prehistoric reptile. Its head alone was certain to provide nightmare material for months to come.

A snake-like and whipping tail propelled the beast forward, cutting a sharp line through the thick swamp water. Its white teeth shone like steak knives in the filtered moonlight. They jutted out along the creature's closed jaws, clearly visible against the dark scales.

"Uh, is that a Grundel?"

A not-so-gentle shove to the back gave me my answer.

"I think so," Kaylee the Swamp Witch said, leaning against her staff. "Gene, are you feeling that?"

I tightened my grip on the spear. "The overwhelming sense of soul-crushing defeat and disappointment at a life unfulfilled? Completely."

"No," Kaylee tilted her head as if she were tasting the air, "there, do you feel it now?"

"I don't feel any—"

A lancing cold sliced straight through me, cutting off my words mid-sentence. Even mostly dried out from the previous fire dangling experience, I wasn't ready for the wildly unpredictable Magick of a Thinning.

Florida's precarious position at the geometrically perfect center of the real world and the supernatural one made it an excellent home for all manner of non-native flora and fauna, and we weren't talking transplants from New York either. Only in the Strange Shine State could a single night include Alligator Men, Bridge Trolls, Midnight Riders, and even a late-nineties-era Mailstation—but there was something else Florida had in abundance: Thinnings.

Those supernatural bald patches served as a bridge between our world and the great beyond. They appeared at random and had a habit of flooding the surrounding area with Wild Magick. Sometimes they'd go completely unnoticed, appearing and disappearing just long enough to eat a sock from your dryer or run a cold chill down your spine, but other times they'd appear at the most inopportune moments, such as when you were face to snout with a mythological super-gator you'd only just discovered was a thing.

"Crap, that's so not what I need right now," I said, pointing to the advancing dinosaur. "Dance card is kinda full and all."

Another poke to the ribs pushed me closer to the water's edge and refocused my attention on the throwback opponent from the Cretaceous period. Grundel would have made even the largest of alligators question their place in the food chain. He was bigger than the Dad Wagon and most likely did not leak oil.

The monster hissed and took the wind right out of my already drooping sails. I tightened my grip on the spear and tried to remember those episodes of American Gladiators I'd watched when Cathy was little.

How do they swing these things?

"Use the pointy end, sir."

Private Petty's spectral form appeared next to me, his fatigues traded out for a more Rambo-like black tank and red bandana.

"Sly? Really?"

"It was a favorite movie as a kid."

"Great. Listen, I'm all for hearing about your childhood—I really am—but right now I'm trying to keep us alive."

Petty shrugged. "I'm already dead."

The Grundel opened his massive jaws and hissed again, this time sending the Alligator men into a tizzy—they'd clearly bet on the home team.

"Don't be smart with me, Private."

"Sir, yes, sir," the ghost said with a very visible smirk.

"Do you know how to do a possession?"

"A what?"

"A possession," I said, holding the spear between myself and the oversized gator. "You know, where you go into my body and take over my consciousness to fight off this Dinosaur World showpiece."

Grundel's tail flicked in the water, sending a wake rolling toward the far shore.

Private Petty frowned. "That sounds immensely dangerous."

The prehistoric alligator reached the banks and pushed his bulk forward. Massive claws cut deep grooves in the muck.

"For me maybe, but not for you. You're dead, remember?"

"Jump!" Private Petty shouted, scaring the crap out of me just in time to kick on my survival instinct and send me lunging out of the way of Grundel's snapping jaws.

The assembled Alligator Men hissed and growled in what I assumed was high praise for their champion.

"Faster than it looks," I cried, slipping in the soft mud and scrambling to my feet before the beast's claws prematurely ended my evening.

Petty pointed to Grundel's bright golden orbs. "Go for the eyes."

"Could you find a harder spot to reach?"

I jabbed the off-balance spear at the beast's head, but instead of catching one of those glittering eyes, the spear missed badly and bounced off its rock-hard scales.

"I think they gave me a bum spear," I said, high-stepping back to avoid the beast's jaws.

"I would recommend an M4, or at worst a decent sidearm, sir."

I jabbed with the spear again, missing badly. "This from the kid who carries a saber."

Kaylee's high-pitched voice cut through the guttural chants of the Alligator Men. "Who the hell are you talking to?"

I dodged another swiping claw, but not before it sliced a few crisp lines through my borrowed flannel.

"Private Casper!" I shouted back, not willing to take my eyes off the scaly beast. "I'll explain later."

"Eye, sir. Jab now!"

"You're State Fencing Champion and the best you can come up with is 'go for the eyes'?"

"Sir!"

"On it." I tucked the Alligator Man's spear under my arm and drove it forward like a lance.

What the hell am I doing?

One thing became very clear immediately—I was *not* the State Fencing Champ, nor was I apt to become one any time soon.

The spear tip missed Grundel's eye entirely, and instead slipped between its open jaws, bouncing off those ferocious teeth like a pinball before careening out the other side.

"Don't let him pull you—" Kaylee shouted, but her shrill voice didn't survive my sudden and graceless splash into the dark water. The butt of the spear had hooked itself on the tail edge of her ex-husband's flannel shirt, and that borrowed clothing had now tied me to a living boat anchor.

"Gene!"

I couldn't tell who shouted that one; with the swamp water swirling around my ears it was impossible to discern much beyond the frothing bubbles. Thankfully, I did have the foresight to grab one very large gulp of air before being dragged under.

And this morning had started out with so much promise...

If I'd thought Grundel on land was scary, in the water the beast was a force of nature. He pulled me toward the bottom with brain-bending speed while I fought to dislodge the spear. Sadly, the hooked flannel held fast, so I switched gears. I yanked at the buttons of Ed's evil shirt before it became my burial shroud. I had the first few undone when the massive beast took a hard turn, most likely avoiding some obstacle, and failed to account for the Gene Law hood ornament riding shotgun.

I crashed into what felt like a tree trunk with spear-snapping force, leaving me with a splintered stick and no idea which way was up.

I really should have watched those nature shows with Kris when I'd had the chance.

I blinked my eyes and tried to adjust to the dark water. A small amount of moonlight filtered down, but I was still too disoriented to trust it; plus, if I swam for the surface I was sure to die a horrible death at the business end of Grundel's crushing jaws.

That's a pleasant thought.

Then again, if I stayed clinging to this trunk, I was certain to pass out from lack of oxygen, *then* be crushed by those massive jaws.

Way to stay inspired, Gene.

A rush of water roared past my dangling feet, and I pulled them in tight. What air I'd grabbed before being yanked in was starting to run out, the painful thumping in my chest telling me as much.

Come on, damn it. If you are going to eat me just get it over with.

Another whooshing current sent my short hair streaming to the side, and I ducked down just in time for the massive alligator to shoot past my head.

Now you're just playing with your food.

My lungs burned—evolution's handy way of reminding me I did not have gills—and I tightened my grip on the broken spear shiv.

Come on, one more pass. You can do it.

A rush of water hit my chest just as two bright orange eyes lit up the murky water. With my legs tucked under me, I kicked out like a kid at the summer camp pool, using my meager muscles to propel me up and over its wide jaws.

My legs cleared the snout scant inches before it would have shattered me like old china, but somehow the trailing cuff of Ed's too-short jeans ended up caught on Grundel's teeth. The monster chose that exact moment to dive for the bottom, throwing me chest first against his head and costing me the spear shiv as well as a few more precious air bubbles.

No, go the other way!

Monster truck Grundel didn't hear me, nor would he have cared if he had. The prehistoric alligator and I had a date with freshwater version of Davey Jones' Locker, and he wasn't interested in showing up late.

My ears popped and my lungs screamed as the dark water raced past, and in my oxygen-deprived haze I wondered if borrowed pants were going to do me in. I'd survived countless clashes with supernatural monsters, Demons, and the Restless Dead, but it certainly appeared for all the world that I would meet my end thanks to some annoyingly undersized denim.

Stupid pants.

18

STAND IN ME

We hit the bottom—hard.

Grundel wasted no time going into a spectacular death roll. Traditional alligators have a tough time with large prey, and while there was very little about me that Grundel would find large, it was safe to assume basic instinct had taken over. The death roll was aptly named in that it was the moment the gator took you to the bottom and rolled, effectively pinning you to the ground until you ran out of air and promptly drowned.

That last part I was keen to avoid.

Grundel spun, slamming me against what felt like an old metal car door. A flash of reflection as the mud washed away from the side-view mirror confirmed my suspicion.

My lungs were quick to remind me they'd been working overtime and were just about at empty, when something appeared in the mirror.

That something was small, purple, rubbery, and all together annoying.

Stewart!

The Imp's words echoed in my head as if we were talking.

"Boss, what are you doing? Oh, wow, is that Deinosuchus? I haven't seen one of those since the late Cretaceous period. Would you look at that? I mean, had to be Florida, am I right?

Stewart, this isn't the time.

"Yeah, I can see that. Did you go for his eyes?" the tiny Imp asked, his reflection pointing at Grundel's bright, orange reptilian pupils.

Again with the eyes! I swear you and Private Petty are going to be the death of me.

"Who's Private Petty? You didn't get another Imp, did you? Oh I'll be so—"

Stewart! Can you get me out of here or not?

"Oh, yeah, no. I'm sorry, I can't. I'm just using this lovely Thinning to make it a little easier to talk to you. Listen, so, I've got some great news."

I fought to hold on to the last bits of precious oxygen.

What?!

"I know where Cathy is."

My heart skipped a beat.

Where?

"Okay, so she's at the Tower of Unceasing Torment. Now, it sounds worse than it is. Well, no, it really is that bad, but... at least I know where she is, so, there's that."

Argh!

"Right. Listen, we're going to get it figured out, but if you should have some sort of army that would be really good. Or perhaps just your Magick—hey, where did your Magick go?"

Soul... split...

"Damn. No fooling?"

I kicked at Grundel, but his massive bulk kept me pinned to the car door.

No... fooling...

"Well ain't that just a pisser. Oh, crap." the tiny Imp looked away briefly before returning to me. "Looks like I've got company. I'm sure you have this well in hand..."

Save... her...

"Yes, boss. That's what I'm doing. Gotta run. Oh, one last thing. Why don't you try using the Thinning? It's Wild Magick, but it beats drowning—gotta run!"

With that the tiny Imp vanished from the mirror.

The Thinning... Wild Magick.

You didn't just go using Wild Magick without consequences, or at least without making sure your will was up to date.

My lungs let me know it was this or sprout gills, so I did what any other self-respecting Magician in my situation would have done. I shoved my hand in the pocket of Ed's jeans and wrapped my fingers around the remains of Private Petty's road-side marker.

"Infestous!" I shouted, giving up all but the last of my air in a single burst.

The Wild Magick of the Thinning surged through me. I tried to control it, but Wild Magick was wild for a reason, and it wanted very little to do with my attempts to coerce it.

Just like Stewart before him, Private Petty's voice boomed in my head.

"Sir, what is going on?"

Possession... stab... gator... please.

"This is very unorthodox and I can't say I'm in agreement with your chosen course of action—"

Die... together... then.

White-hot anger surged in my arms and I found them grabbing the side-view mirror, then yanking the entire assembly out of its rusted frame. It was a strange sensation having Private Petty running the show, but I had to admit the kid was effective.

Wild Magick roared as together we slammed the metal arm of that mirror down on Grundel's head. It skipped across his boney scales before plunging deep into a glowing golden eye.

Nice...

Private Petty wasn't done. He unbuttoned the loaner jeans and shimmied out of them, then kicked with whatever we had left to drive the spike deep into Grundel's tiny gray matter.

Wait... reconciliation... wheel.

I fought to get control away from the Private, willing him to go back for the pants, the pocket of which held the burned remnants of the picture disc from the Viewmaster that split my soul.

"Those photos or your life. We don't have enough oxygen for both."

Wheel... is... life.

The Private kicked off, pushing us toward the surface, but I wasn't willing to let the pants go without a fight.

Animus...

The Wild Magick fought me, resisting my efforts, so I pushed harder, even as the denim faded from view below me.

Animus.

The Thinning was closing—whatever I hoped to achieve I wasn't going to succeed if I didn't hurry.

Animus!

For an instant, I thought I saw the pants move, but Private Petty turned my attention to the surface and the silvery moonlight that broke through large lily pads. We erupted beneath the thin layer of algae that covered the swamp water, gasping for breath in the cool night air.

Private Petty's rugged determination had been enough to get us to the surface, but it took our combined efforts to dog paddle toward the shore.

"Gene!" Little Ed shouted, his voice breaking the stunned silence of the Alligator Men.

Private Petty urged my body toward the young Demon Hunter's voice, pushing me forward with each stroke.

"You can do it, sir."

Thanks, kid.

Together we half-swam and half-crawled the last few yards, then collapsed on the bank gasping for air.

The Thinning waned and took with it the Wild Magick fueling my control over the deceased Private.

"Time… to… get out," I said, urging the ghost toward the mental door.

"There are still too many threats, sir."

"Private!"

Before I knew it Private Petty had me on my feet. Sure, I had no pants, but the young fencing champ made sure I had a perfectly balanced ghostly saber in my hands.

"The chief represents our main threat, and once he's neutralized then we can move to the next step."

I shook my head and fought against the stubborn spirit. "No, he lost his children."

Private Petty raised my hand and the saber with it. "He is a threat and must be stopped."

For his part the Bull Gator appeared stunned. It's not every day your champion gets beaten in his own lair, and you're left with a pantsless ex-Magician.

"Private, stand down."

My words fell on deaf ears. The young soldier pushed me toward the Bull Gator, imaginary lines of possible thrusts and feints filling my vision. With the last of the Wild Magick fading it took with it any chance I had to push the ghost back out, and it didn't take long for Private Petty to figure that out.

"Stop fighting me," the spirit said. "You know this is for the best. I will save us both, and then—"

"And then what? Then you go on a murder spree? No amount of death is going to bring your wife and daughter back."

The young soldier slowed, his will slipping.

"You aren't safe. I can make you safe. I can make all of you safe. I…"

"Private, stand down. That's an order."

"Sir." Private hesitated and with it his saber drooped. "All I ever wanted to do was keep them safe. You have to understand that."

"I do, Private. I do. I had a family too once. I know what sacrifice is."

The pit of my stomach collapsed as the sorrowful spirit of Private Petty let go. Without the strong soldier's will to keep me upright, I dropped to my knees in front of the Bull Gator and did my best to not look completely helpless.

The last of the Thinning dissipated like fog burned off in the sun, leaving me pants-less, sword-less, and without my Magick in front of the Bull Gator.

Well, Private, I hope to hell this is the right call.

"I do too, sir."

19

MAIL TIME

"I still can't believe it, and I was there!" an excitable Little Ed said, pushing apart a stumpy clump of saw palmetto so I could get by. "I thought for sure you were a goner."

"So did I." I willed my exhausted legs to take me past the little green palm bushes without further damage to the loaner jeans.

"Mom, did you—"

"Yes, Eddie." Kaylee's voice was sharp and more than a little stern when she cut off her son mid-sentence. "I was there. I saw the pants rise out of the water and walk their way up the shore."

"That was amazing! Scared the heck out of the Alligator Men, and me… but only for a few seconds."

I smiled—it was pretty damn impressive, even for me.

Right from the beginning I'd figured there was little chance of reasoning with a very pissed-off chief, but I hadn't been about to let Private Petty cut him down. He may have been scaly and terrifying, but he was also a dad, and that's a pain I knew all too well.

"You channeled Wild Magick from that Thinning," Kaylee said, her stern voice tightening up a few notches. "Do you know how insane that was?"

"I do."

The Swamp Witch turned back to face me, fire in her eyes. "I don't think you do. That was Wild Magick—you had no idea what it could have done. Just because you did it once, and made yourself a pair of walking pants in the process, doesn't mean it won't blow up in all our faces the next time."

"There won't be a next time," I said, carefully avoiding a series of large mounds certain to be riddled with sleeping fire ants.

"And how do you know that?"

"I know that because I still have this," I said, holding up the burnt and soaking photo wheel. "I'm going to put my soul back together, and when I do, I won't need to hunt and peck for Wild Magick. I'll be *me.*"

I checked the images again. I didn't know exactly how, but I'd gained a square on my evil half. Nine memories against seven black squares—I'll take it.

"You lost the Viewmaster. You said it yourself. They were destroyed by your Darkling, unmade in the truck bed of the peanut hauler."

"I've got a couple options. Don't worry about me."

Just get here in one piece, Adam...

Kaylee rolled her eyes and slapped aside a dense rosemary bush with her staff. "I don't."

We continued to trudge through the scrub-brush swamp for what felt like hours. It was exhausting work, even with the spring in my step provided by the Magickal capris. I was all but spent from my fight with Grundel and with Private Petty, but to the victor went the spoils, I had my life, the picture disc... and Ten Spins' book.

When the possessed pants had risen out of the swamp water like a B-movie monster, the Alligator Men scattered. Maybe it had been the possessed denim, but more likely it had been the sudden loss of Grundel that rocked their reptilian world.

Either way, none of us had hung around long enough for a post-mortem briefing.

I squeezed the dense book under my arm. It was more than a treatise on terrifying Magick of nigh-epic proportions—it was also my link to Tristan Shelldeck. Once I had my power back the first order of business was going to be tracking down that kid, and I was going to use the book to do it.

Little Ed scampered across a fallen cypress that formed a makeshift bridge above the muck before stopping to confront his mom. "Where did you go?"

"What do you mean where did I go?" the Swamp Witch said, crossing the log and using her staff for support when needed. "I was there the whole time."

"Not at the house you weren't. I set Gene up with the Mail-station and by the time we turned around you were gone."

"I had something to attend to, that's all."

"Did that something have anything to do with all those plastic pink flamingos you have on the porch?" I asked, easing over the slippery tree with mud-covered feet.

"It's not your concern."

"Like hell it's not," I said after reaching the other side, damn happy to not have fallen in. "I've seen flocks like that before. I know how they happen, and I have the distinct impression you don't."

Kaylee pressed forward, knocking aside low branches in the process. "I do not need, nor want your help. They're trash, that's all. Some kids must be playing around in the deep swamp and they left those damn things behind."

"Oh yeah? Kids bring plastic birds to the Green Swamp now? Is that a thing?"

Kaylee ignored me, and instead stomped through the under-brush, laying waste to a small patch of ghostly, green deer moss.

"I'm going to guess that's a no," I said, happy to have what remained of the soft and spongy moss under my tired feet. "If it is the Flock you're going to need to tread lightly."

We broke through the last line of vegetation and arrived at Kaylee's swamp house for the second time tonight.

"Eddie, go get a fire going. Gene's soaked and he's going to need to dry out. Also see if you can find another pair of—"

"No," I said, interrupting the Swamp Witch. "No more brotherhood of the traveling pants. I'll keep these."

"Fine. Eddie, go get him a new shirt and start that fire."

"You got it, Mom."

The lanky Demon Hunter scrambled up the steps and into the house before Kaylee turned her attention to me.

"I need to know everything you know about those flamingos."

"Whatever happened to 'it's none of your concern,'" I said, feigning disinterest and walking past her toward the house.

The Swamp Witch's staff slipped under my chin and blocked my way to the steps. "I'm making it your concern now."

I placed a hand on the staff. Kaylee might not have been the most powerful Witch I'd ever met, but that staff had more than a little Magick built up in it, and I was in no position to be on the business end of it in my present state.

"Delia."

"Who?"

"Sangre Reina... it was a long time ago."

Kaylee tilted her head. "What the hell are you talking about?"

"Word really doesn't make its way in up here does it?"

The Swamp Witch pressed her staff deeper into the soft fleshy part of my neck. "Who is Delia and what is she doing in my swamp?"

"She was a deplorable human being—if you could even call

her human. Insatiable blood lust and cruelty really takes away from the whole 'human spirit' sort of thing."

I tried to push past her, but Kaylee wouldn't pull back the staff.

"What do you mean 'was' a deplorable human being? What is she now?"

"Well, I Soul-Split her, so much like me she was reduced to a shell of her former self. Unlike me, however, her Darkling was expertly trapped."

"You Soul-Split another Magician? That's a capital crime!"

"You don't think I know that? The woman was murdering innocents and drinking their blood."

"Why would she—"

"To keep herself sexy and vibrant, among other things. Delia was hundreds of years old, but when I knew her she still looked like a cover-girl model."

Kaylee's staff dipped slightly.

"Then why is she in my swamp?"

I placed a hand on the staff and pressed it down gently, looking Kaylee directly in the eyes. "She's not, trust me. She'd be far too old now. Still, she was my first exposure to the Flock. Those birds are enigmatic and tricky. There's a lot of baggage there. My expert opinion is that you should stay the heck away from wherever the Flock is."

"And if I don't?"

I pointed to Kaylee's head. "Then you better hope your mental muscles are up to snuff."

The Swamp Witch tilted her head. "Huh?"

"I'll explain it to you in the morning. Right now I'm going to eat, sleep, and find out what the hell the person who stole this book was looking to do with it."

"Hey, Gene!" Little Ed's face appeared at the door. Already, the first hints of roasted alligator wafted out to greet me.

Alligator? Really?

"I've always wanted to say this."

"What?"

"You've got mail!"

20

FLAPJACKS AND FAMILY

*T*he mouth-watering smell of fresh eggs cooking on a well-seasoned griddle did little to diminish the tiredness that had settled in my bones. One of the downsides to staying with Kaylee and her son in the middle of the Green Swamp had to have been the nighttime noises. First, I had no idea there were that many species of frog, and second, I hadn't known that if you put enough of them together, they could go toe-to-toe with a commercial jetliner.

"More coffee?" the pleasant young waitress asked, holding out a steaming silvery pot.

"Just keep it coming," I said, my hand doing its best to keep my head upright. "Thanks."

"Sure thing." She smiled, then worked her way back to the counter to check on our breakfast.

While I might not have been the most agreeable person in the morning, the Swamp Witch was nigh unbearable. "We could have just eaten at my house. I don't understand why you had to drag us all the way to Lacoochee."

Sigh.

"First," I said, squinting at the local paper before setting it aside. "I didn't want last night's leftovers for breakfast. I like your son's cooking as much as the next guy, but I think I've had enough alligator for one lifetime."

Kaylee frowned and poked at her coffee with a spoon.

"And second," I said, not taking the bait. "Adam indicated he'd meet me here, and if there's a chance he's going to show up, then I'm not going to miss it."

The Swamp Witch toyed with a long braid she'd decided to wrap around her forehead like a crown. It seemed like a decidedly younger woman's style, but seeing as I had no idea what worked in the world of women's fashion I thought it best to keep my mouth shut.

"Fine, while I'm waiting for you to stuff your heart full of grease, mind telling me what you can about this Delia character?"

I fought down a scalding sip of the motor-oil-grade coffee before responding. "You should be asking me about the Flock, not some long-dead Skeeter."

Kaylee tilted her head.

Sigh.

"There's not much to tell. You watch many vampire shows?"

Ed's ex-wife shook her head. "I don't have a television."

"Well that would be a 'no,' then. Okay, what about books? You ever read any vampire fiction? I could have sworn we had to read Dracula in school."

"I was home schooled."

Of course you were.

"Right, okay. So, you know about mosquitos, right?"

"Yeah."

"Okay, so imagine a twisted mosquito woman who—while stunningly beautiful when she chooses to be—uses her power to drain the blood from young men and women. Ostensibly does it to stay alive, but also to keep her beauty."

Kaylee bit her lip in thought.

To be honest, she wasn't an unattractive woman, and that little move certainly won her a few looks from the other cowpokes in the restaurant.

Ah, Ed, now I see it.

The more time I spent around the Swamp Witch the more I understood why my old roommate had fallen for her. She was just his type, and that hadn't changed since college. While he never mentioned it directly, I knew he'd had a thing for Morgan the very first time we met her.

The old Demon Hunter had hid it well, but I knew better.

So he found himself a safer and generally better all-around person, then lost her. Oh, Ed...

"I don't get it." Kaylee tore a sugar packet and dumped it's contents into her coffee before leaving the paper carcass with the rest of its fallen comrades in a growing pile on the table.

"What don't you get? Think vampire-like. Basically Dracula, but since vampires aren't real, not Dracula. How can I make this any more clear?"

"No, I mean, what's the point of fighting getting old?"

It was my turn to be confused. "Huh?"

The Swamp Witch sipped at her coffee-tinted slurry. "Well I mean, what's the damn point? We all get old, we all die. Why get so hung up on how you look or who likes you? It's kind of a pointless game isn't it? I mean, let's take that waitress. She's got to be, what... eighteen? Sure, she looks great today, but what about five or ten, or even twenty years from now? While we can't say for sure, we know for sure she won't look eighteen."

"Right..."

"Well, that's the thing, isn't it. Who the hell cares? If she's found what she's meant to do with her life, if she's found her passion."

"Slinging motor-oil?" I said, gesturing to my half-empty cup.

"If that's what brings her joy, yes."

"I don't think that—"

Kaylee brushed me off. "See that's just it, Gene. She shouldn't need to know what you think, or I think, or frankly what any of us think about her. She should be her own person and do what brings her joy."

"And pays the bills."

Kaylee frowned and turned her attention back to me. "Yes, and pay the bills, but maybe she'll be smart. Maybe she'll find a nice quiet place in the Green Swamp that no one pays any attention to, and homestead it."

"Ah... So, go be a squatter? That's a passion to aspire to."

The subject of our debate returned with a beautiful platter of scrambled eggs, bacon, grits, and a short stack of golden pancakes. I couldn't be sure, but part of me wanted to believe this was what they were serving in Valhalla.

"Can I get ya anything else, honey?" our waitress asked.

"Nope, just find your joy."

"Huh?" she said, kicking her hip out to one side.

"He's fine." Kaylee slammed a boot tip into my shin. "Thank you."

"No problem."

I reached for the silverware and hadn't sliced into the first glorious pancake before the old cowbell tied to the front door clanged and Little Ed pushed his way in.

"Hey, you told him to come to TJ's right?"

Sigh... so close.

I placed the fork down. "Yes, you saw me write the message. Remember?"

"Yeah..."

"What is it, Eddie?" I asked, keeping one eye on the slowly dissipating steam of my hot breakfast.

"A car circled a few times, but they haven't stopped."

"They?"

"Yeah, it's two people."

"What kind of car is it?" Kaylee asked.

"It's some sort of sedan," Little Ed scrunched up his face in thought, "I don't know cars. It's got four doors, it's silver, and it's got one of those little metal thingies on the hood."

"Cadillac," Kaylee and I said in unison.

"Uh, sure. That."

"You know anyone who drives a caddy, Gene?" the Swamp Witch asked, pushing back from the table.

"No, but it could be anything. I mean, this is a town and all—"

Kaylee was on her feet in seconds and motioning for the door. "Throw your cash on the table and come on. I knew this was a bad idea from the moment you told me."

The steam was fading fast on my glorious repast and I had to fight to tear myself away from it. "Wait, you said 'they,' Eddie. Who was in the car?"

"I couldn't really see the driver from where I was. There was an old woman in the passenger seat, all done up with make-up and stuff."

"Could it be the vampire?" an already clearly concerned Kaylee asked, her body giving all indications it was only seconds away from grabbing her son and running out the door.

"There's no such thing."

"But I thought you just—"

"Long story. Listen, it's not Delia. There's just no way. Now, everybody sit back down and we can eat."

Crisp bacon called to me from the platter.

Don't let our sacrifice be in vain, Gene. Eat us, the bacon compels you!

"Well, I'm not hanging around long enough to find out. Come on, Gene. Eddie, you start the car."

Little Ed turned back to the door and froze. "Too late, Mom. They're out front."

Kaylee tightened her hand down on her staff and pulled her son away from the glass door. "Get behind me."

The Swamp Witch yanked her young son and focused all her attention on the door. I still didn't know what that damn staff did, but the Magick rolling off of it had me more than a little concerned.

"Come on, you two. It could be anything—"

The cowbell over the door clanged and a matronly woman in a velour running suit pushed her way into the diner. Long navy sleeves with thin white lines adorned her arms and the same pattern traced the fabric-covered curves of her ample thighs. Little Ed was right, she *was* all done up—her makeup had its own makeup.

She clutched a monster purse under her arm and fanned at the sweat on her face.

"Adam, is this where your old boss is now?"

Adam?

"He said to meet him here, Mom."

Mom?!

The equally large but far more bearded Adam Grayson followed his mother into the diner. His eyes panned the restaurant until they fell on me and the swamp people.

"Gene?"

"It's me."

Adam's cherubic face lit up like a Christmas tree. He bounded across the diner and threw his thick arms around me. "Holy crap, Gene. I didn't think I was going to see you again."

"Yeah," I said, a couple of rogue tears stinging at the corner of my eyes. "I missed you too, buddy."

Adam let go and looked down at my platter.

"Oh man, you even got me breakfast. Best. Boss. Ever."

21

BREAKFAST BEATDOWN

*A*dam didn't wait for me to respond. He took a seat at my place and immediately cut into the short stack of pancakes. "Wow, these are really good. You should get some."

"I did... never mind."

"Adam." His track-suited mother placed her saddle bag on the open seat next to him. "Is this your boss?"

"Uh, huh."

"Oh, it's such a pleasure to meet you, Mr. Law. Adam has told me all about you."

"He has?" I said, extending a hand.

The prosperous woman brushed it aside and threw her own thick arms around me. "Oh, I just can't tell you how happy I am to see someone take a chance on my Adam. He's such a smart boy, even if he can be a tad bit unmotivated from time to time."

"Uh, sure thing, Mrs. Grayson."

"Please, call me Angela."

"Um, Gene?" Kaylee said, her head tilted so far sideways I thought she might fall over. "And this is?"

"Oh, and this has to be your wife. Mrs. Law, I'm Angela. Adam's mother."

"No! I'm not his... we aren't... no ma'am."

Little Ed and his mother returned to the table just as our waitress replaced the silver coffee pot. "Will this all be on one check?"

"No!" Kaylee and I said in unison.

"Oh, I'll cover it, dear," Angela said, removing her purse and sitting down next to her son. "What's the sense of having a nice cash settlement if you aren't going to use it. Am I right?"

The young waitress didn't appear to know what to make of our motley crew, but her apparent desire for tips outweighed any tangential concerns.

"Works for me. What can I get ya?"

Angela surveyed the table and then the counter. "Do you have a boyfriend?"

"Excuse me?"

Angela nudged Adam with her elbow as he vigorously consumed what had been my breakfast. "My son's single, and he's quite a catch. Senior Vice President of Information Technology."

The waitress appeared more than a little confused. I jumped in to get us back on track. "She'll have what I was having, in fact we'll get two—"

"Three, actually," Little Ed said, jumping onto the free food train with gusto.

The waitress scribbled down our orders and beat a path to the counter before Angela could potentially ask about her family lineage or comment on the childbearing potential of her hips.

"Adam," I said, scooping a hand under my apprentice's arm. "If I could have a word with you at the counter."

"Uh, yeah sure. I just need to—" Adam didn't get the bacon slice to his mouth before I had him up and moving to the largely empty bar.

"I don't even know where to begin. Your mom? You brought your mom to… to… Lacoochee?"

"You said it was dangerous, and you told me to get the"—Adam glanced over his shoulders to check the few patrons loitering about—"big box from storage."

"But your mom?"

My apprentice shrugged. "You said it wasn't safe. I'm not leaving my mom in Tampa if it's not safe."

You'd do the same thing. His family doesn't have a protection guarantee from the House.

"Right, okay. Let's put a pin in that for a moment," I said stealing a glance at the table. Angela was already talking the ears off of Kaylee and Little Ed. "Did you get it?"

Adam nodded. "Yeah, it was in the back. We really need to clean that place up."

"Do you think you were followed?"

"What am I, a secret agent? I don't know."

"Right, I'll deal with that later. First, I need to know if you checked on my family."

"You do know they have this thing called the internet, right? I mean, you did go so far as to send me an email. Why didn't you just look on their social media pages?"

Damn you, Mailstation.

I brushed him aside. "It's a long story."

"Well, they aren't."

"What do you mean?"

"I mean Porter isn't much for posting, and Cathy isn't either. She appears to be doing good in school."

"Is she still doing jiujitsu?"

"No. She plays the violin now."

"What?!"

"Yeah, surprised me too, but there are a few videos out there with her in them at some recital. Your daughter's got some talent."

You've got to tell him.

"It's not Cathy."

Adam nodded. "Yeah, it's not the Cathy I knew, but kids grow up, man. Their interests change. I remember when I was younger I had a real soft spot for the Xbox, but now I'm more into vintage gaming. You know, like the old Nintendo."

"Adam," I said, grabbing the sleeve of his hoodie. "Stewart came to visit me."

My wide-bodied apprentice froze mid-sentence. "What do you mean he came to visit you? I thought he was in, you know…" Adam again checked over his shoulder. "Hell?"

"Damn it, Grayson, he is. That's what I'm telling you. He's in Hell and Cathy's there with him."

Adam pulled out his phone and scrolled through the screen. "No, she's not. Look here's a video of her."

Catherine.

Even with the Imp's words echoing in my ears, and the fingerprinted haze of Adam's phone screen, it was all but impossible to deny.

It's not her.

I could tell myself that again and again, but it just didn't want to stick. There she was, my Cathy, coaxing soul-shattering notes from a violin.

My daughter would never have had the patience for an instrument…

"Adam!" Angela shouted from the table. "Your food is getting cold."

My apprentice shoved the phone in my hand before joining the others. "I'm coming."

The video looped as I scrolled through the comments.

"Impressive." The waitress looked over my shoulder at the graceful moves of someone that may or may not have been my daughter. "See how much better she is without you in her life, Gene?"

"That's not my daughter and you know it."

The waitress-shaped House adjusted her apron. "We really seem to be doing the servant look a lot here. What is it you aren't telling me?"

The young woman ran a soft hand down the side of my face. Her fingers sent waves of pleasure through my body. "Feels good, right?"

I tried to look away and turn my attention back to the phone, but the House was too strong.

"Listen, Gene, I get it. I do. It's hard to believe your daughter is alive and well, let alone thriving without you, yet as you can clearly see from that video, she's doing exactly that. I'd love to say the same for you, but I'm not sensing you've gotten your Magick back. Nor am I sensing you have a plan for doing as much."

My hands shook in frustration, tightening down on the phone and turning off the screen.

"I'm working on that."

"Right, right, 'working' on it while you swim with Alligator Men and slum it up with Swampwater Sally?"

I tried to get some distance between us, but the waitress closed the gap quickly, pressing her thigh against mine and catching me off-guard.

"It's a process," I said, trying to regain my composure. "It's going to take time. Adam is here, and he brought what I need and—"

"This sounds like a lot of talk," the waitress said, holding her hand up like a puppet. "You're doing a lot of this, when you should be doing this." She clamped her fingers shut—hard.

"I've got a plan, and a backup option—"

The waitress shook her head. "Think again, Gene. Check your reconciliation wheel."

I pulled the paper disc out of my pocket, two memories had vanished, replaced with opaque black squares. "What the hell?"

"You're losing yourself to this obsession." The waitress held up her open palm. "I'm starting to think you aren't properly motivated."

"No. It's not that. It's—"

She snatched Adam's phone out of my hand and clicked the screen on, then returned it to me. "You might want to check your daughter's feed now."

The black screen flashed to life and a whirlwind of messages scrolled by.

She's been in an accident.

Is it serious?

The doctors don't know.

Oh my God, Cathy. I'm so sorry about your mom.

"What have you done?" I said, my stomach curling in on itself.

"I don't know, Gene. You tell me. What have I done? Are you going to get back on track, or is Porter's accident permanent?" The waitress pressed her hands to her face. "Oh, the anticipation."

"I'll do it," I said, unable to tear my eyes away from the tiny phone screen.

"You'll do what?"

"I'll get my Magick back."

"First, it stopped being yours when I gave it to you, and second, I'm just not feeling it. Sounds to me like Porter might not pull through."

The waitress picked up the tray and headed toward our table.

"Stop, wait! I'll do whatever you want."

She paused, turning to look back at me over her shoulder. "Say it again."

My shoulders fell, and with them went my will to fight the House. "I'll do whatever you want."

Adam's phone chimed in my hand.

Okay everybody, I just talked to the doctor, he says she's going to be fine, it's a miracle!

"You okay, honey?" the waitress said, her voice once again her own. "You look like you've seen a ghost."

22

MADE UP MATRIMONY

I sat in relative silence at the table, my appetite gone. Thankfully, with Angela there, my silence was the least of our worries. Within a few minutes of my return, she'd counseled Kaylee on her look and recommended no less than half a dozen different shampoos and body washes. The Swamp Witch was clearly fuming but held her tongue—the real question was how long that would last.

Little Ed was only halfway through his eggs when Angela began asking him very detailed questions about his love life. Those questions culminated in a brief yet very awkward exchange between Adam and his mother regarding his gender preferences. This family squabble only ended when Angela elected to discuss it at a later date.

I kept a firm grip on my coffee cup and let the rest of the breakfast action play out in the silver pot's reflection. That convex mirror gave me a way to keep tabs on the waitress, who continued to be herself and not my least favorite piece of real estate in all the world.

Angela had found a new bone of contention to pick with her son, but was interrupted when the door's cowbell clanged again.

Thanks to that reflective pot I got a look at who was arriving for a mid-morning breakfast, and it sent the hairs on my arm straight up.

Short, red-haired, and wearing a thin linen white shirt, the Leprechaun I'd worked a deal with last year waltzed into TJ's like he owned the place.

"Kelly! How are you today, sweetheart?"

"Morning, Mr. Tally! I didn't know you were going to be in town this week. Usual table?"

The Leprechaun caught my eyes in the pot's reflection. "No. I'm going to sit at the counter today."

"You got it," the young waitress said before scooting off to another table.

"Adam," I whispered, trying to get my young apprentice's attention. "I've got to get out of here—now."

"Huh? We just got here."

The Leprechaun's reflection eyed our table, and I tilted my head at his distorted form in the silver pot. "That's the fairy I made the deal with for the spike."

Adam nodded. "Okay, you never told me what the deal was for?"

"A year of memories."

My apprentice pursed his lips. "Well life hasn't been very good to you lately, right? Wouldn't be too hard to give up the last year would it?"

"No, damn it. *This* year of memories with my wife."

Adam's eyes widened. "But you haven't had any... Oh, crap."

"Right."

"What if we—" my young apprentice's words were cut off by the diminutive man's arrival.

"Eugene Law, it's great to see you. I heard all about that nasty business with the spike last year. So happy you could get some value from it."

I took a deep breath and feigned pleasure at seeing the

Leprechaun again. "Good morning to you as well. What are you doing in Lacoochee?"

"I visit the Green Swamp every year. Lots of good finds around these parts—a purveyor of exquisite artifacts has to be on the lookout year round. So, are you going to introduce me to the family?"

"Uh..."

Angela sprung to attention and extended a hand to the small man. He accepted it like a prized treasure and kissed her knuckles. "And who might you be?"

Even in her advancing years, Angela could still channel a decent schoolgirl giggle. "Oh my, I'm Angela Grayson."

"Angela, I've not met angels half as fair."

Ms. Grayson blushed and fanned her face with a spare menu. "Such a charmer—oh my. Who might you be?"

"Yeah," Kaylee said, her face the polar opposite of Angela's. "How many people *do* you know here, Gene?"

With the Leprechaun's back to me I made eye contact with Kaylee and slowly shook my head, mouthing to the Swamp Witch a single word. "No."

"Just call me Mr. Tallow," the Leprechaun said with a flourish before taking a moment to admire Kaylee's staff. "I didn't know Gene was going to be in town, nor that his wife had the same occupation."

Kaylee started to respond, but my vigorous head shaking stayed her tongue. Angela, however, didn't waste a second before chiming in. "Oh, that's not his wife."

"It isn't?"

"That's what he told me. It's a shame, really, cause they look like such a good couple."

The Leprechaun turned his attention to me. "So your wife is..."

"Right here," I said, pointing to Kaylee. "It's a joke! I was just having fun with Angela. Right, *sweetheart?*"

Kaylee's eyes narrowed. "Uh…"

"We play that little prank all the time," I said, getting up from my seat and stepping around to place a hand on the Swamp Witch's shoulder. "But seriously, we are so very married—yes, completely married. We share *everything*." I leaned down next to her ear; to everyone else at the table it looked like I was leaving an intimate kiss, but that wasn't what I was doing.

"Think of me, last night—without pants."

"What?!" she whispered, her voice barely audible, but full of righteous anger.

"At the water's edge. Make it funny."

"Why the hell should I—"

"Because he's a Leprechaun and if he gets wind that I can't come through on my deal he won't stop at me. Do this and I'll solve your bird problem."

The Leprechaun tilted his head to one side, giving Kaylee a very deep once over.

"Just do it or we're toast," I quietly pleaded.

Kaylee placed a hand on my arm. "He's such a kidder, but I love him."

The Leprechaun leaned in closer, his presence picking at the edges of my mind. Those little mental fingers poked and prodded, then left as quickly as they arrived. Kaylee's thoughts must have been far more enticing.

"Oh, ho, ho," the small man said, placing a hand on his stomach. "My, my, you two *do* have fun. I don't know why, but I always thought your wife was a brunette. No matter, I must have been mistaken."

The waitress called from the counter. "Order up, Tally. Adam and Eve on a Raft with a spot of lemon."

"That'll be me," the small man said before taking a moment to pause in front of Angela. "I'm going to be in town for a few days doing some prospecting at the finer antique establishments in north central Florida. I would be honored if you would accompany me."

"Mom, I'm not sure that's a good—"

"I'd love to," Angela said, smiling wide-eyed at the inscrutable fairy. "Adam, you'll be fine for a little while. My goodness, you'd think the boy couldn't function on his own."

Adam squeezed his lips together so tight that they vanished beneath his beard.

"Wonderful, my angel." The Leprechaun turned to Adam. "I swear to you with the utmost of sincerity that no harm shall befall your mother in my company."

"I guess it's okay—"

"You're darn tooting it's okay," Angela said, again talking over her son. "Now, Mr. Tallow, shall we adjourn to your table?" Angela said, rising from her seat and taking the hand of the much smaller man.

"Certainly. Oh, the sights you'll see today. I guarantee it."

"Gene…" Adam said through clenched jaws.

"Mr. Tallow, we have your word that you will return Angela Grayson to us unharmed?"

The Leprechaun ushered the older Grayson toward the counter before turning his attention back to me.

"You do, just like I have your word that you will deliver exactly what I expect when it comes due…"

Kaylee's hand gripped mine tighter. If I could feel it, so could she. Leprechauns hold power, a lot of power, and if Mr. Tallow had wanted us gone, he could have done it with little hesitation.

"I will…"

Kaylee's nails dug into my hand and for a moment I wondered if this was the right move.

No going back now, only forward from here on out.

"Excellent!" The little man practically leapt out of his sandals. "Well, you love birds have a wonderful day. We'll scour the markets today, my angel, but first, breakfast."

They'd adjourned to their own table, but Kaylee didn't release my hand; if anything the Swamp Witch let me know just how much grip strength she had.

"I don't know what you just made me complicit in, but I don't like it. If you don't get this resolved—and fast—I swear to you, Eugene Law, I will introduce you to each and every member of Stinkstone's family."

23

LONG DISTANCE

*A*dam had his mother's car keys. I offered to drive the whole gang back to the clearing closest to the Swamp Witch's house, but Kaylee and her son declined. I had the distinct impression she needed fresh air and a good bit of time to clear out the visuals she'd put in her head on my account.

Because of that, it was Adam and I rolling out of town in his mom's Cadillac. Just like the other night, we couldn't get very far down the road before the soft ground turned to muck and forced us to pull the luxury car off into a wide clearing.

I pulled the photo wheel out and held it up to the light, my gut churning at the new score. I didn't know how it happened, but the Darkling now owned all but five squares. These remaining still frames of my life were all that stood between me and a lost reconciliation with my other half.

If he brought the mirror, then none of this matters.

I took a deep breath and tucked the paper disc back in the folds of my borrowed denim. There were plenty of things I wanted to discuss with my young apprentice, but I really didn't know where to start. For his part, Adam appeared lost in thought as well, trying to decipher just what sort of threat the Leprechaun posed to his mother.

"You don't think he'll do anything to her, right?"

I shook my head. "He can't. Fairies have rules—so many damn rules. If he said no harm would befall her, then he means it."

Adam pursed his lips and let them vanish beneath the illustrious facial hair that adorned his face. "Right, but isn't that the whole point with wee folk? They are sneaky tricksters. They screw with things."

"You're right, Adam. You should go track him down and demand he release your mother this instant."

Adam's eyes widened. "I…"

"Yeah, you wouldn't do that, because you know you don't stand a chance against him."

"But what about you?"

"What *about* me?"

The young apprentice pointed a finger at my chest. "You work for the House now. Nigh infinite power and all, right?"

He didn't understand—damn you, Mailstation.

"Wrong," I said, pushing open the door. "Open the trunk."

Adam popped the trunk release and scrambled out of the car behind me. "What do you mean wrong? Did you find a way out of the deal? Are you free?"

"No."

"I don't understand—"

I flung the trunk lid up and cut Adam off. "My Magick is gone."

"What do you mean gone?"

Sigh.

"See for yourself," I said, pulling out an old pair of paper-thin 3D glasses from the box of oddities in the trunk and slapping them against Adam's chest. "Tell me what you see."

Adam shook his head. "I'm not looking at you with Jerry's Nine-Dimensional Glasses—I'd fry my brain."

"Try again."

"Gene?"

"It's gone, Adam. All of it. I'm about as useful as man nipples."

My apprentice raised the paper and plastic lens to his face slowly, his hands shaking ever so slightly. "Gene, I'm not feeling any—"

"Magick? Yeah, what part of 'I have no Magick' isn't getting in your head?"

Adam placed the paper glasses to his face, his eyes closed. "If you're joking I'm going to end up like that guy from Raiders of the Lost Ark."

"Yep."

"You aren't joking?"

I started pulling items out of the box one at a time and laying them out on the plush carpeted interior. "Nope."

I dug past an old blender and set it to the side. Mindy's Brain Freezer whipped up frozen concoctions that could chill a person to the bone.

Temping, but not what I need.

Adam opened his eyes. "Gene… Where's your Magick?"

"It's with the evil bastard looking for this," I said, holding up a simple woman's compact with tiny sigils scratched along the edges.

Adam yanked the Nine-Dimensional glasses away from his face before risking even a glance at the nondescript plastic disc. "That's Delia's Darkling," he said in hushed tones.

"I know, but it's more than that."

"What do you mean?"

"It's a very long story, but this isn't just a Darkling trap—it's a piece of unbridled potential. With the right Magick I could use this to reunite with Evil Gene and get my life back."

"Gene, I don't know if I could—"

"Not you, but I appreciate the thought. No, this is far more subtle than either of us are remotely capable of—this has the Swamp Witch written all over it."

Adam slid the glasses into his pocket. "Wait a second. If you have a Darkling… You've been Soul-Split?!"

I nodded.

"Holy shit, Gene. Someone Soul-Split you while you were basically a fully evolved Mega Pokemon?"

"I have no idea what that means."

Adam slapped a hand to his face. "Someone Soul-Split Super Gene."

"Yeah, a couple of someones, actually. Demon Hunting peanut vendors."

Adam exhaled and placed both hands on the edge of the trunk. "So that's why you wanted me to get out of town as fast as I could go and bring you this box."

I nodded, dropping the malevolent compact in my pocket without a second thought. "Yes, but I also needed you to bring it here for another reason."

"What's that?"

"I knew the Darkling would follow you, and I need him back here."

"You want him here? Why?"

I shook my head. "No, I *need* him here because I have a much bigger problem."

"What's that?"

"Cathy is still in Hell."

Adam shook his head. "No she isn't. We went over that— Cathy's fine. I showed you the video on my phone. Besides, don't you think we would have noticed something if she wasn't? I mean, you may have lost your Magick, but I haven't. She's your daughter. I'm sure of it."

I dug into the box and continued to place items on the floor of the trunk. My hands touched the cool silver sides of a two-slot toaster and I snapped them back. Memories of a long-forgotten morning flooded back at the barest touch of its shiny metal. The power inside that simple appliance was enough to burn down half the Green Swamp if left unchecked. I gently pushed it aside and found a small bag of at least a dozen different-sized buttons beneath it. I set them aside carefully as well.

"What are you looking for?" Adam asked.

My hands grazed a slender bronze rendering of Bastet, the Egyptian cat woman from long before a character with the same name had become popular in comic books. A feline head was perched on the bare neck and chest of a strong and capable woman. The statue's tiny eyes were covered by a twisted plastic bag of blindfold. I breathed a quiet sigh of relief knowing we'd all be safe, provided they stayed that way. I imagined the nubile woman's feline eyes staring up at me from beneath that twisted plastic, their chilling gaze feral and hungry. I set the statue back in the box, careful to not let the blinder slip.

"Have you been able to open a decent-sized Hellgate?" I asked, relieved to not have Bastet in my hands anymore.

My young apprentice shook his head. "No. You know that. We both tried multiple times after—"

"After I slammed the last one shut outside the Brighton 8 and trapped my daughter inside." My stomach curled at the words.

"You didn't have a choice. It was that or let The Defiler come through. You made a sacrifice and saved a lot of people."

Visions of Cathy's final moments set my heart beating faster beneath the borrowed flannel. "I abandoned my daughter."

"You didn't abandon her! You sent Stewart as protection. I don't get why we're even having this conversation. You did the unthinkable—you struck a deal with 69 Mallory Lane. Your family is safe now."

I fished an old soup can, open on one side, out of the box.

The can held a string on the other end which had been cut after only a few feet.

"Are they?" I asked, wiping some dust off a sigil embossed on the side of the can.

"Last we checked," he said, holding up his phone. "I wasn't going to tell you this, but Porter was in a massive car wreck and walked away with only a few bruises. The House has been true to its word—if there even is such a thing. You've got to drop this whole 'Cathy is still in Hell' talk, because it's going to drive you crazy."

I cleared away a small patch of dead leaves on the ground with my foot.

"Don't do it, Gene."

Satisfied the sand was without blemish, I began tracing the designs of an elaborate sigil in the newly blank spot.

Adam bent down next to me. "Gene, I've seen this before. It's obsession. Mom got this way after Dad died—it's not healthy. You've got to get past it. Your daughter is fine, your family is fine, but *you* aren't. I can't begin to know what it's like to be Soul-Split, but I'm telling you it's screwing with your head."

I put the finishing touches on Marvin's Long Line, then paused to verify all of its curving lines and connecting paths. We were about to make a very long distance call and I had no interest in paying the charges if I got the wrong party on the other end of the line.

"I need your Magick," I said, pushing the cut string into the middle of the sigil.

"Gene," Adam said, his voice softer. "I shouldn't be doing this. It's just enabling you."

I set the can on the ground outside the Long Line sigil. "You think Cathy's fine. I think she's still in Hell. So, if you are right, this is going to go nowhere."

"Gene, we tried all this before, don't you remember?"

"I know more now than I did before."

"How could you? You don't even have your Magick." My apprentice was clearly torn.

"I just *know*. Listen, here's the deal. You do this for me now. If I'm wrong, I'll accept everything you say. Cathy's safe and sound in Tampa, and I'll drop this whole thing, but if I'm right—"

"If you're right, I'll do whatever it takes to help you get her back. I'm telling you though, she's fine."

"Do it... please."

My apprentice sighed and placed a hand on the can. "Is there anywhere in particular I should be calling? I mean, other than the limitless expanse of eternal damnation?"

I placed a hand on top of his. "Yes."

"Well?"

"The Tower of Unceasing Torment."

Adam tilted his head slightly. "The *what*?"

"Just do it."

Magick erupted from my apprentice's fingers. He'd gotten a good bit stronger than I remembered, or perhaps it was just my complete lack of power, but whatever the reason, Adam wielded a good bit more juice than I'd expected.

"Connect parenthesis port six, six, six, close parenthesis."

"Still haven't switched to Latin?" I asked.

"Meh, this works."

The tin can crackled and a whoosh of static flooded the clearing. "See, I told you, it's not going to work because there's no one there to—"

"Hello?"

My heart shattered all over again. It had been so long I was afraid I would have forgotten, but there it was, a voice that shattered my heart into a thousand tiny pieces—a frail, frightened, and familiar voice.

"Cathy?" I asked, holding my breath as the static roared again.

Please... please...

"Dad? Can you hear me?"

24

IDENTITY UNKNOWN

I flinched as another burst of static from the soup can made it next to impossible for me to respond. "Cathy, I can hear you."

"Dad?"

Adam squeezed his eyes shut. I could feel the concentration needed to hold open that connection—it wasn't easy, and he wouldn't be able to hold it open for long.

"Dad? You're fading."

"Are you okay?" I shouted over the waves of static.

"I'm scared."

"I know, sweetheart."

The fear in my daughter's voice was gut churning. Even with only half a soul I felt every ounce of it in full and living color.

"What do you see? Where are you?"

My daughter's words broke up, lost in the garble of another wash of extra-worldly static.

"Hold on to her, Adam!"

"It's… hard…" my apprentice said, sweat beading along his furrowed brow. "She's different, something's not right. I don't understand."

"What don't you understand? The House lied." I grabbed the young man's hoodie and brought his face next to mine, almost breaking his link to my daughter in the process. "The damn House lied. That's Cathy, I know it's her, and she's still lost."

"Dad…"

Cathy's voice was faint now, barely registering above the collapsing connection.

"Don't lose her!" I shouted, letting go of Adam's hoodie and placing my hands on his to will Magick I didn't have into the can.

"Something's wrong… Are you sure this is her?" Adam said, clearly fighting to keep the connection open. "It's confusing and jumbled. There's a lot of anger…"

I know my blood.

"Cathy, don't go!"

"I…"

"I'm coming for you! I promised you I would and I meant it. I'm coming for you and I'll tear this world to pieces if I have to."

"Love…"

"I love you, Cathy," I cried, no longer able to hold back the tears.

A subtle red glow enveloped the can, like the insides of a toaster, but just like those bread-cooking metal rods, it got brighter, a lot brighter.

"Gene," Adam said, the hot light slipping out between his fingers. "I've got to cut the call."

"No! Cathy, can you hear me? I need you to find Stewart. I sent him to help you. He's bound to me and will do whatever I tell him to do. Stay quiet and stay safe. I'm coming for you. Cathy, do you hear me? Cathy!"

Angry red light poured out of the tin can, casting us in fiery hue.

"Gene… That's not Cathy! There's too much anger."

"What do you mean it's not—"

A hard-edged and gravelly version of Cathy's voice spoke, sharp and oddly pitched, like a distorted piece of audio stretched nearly to the point of breaking. "I hear you. I'm here waiting for you. Come save me."

"Cathy!" I shouted into the can.

"That can't be her." Small wisps of smoke rose from Adam's fingers. "I'm telling you something isn't right."

"Dad?" Catherine's voice was back again, without the terrifying edge. "Dad, I love you. Please help me."

"I will, I'm coming for you."

"Stop," Adam cried, the smell of burning flesh filling the surrounding air. "It's using you. Whatever that is, it's not your daughter."

"It's me, Dad."

"I know, sweetheart."

Adam's hands shook, his fingers holding tight to the bending metal. "I've got to let it go. It's going to pull me in!"

"No... Cathy!"

The twisted voice returned. "Find me—"

I didn't hear the rest of her words. They were lost in a burst of static.

"Cathy!"

"Gene, help me," Adam pleaded, his own voice breaking.

"Cathy!"

My apprentice struggled to release the can and its hold on his Magick. "Please!"

In a fit of frustration I raked my fingers through the sigil, cutting Marvin's Long Line and closing the door on my only daughter all over again. Adam fell forward, shoving his hands into the sand and puffing through the pain.

"I... I wasn't sure you would do that," he said, burying his fingers deep and blinking back at the tears in his eyes.

I kicked the can away, letting it tumble across the clearing before ending up in a shallow pool of swamp water. The bright red metal sent a blast of steam into the air and took with it what remained of my patience.

"Neither was I."

Adam flexed his fingers beneath the cool sand. "Gene, it wasn't her."

"Like hell it wasn't."

My apprentice shook his head. "You don't have your Magick, you couldn't feel what I felt. I'm telling you it wasn't her."

I got up and slammed the trunk shut then spun around on him. "Oh yeah? Well, then tell me what that was, Mr. Master Magician?"

"Gene..." Adam's shoulders slumped in his navy hoodie. "I don't know, but I do know what it looks like—"

"You do? So enlighten me, what does it look like, Merlin?"

My apprentice removed his gently roasted fingers from the sand to examine them. "It looks like obsession," he said, his voice soft and without malice. "Like I said before, after my dad died it was the same thing. My mom didn't want to believe it. She kept thinking he could hear her, that somehow he was still there."

"This is nothing like that," I yelled, slamming my fist against the trunk lid. "Cathy isn't dead."

"You're right, Gene. She's not. She's alive and well in Tampa with her mom and brother. She's growing up and learning new things. You aren't in her life anymore, and that's because you *chose* not to be."

Had I still had my Magick I wasn't sure what I would have done at that moment. I wanted to tear him apart. I wanted to hold my daughter again. I wanted to make all of this right, but my power was gone, and with it had gone any chance I might have had to get to her.

"I did what I had to do."

Adam blew on his pink fingers. "I know you did. I also don't know that I would have been capable of doing the same in your place."

"I'm not going to argue with you anymore. I'm simply going to tell you how it's going to be," I said, willing my voice to a level tone. "You are going to help me get a Hellgate open and afterwards we can go our own way. You won't be my apprentice anymore; you'll be on your own."

Adam's face fell, this time he left no doubt that there were tears forming in the corner of his eyes. "Don't do this, Gene."

"I'm afraid you haven't left me much in the way of a choice. You don't believe that was my daughter, do you?"

Adam hesitated, his face a mess of emotions. "I…"

"That's all I need to know."

The sound of dry leaves cracking and snapping twigs drew our attention to the edge of the clearing. Little Ed and Kaylee broke through the tree line, the Swamp Witch holding up her son. "We interrupting something, boys?"

"No," Adam and I said in unison.

"Good. You promised me we'd deal with my bird problem."

"I did—we need to go to where you found the flamingos."

Adam wiped his eyes with his sleeve. "You mean like from the movie theatre last year? There are more of them?"

"Yes," I said, acknowledging my apprentice perhaps more curtly than I intended. "Where are they?"

Kaylee tilted her head slightly, perhaps noticing the tension between Adam and I. "Sturkey."

"Isn't that a restaurant?" Adam asked. "I could have sworn we stopped at one on the way over."

"Not Stuckey's," Little Ed shook his head, "Sturkey. It's a derelict mining town deep in the swamp: old, abandoned, and overrun with limestone."

I pressed a hand against the compact in one pocket while I thought of the photo wheel in the other.

I'm going to get my Magick back, and when I do I know exactly where I'm headed.

"We better get going," Kaylee said, pointing toward a path leading away from her house. "I'd like to get there before the evening service."

"Evening service?" Adam and I asked.

"Yeah, did we forget to mention? Sturkey's sacred to the Bridge Trolls."

The color drained from my apprentice's face. "Wait, you never said anything about Bridge Trolls in your email, Gene."

Kaylee brushed him off. "You'll manage. You don't eat rocks, do you?"

"No…"

"Then you'll be fine."

Adam didn't appear convinced. He fished out his mother's keys and unlocked the trunk, then gathered up a number of different items from our dangerous Magickal collection before shoving them in a comically tight backpack. He slung the purse-like pouch over his shoulder and locked the trunk back up.

Kaylee led us out of the clearing and into the dense swamp. We hadn't gone more than twenty feet before Adam placed a hand on my shoulder. "Gene, what about the compact and Delia's Darkling. It's trapped in that mirror. Shouldn't we leave it in the car?"

"And risk Evil Gene finding it first? No, it stays with me. The mirror is safe inside that compact. Back when I had Magick, I encased the sides with Quigley's Quagmire. No one is getting past that—no one short of my Darkling."

Adam nodded. "Gene, what if she's there?"

"Delia?"

"Yeah…"

"Having walked around without my Magick for a day or so now, I can attest that there's little chance she's still alive. Besides, that was a long time ago."

"Okay…" Adam fiddled with this tiny backpack straps. "Listen, about Cathy, I just—"

"Stop. I'm done discussing it. I'm going to save my daughter, with or without your help."

"You didn't feel what I did. I'm telling you, something isn't right…"

"Without it is," I said, shaking off his arm and pushing ahead into the scrub palmetto.

25

THE MUSCLES THAT TUSSLES

*K*aylee hadn't been lying; then again, I didn't believe subterfuge was a move she understood. The trek to Sturkey was anything but short. The majority of the day had been spent pushing our way through dense scrub palmetto and trudging across sugar-white sand. Large pines blocked the path from time to time, forcing the Swamp Witch to pause and consult what appeared to be some form of mental map.

Adam for his part stayed quiet. I could tell he was brooding, but I didn't care. His happiness was not something that I was interested in worrying about at the time.

I snuck another look at the reconciliation wheel and really wished I hadn't. According to the picture disc I was paying a hefty price for my conversation with Adam. I'd lost five squares thanks to that little maneuver.

You have the mirror now; you don't need the stupid disc. You can force the issue.

"Please don't tell me you're lost," I said, shoving the photo circle back in my pocket before scratching at a fire ant that had decided to chew on my exposed ankle.

Kaylee turned a very slow three-sixty following the horizon with her eyes. "I'm not lost…"

"You aren't inspiring confidence."

Little Ed took a seat on a fallen log and removed one of his shoes, then turned it over to pour the fine white sand in it on the ground. "Just like the hunts with Dad."

"Except your father never knew what he was doing—I do."

Little Ed stifled a smirk and tugged his sneaker back on. "It's that way, Mom."

The Swamp Witch tilted her head. "Are you sure? I could have sworn it was this way?"

"Nope. If we go that way we'll end up neck deep in an old Timucua burial mound full of Restless Dead. Don't you remember? That was the hunt both of you went on, back when we were a…" Little Ed's voice trailed off. His mother didn't press him to finish his statement.

"Restless Dead?" I asked, getting a good look at the dense cypress swamp leading toward the burial mound. "I'd just as soon avoid that if I can help it—no Magick and all."

"Agreed. We'll keep clear of it as best we can, but we should be fine, provided there are no Thinnings," Kaylee said, pulling her long auburn hair back and tying if off in a rubber band.

"Oh yeah, you keep track of those do you?"

The Swamp Witch shook her head. "You can't. It's impossible to track Thinnings—they just *happen*."

Adam dropped his hoodie's zipper to half-mast, exposing us to a number of dark sweat stains expanding along his chest and arms. "Uh, that's not entirely true."

"Oh really, please tell us, Mr. Master Magician," I said, not bothering to remove the irritation from my voice.

"Well, ever since your… ever since you've been gone, I've been studying them. I managed to amass a considerable amount of data and I believe I can predict when they'll appear."

It was Kaylee's turn to appear incredulous. "Magicians have

been trying to understand Florida's Thinnings for hundreds of years, yet you're telling me you figured them out all on your own?"

Adam played in the sand with his feet. "Uh, sort of."

"What's the big deal, you two?" Little Ed asked knocking his heel against the ground a few times to push his foot back into the hard rubber sole. "Dad used to talk about the possibility of doing that, maybe Adam here solved it."

"Well, it wasn't just me…"

Both Kaylee and I raised an eyebrow and turned our attention to the junior Magician. "Who helped you?"

"I wouldn't say it was a who, more a what." Adam continued to draw in the sand with his feet.

Now it was time for the resident junior Demon Hunter to get concerned. "You didn't make a deal with a Demon, did you?"

"No," Adam said, suddenly perking up and shaking his head. "I used the cloud."

Kaylee looked up at the thin stratus clouds high overhead. "Odd, I would never have thought clouds were tied to Thinnings."

"That's not what he's saying," I said, marginally surprised at how little technical knowledge the Swamp Witch possessed.

"No?"

"No. He's talking about massive computers as large as whole city blocks."

"Gene's right," Adam said, now much more interested in explaining his theory. "Specifically, I've been working on a simple artificial intelligence and merging it with a golem spell to produce a—"

Kaylee sprung at Adam so fast I could barely get between her and the pudgy young man. "*Who* told you it was safe to build a golem? Who?"

Adam's face lost most of its color and he took a few steps

back, clinging to his backpack straps like a life preserver. "I… I didn't think it would be a big deal."

"Well, it is a big deal—a very big deal."

Even though I was remarkably unhappy with Adam, I wasn't about to let the softy get brow beat by Kaylee. I stepped in to talk her down.

"Golems are technically allowed if your master does not expressly forbid them. Did I expressly forbid self-directional, autonomous, animated non-living tissue?"

Adam scrunched up his face as if processing my choice of words. "No…"

"Then you may make a golem."

"Well I already did."

You aren't making this easy.

Adam retrieved a small, rubbery action figure from his backpack. The muscular little man had thick corded legs and arms like tiny tree trunks. He wasn't much for clothing, instead preferring a tightly wrapped set of what looked like performance swimwear.

"What is that?"

Adam beamed. "This is—"

"That is the single greatest wrestler in the history of televised bloodsport…" Little Ed said, his words dripping with reverence.

"You turned a wrestling doll into a golem?" I said, not sure whether I was impressed or mortified.

Adam shook his head. "No, I turned an *action figure* into a golem, and I pumped him full of calculations on Thinnings I created from the cloud."

The Swamp Witch shook her head. "Does anyone have a clue what he's saying?"

"Look, it'll make more sense if I show you." Adam adjusted the arms and legs of the tiny muscle man into position.

Kaylee frowned. "Please tell me this is PG."

Adam nodded. "Of course. This is 'The Muscles That Tussles.' He's strictly above board."

Somewhere inside this half of my soul a small piece of my childhood died a terrible and horrifying death.

Apparently satisfied 'The Muscles' was in the right position, Adam placed him on the ground.

"Oh man," Little Ed said, leaning forward. "Don't tell me you start him with the catch phrase."

Adam nodded vigorously.

I need to get these two a room.

"May I?"

My apprentice spread his arms wide. "Go for it."

Kaylee placed her staff against the young Demon Hunter's chest. "I think not."

"Why? It's no big—"

The Swamp Witch's eyes reminded me of Porter's for a brief moment. "Golems are not something to fool around with. I'm not going to have any child of mine even hinting at such a thing."

Little Ed's face turned bright red. "You don't wanna tussle with these muscles."

The Magick was subtle, but it was there. Adam had clearly been practicing since we'd last been together, and his little rubber doll was proof of that.

"You know what time it is?" the remarkable little wrestler rumbled from deep in his Magickally enhanced belly. "It's time to party!"

Not a one of us moved.

Adam smiled like the cat that ate the canary. "That means there're no Thinnings nearby."

"I could have told you that," Kaylee said, throwing her arms in the air.

Adam deflated like someone had let the air out of his hoodie. "Well, it's a work in progress. The algorithms aren't perfect yet, and the neural network hasn't converged on a perfect set of weightings for predictive analysis—"

Kaylee shook her head and turned back to the path. "You keep that creepy little thing far away from me."

"It's not creepy," Little Ed said, following his mother toward Sturkey.

"I wasn't talking about the doll."

Adam picked up his action figure and tucked it in the center of his hoodie, where it hung out like a kangaroo's joey.

"That really is kinda creepy," I said, still mad as hell at the kid, but impressed just the same.

"Do you think?"

"Oh yes, *very.*"

Adam's shoulders slumped. "Okay, I'll unmake it when I get home."

"Who said anything about unmaking it?"

"Wait... so you like it?" Adam said, perking up slightly.

"Nope, still spooks me out."

"Oh."

"But what I *do* like, is that you took some serious initiative while I was gone, and that is impressive as hell."

"Really?"

It was hard to not chuckle at the oversized hoodie pouch with a pair of rubber wrestler feet hanging out on one side.

"Couldn't have used like some army men or something?"

"Um, well…"

"Or even a rubber snake?"

Adam shook his head. "I hate snakes."

"Well, at least we can agree on that."

Adam smiled. "Does this mean you'll reconsider what I said about Cathy?"

"Nope."

"Gene, it wasn't—"

"I'd stop while you're behind."

26

STURKEY

*W*ith the sun having moved past midday and into the afternoon, marsh mosquitoes woke up and found the bare spots around my ankles with expert precision. Those little bastards dug in like a wild pack of cannibals, and in short order my fire ant bites had been supplemented with the rage-inducing itchiness of at least half a dozen red welts.

"Please tell me we're getting close."

Kaylee didn't respond, but I did get a nod from Little Ed. I checked on Adam, only to find the 'Muscles that Tussles' bobbing along in his pouch, now adjusted so that the doll's angry little face stared at my back.

Great.

The meandering path to Sturkey had actually gotten a lot worse after that clearing. Sure, we were in a swamp, so the term 'path' had to be used with the utmost of creativity, but it had quickly descended into a loose smattering of old cypress stumps and wide mud fields that didn't dare run in a straight line. The sun was low in the sky, bringing with it a strange coldness that tumbled down from the tall pine's shadows.

"That's the mound," Kaylee said unprompted. She'd been

stealing glances in the general direction of the Timucua mound for the last thirty minutes.

"I thought you and the Eds took care of it," I said, focusing all my attention on finding the best patch of bare earth for my tired feet.

"We did," the young Demon Hunter said. "We locked it up tight as a drum. What you are feeling now is nothing compared to what it was."

I raised an eyebrow. "Really? Cause its sure got a 'primal murder' vibe going."

"It's just because we're getting close to Sturkey," Kaylee said, testing the mud depth with her staff. "There's a history."

Adam flipped his hood around to wipe the sweat from his face. "Should we know it?"

"I'm guessing the mining town and the natives didn't get along? I'm going to take 'stealing their land' for two hundred, Alex," I said, leaning against a narrow sapling's trunk to avoid falling in the mud yet again.

The Swamp Witch stopped. "Who's Alex?"

"Forget it. Am I right?"

"Yes, for the most part. The mining town is long gone now, almost completely absorbed by the swamp, but there's still a rich vein of limestone there. That's what brings the Bridge Trolls."

I shook my head. "And that's why you don't leave food out on the counter—never know what sort of pests you'll get."

Kaylee clearly bristled at that last comment, but she didn't have time to chastise me before Little Ed announced our arrival in Sturkey.

"How can you tell?" I said, stepping off a slippery cypress nub and onto a patch of dry land.

"Take a deep breath," the junior Demon Hunter said.

I did, and immediately coughed at the pungent smell of rotten eggs. "What is that? Sulfur?"

Little Ed shook his head. "No, that's limestone. When it's ground up, though, it produces a sulfur-like odor."

"Well that's just great," I said, swatting at a rather large mosquito that had set up shop on my ankle.

"Why?" Kaylee asked, after she, along with Adam and the rubber wrestler, joined us on the shore.

"It might make it harder to draw them out."

The Swamp Witch tilted her head. "Huh?"

"Show me where you found the flamingos."

"Follow me," she said, leading us into a dense pine patch just off the shore. "Trust me, you can't miss it."

KAYLEE NAVIGATED the pine scrub with zero effort. It was clear the Swamp Witch, and her son, were veterans of the Green Swamp—Adam and I weren't.

We hadn't traveled ten feet before my apprentice tangled himself in a patch of thorny briars. "Uh, Gene, a little help here?"

Mercifully our guides waited while I unhooked the young Magician and his beef-cake golem from the local flora. Kaylee gently pulled aside a large palm frond and directed us past. "Welcome to Sturkey."

"This is it?" I said, more than a little underwhelmed. It may have been classified as a mining town at one time, but right now it would have been hard pressed to be considered much more than a campsite.

"You were expecting more?" the Swamp Witch asked, knocking some mud off her staff against a discarded sheet of rusting metal.

"I was expecting... something? This is just junk."

The town of Sturkey appeared to be nothing more than old steel buildings, long since reduced to rust, that jutted out of the ground in ramshackle fashion. It was hard to see much beyond the dense trees, but it certainly wasn't going to make the tourist guidebooks.

"Use your imagination, Gene," Little Ed said, pointing at one of the collapsed tetanus factories slowly being consumed by the swamp. "I'm guessing that was where they ground the limestone."

I tilted my head. "Are you sure it wasn't the brothel? I mean it was a mining town, right?"

That comment earned me a sharp rap on the head from Kaylee's staff before she stomped deeper into the derelict town. "Come on, the flamingos have been appearing over here."

The Swamp Witch led us past at least a dozen more rust buckets before stopping outside what had to be the only concrete structure in the whole town. Simple and nondescript, the building's steel roof was still intact, but just barely. Thin shafts of sunlight, not already filtered out by the pine forest overhead, wormed their way into the structure, giving it an eerie half-light. Bright pink plastic flamingos surrounded the concrete box in almost absurd numbers. The birds sat on thin metal rods, giving them the appearance of flocking around the creepy old building.

"Wow," Little Ed said, reaching down to pick one of the yard ornaments up. "What is—"

"Stop!" I said, grabbing the junior Demon Hunter's hand. "Don't touch them."

Little Ed pulled his arm back like he'd seen a water moccasin. "Why? Are they dangerous?"

"Only if you like your fingers."

Little Ed backed away from bright pink yard birds.

"I'm kidding," I said, picking one up and pressing its beak against my fingers. "See, there's nothing to be afraid—argh, my hand!"

I snapped my hand back and dropped the flamingo.

"Gene!" Little Ed shouted.

"He's faking." Kaylee pushed past her son and scooped up the flamingo in her arms. "I've been doing this for days, there's nothing dangerous about them."

I chuckled and grabbed another plastic bird, then offered it to Ed's son. "She's right, these won't hurt you."

Little Ed held up his hands, clearly wanting nothing to do with the yard art. I chuckled and turned my attention back to the Swamp Witch. "I have got to question your mom-game, Kaylee, that was an opportune moment to mess with his head."

Ed's ex-wife ignored me, and instead navigated a path through the derelict yard ornaments to a door-less entry into the mildew-covered building. "There are more inside."

"Take me to the source."

THE SWAMP WITCH hadn't been kidding; that didn't surprise me, as I'd already determined she was about as jovial as a post-operative infection. What I didn't expect was just how much she'd meant by 'more.'

Thin shafts of sunlight filtered through the steel roof and shined upon the bright pink bodies of hundreds if not thousands of plastic flamingos. There were so many inside that they couldn't stand in the ground—instead, they were strewn above in heaping piles, their plastic eyes following us.

"Is this normal?" Ed's ex-wife asked.

"No. Well, I've only ever seen it once..."

Kaylee turned to face me, her eyes glaring in the half-light. "Something you care to enlighten me with?"

Not particularly.

"It's nothing," I lied. "I'll talk to them and see what's going on..."

If they'll let me.

Kaylee threw up her hands in disgust. "You mind filling me in on what's going on here? This is my swamp and I don't appreciate being kept in the dark."

"Don't worry," I said, rolling up my sleeves. "I've got it."

The Swamp Witch shook her head. "I swear, we might as well be married."

"Huh?"

"You are no different from Ed—always have to have all the answers. I swear it would kill you to admit you might not know everything."

"Are you kidding?" I said, pushing aside a pile of plastic birds with my foot. "My life is basically a testament to my lack of knowledge. Let me total it up for you. I have a daughter trapped in Hell, or at least that's what I think, but go ask my apprentice back there and he'll tell you I'm wrong. Heck, ask anyone and they'll tell you my daughter is still safe in Tampa."

"Why don't you just—"

"Ask them? I'd love to, except I made a deal to save my daughter and in exchange my family cannot see me anymore. I don't exist to them. So, yeah, not knowing what I'm doing is totally my thing, and I do it better than anyone else."

Kaylee stared at me, and for a moment I thought I'd found a way to melt a little of that icy demeanor. "What are you going to do?"

I cleared out a space on the sandy floor. "I'm going to join the Flock. Again."

Ed's ex-wife shook her head. "Not in my swamp. I'm the one doing whatever that entails."

"No." I said, my flat denial sending the Swamp Witch into a tizzy.

"You told me—"

"I told you I'd help, and that's what I'm going to do. The Flock is nothing to sneeze at. It's dangerous. These little pink birds look harmless, but what they do in here," I pointed a finger at my head, "is decidedly not. I'm not doing that to you. I've been through it twice now, and I know what I'm up against."

I knelt down in the open spot between the stacks, my knees sinking in the soft sand.

Kaylee fumed. "Is this because you're a *Magician*? You don't think I wouldn't understand? I'm just some stupid woman, is that it? You are so like Ed—so very like him."

I placed my hands in my lap, one inside the other, and took a deep breath. "You're gonna want to save up all that anger, especially if I screw this up and you end up with an invisible monster."

"What?!"

"Exactly," I said, releasing the tension in my shoulders. "Just hold on to that."

27

FOWL PLAY

Kaylee paced in front of me, randomly stopping to kick plastic flamingos against the distant walls. "Well?"

I opened one eye. "That isn't helping."

Ed's ex-wife threw her hands up in the air. "I'm sorry, is this disrupting your navel-gazing?"

Sigh.

"I'm trying to do you a favor. When they come, they can get aggressive, so just stay out of the way."

Kaylee sulked. "I don't see anything happening."

"Exactly, that's the point. You can't see the real ones. These are just the duplicates," I said, trying to regain my focus.

"Duplicates?"

Sigh.

"Yes, the duplicates. That means one of them might be nesting, and if that's the case, then that's a lot more than you want to be involved in, trust me."

Kaylee surveyed the concrete block room. "Still no movement."

I closed my eyes and tried to ignore the woman's predatory pacing.

Where are you hiding?

My mind went back to the first frightening time I had joined the Flock, and the confusion, panic, and bone-chilling fear that came along with that memory. Oddly, none of that had anything to do with those enigmatic birds.

Don't think about that...

I took a deep breath and pushed those thoughts out of my head. Stacks of plastic flamingos didn't just show up in the middle of the swamp; the Flock had to be here, but where were they?

"Does it normally take this long?" Kaylee asked, more than a hint of frustration in her voice.

"Good grief, woman, are you sure Little Ed's your son?"

The Swamp Witch slammed the end of her staff against the ground, Magick bubbling up like hot magma. "What did you say?"

"It was a joke—kids, impatience, you know." My words were interrupted by a subtle shifting of the stacks.

"What was that?"

"Ssh," I said, holding up a hand. "You don't want to spook it."

"Hey!" Adam's voice came from outside the concrete bird house. "One of those plastic birds just shot through my legs. It's headed your way, and fast."

"If the bird was outside, then what is that?" Kaylee pointed to the shifting mound of plastic yard art.

"I don't know, but here it comes," I cried, getting back in position.

The Swamp Witch backpedaled, her Magick swirling just outside the confines of that oaken staff. "What do I do?"

"Nothing. It will come to me."

The plastic pink bird picked its way through the stacks. Its narrow legs slipped between the hard bodies with careful precision. Coal-black eyes darted back and forth between Kaylee and I, unsure and calculating.

I closed my eyes and took a deep breath, extending my mind and reaching out for the tiny bird.

We are Flock.

The flamingo didn't respond.

"Gene... What's going on?" Kaylee said, fear in her voice.

I snapped my eyes open to find the little bird had ignored me entirely. All of its focus was on Ed's ex-wife, her staff, and the Magick she was putting out.

"It's the Magick. Stop!"

Kaylee shook her head, taking another step backward. "I can't. It just happens sometimes and—"

Crash!

The Swamp Witch slipped on the shifting stacks. Her back hit the pile, and in an instant the bird was on top of her. "What do I do?"

Crap.

"Don't do anything aggressive," I said, trying to keep my voice level.

The plastic bird's long neck worked like a periscope, bringing those black eyes in line with hers.

Kaylee barely suppressed the panic in her voice. "Gene..."

The bird twisted to run its nose along her chest.

"What's it doing?" asked, her eyes wide.

"Sizing you up."

Kaylee's hands opened and closed. I could tell she wanted to do something, but didn't know what. "Is there anything I should be doing right now?"

"No—well, I take that back."

"What?"

"Don't blink."

The pink bird dug its beak into the Swamp Witch's shirt.

"Damn it, Gene."

"You said you wanted to join the Flock—looks like you're going to get your wish."

The tiny bird jumped onto Kaylee's chest, its metal legs pressing against her skin. Kaylee shifted beneath the flamingo. Her hands shook and she struggled to keep her breath under control.

Crap.

"What did I say about confidence?"

"I'm trying," the Swamp Witch said, her voice cracking.

"You need a display of confidence or things are going to turn on you really fast."

"I'm trying..." Kaylee's body language indicated otherwise.

"Stop trying and start *doing*. That's Ed's Mom, and she doesn't approve of you. You hear me? She doesn't approve of you because you aren't good enough for her son."

The bird's black eyes bore down on the Swamp Witch.

"Are you gonna take that?"

"No..." Kaylee sputtered.

"Don't tell me, damn it. Show that bird who's boss, or things are going to go bad."

"It's a plastic bird," Kaylee stammered. "How bad could it—"

Ed's ex-wife hadn't finished her sentence before the yard art stabbed one of those thin metal rods into her thigh, then pushed its long beak right up to the Witch's face.

Kaylee began to panic and the beautifully subtle Magick she'd been drawing up through the staff started to fade.

"Stop," I said, as the thin line of blood dripped out of the Swamp Witch's leg. "This is it, this is the challenge. Do not break eye contact."

"What?!"

I shook my head. "Listen to my words, but don't look at me, and don't take your eyes off that bird. Stare it down. Focus!"

Kaylee's hands twitched and her Magick fluttered in and out. "I..."

"Do what I'm telling you or the next metal post will end up between your ears."

The Swamp Witch got very still, locking eyes with the plastic bird and barely breathing.

The pile of flamingos on the far side of the room shifted again—this time with far more gusto. Something was unburying itself.

"Gene," Ed's ex-wife whispered, trying to get my attention.

I turned back just in time for the bird to press its beak against her nose.

"Don't stop. Do not let up."

Their eyes remained locked in a furious match of wills. More blood trickled down her leg, the tiny creature twisting the metal rod like a screwdriver.

"Argh..." The Swamp Witch gritted her teeth.

"I don't care how much it hurts. You let up now and I guarantee you it goes for your eyes."

The flamingo pushed itself about as close as it could to her face, then stopped, the Swamp Witch pushing back. Kaylee switched from holding ground to taking it. She seized the offensive and stared down the flamingo's coal-black gaze in the process.

She doing it.

The small creature sighed, removing its metal rod from Kaylee's leg in a single fluid motion. A thin stream of blood trickled down her thigh, dripping onto the surrounding plastic birds before turning the soft sand red.

The flamingo bent down and gently pecked at the oozing blood.

Kaylee slowly sat up, unable to take her eyes off the tiny bird. "What in the hell just happened?"

"Welcome to the Flock."

The little bird shook like a water fowl, then snuggled its beak under the chin of one very confused Swamp Witch.

"I don't get it."

"Just wait."

The pile in the corner shifted again, this time sending an avalanche of plastic yard art tumbling down.

"Gene," Kaylee said, keeping her hands away from the plastic bird. "It's... talking to me?"

"Images and thoughts. Listen, there's going to be a pull—a really strong one—you've got to push past that."

Kaylee tilted her head. "A pull?"

"Yeah, be ready for it. The Flock is going to want to run, to hide, and to take you down a paranoid and dangerous road. You're going to have to fight that."

The Swamp Witch's eyes glazed over. "I'm seeing images, Gene. What do they mean?"

"Potential paths. It's showing you the—"

"Future?"

"Not necessarily."

I'd have been lying if I said I wasn't jealous. The Flock was enigmatic, dangerous, but also beautiful. They were a sword that cut both ways, but to have one of them on your side was powerful and I missed it.

Sorry, Gertrude. You were a good bird.

"What do you see?" I asked, hoping Kaylee wasn't too far gone to hear me. The images would come fast, and they'd be confusing, but that bird might tell us something valuable.

"Eddie," Kaylee cried, jumping up, clearly startled by something she saw. The tiny bird hopped off and nuzzled her leg.

"Remember, it's not necessarily truth. The Flock's images can be confusing and broken."

"We have company, Gene."

"What?"

Suddenly the room felt a good bit smaller than it had only moments earlier.

Kaylee walked past me, her feet sending the piles of plastic birds sliding, until she reached the shifting spot. Ed's ex-wife dug her hands into the stacks, causing more plastic carcasses to tumble down, and retrieved a woman I'd never expected to see —Delia, the Sangre Reine. The Blood Queen was still alive, though not necessarily well, and standing in Sturkey.

"Hello, Gene. Surprised to see me?"

TICKETS TO THE GUN SHOW

The Sangre Reina, the Blood Queen, the hottest woman in South Beach, Delia had gone by a few names back when I'd known her. Back then she'd also taken a lot better care of herself. The old woman fighting her way out of the pile plastic birds looked nothing like the powerful Skeeter who had almost ended my world all those years ago. Spots covered Delia's liverwurst skin, brown, black, and otherwise; her neck alone could have served as a model for one of my son's connect-the-dots puzzles. A tight-fitting tracksuit stretched to its limit against the rest of her bloated body, clearly pushing the load-bearing capacity of velour.

"Delia…"

The former blood royalty frowned, jagged teeth making an appearance behind withered lips.

"Is that you? Is that Eugene Law?" Delia pointed at my slightly rounded midsection. "Somebody grew up… and out."

"You must not have access to a mirror," I said, frowning at her own appearance.

Delia's eyes flashed at the word. "No, why, do you have one?"

"Not for you."

Kaylee reached down to scoop up the tiny bird.

"Stop."

Both women looked at me.

"Kaylee, do not pick up the bird."

The Swamp Witch hesitated, her fingers twitching over the tiny plastic animal. "We are Flock, Gene. You wouldn't understand."

"I do understand, because I've been there before. I warned you about the pull."

Kaylee shook her head. "No, this is different. We need to leave. It's too dangerous here. She's shown me things, Gene. Little Ed is in trouble—"

"She..." the Blood Queen hissed, her own fingers twitching and gaze unwilling to leave Kaylee's bird.

"Kaylee, the images aren't real, or at least they aren't all real. The visions are just potentials—forking paths. It's how they communicate: images, visions, fragments of thought, and potential outcomes. You can get lost in them. It wants you to go, it wants you to pick it up and run away from everything. I told you, the pull is strong—you've got to be stronger."

Delia licked at her lips, a graying tongue playing over cracked lips. "There she is. I've been waiting for you little bird..."

"Yeah, well, you aren't getting it," I said, splitting my frustration between both women. "Adam, get in here. I need your help."

My apprentice bounded around the corner, sweat staining the shirt beneath his unzipped hoodie. Tiny droplets of mist clung to the tips of his thick beard. "Yeah, what do you—"

Adam froze the moment he laid eyes on the Blood Queen. "Is that..."

I nodded. "Yes."

"What is she doing here?"

"She's looking for that," I said, pointing to Kaylee and the tiny bird pressing its head against her bloody thigh.

My apprentice's eyes drifted to the thin trickle of red on the Swamp Witch's leg and he promptly lost a good bit of the color in his face. "What happened to your leg?"

"Long story, Adam," I said, trying to get my apprentice back on topic. "Very long story, and one we don't have time for."

Kaylee's fingers twitched above the fawning bird.

Crap.

"Okay ladies, here's what we are going to do. Adam," I said, turning to my apprentice. "I need you to gently escort Kaylee out of the building *without* the bird. Delia and I are going to have a nice conversation, and then we'll be joining you."

"Uh, Gene?"

"What?"

My apprentice frowned. "Where is Kaylee?"

I swung around to find the Swamp Witch gone.

"Son of a—"

Delia laughed, her voice gravely and deep. "Just use your Magick, Gene. If I recall correctly you've got some serious..." The Blood Queen trailed off, her crooked nose sniffing the air like an ancient bloodhound. "Wait..." She took another deep breath. "Gene, I don't smell your Magick. Where is that churning little cauldron of power?"

I ignored the Blood Queen. "Adam, get Jerry's Nine Dimensional glasses. You won't be able to see Kaylee, but you should be able to pick up a trail."

My apprentice swung his backpack around and unzipped it. "Got it."

Delia's eyes sparkled from beneath that wrinkled skin. "It's gone—your Magick is gone!"

This was not going how I'd planned it, but then again, I really hadn't planned this happening at all.

"Adam, get the glasses!"

"I'm trying." My apprentice fumbled through the contents of his bag. "Are you sure we put them in here?"

Delia clapped her spotted and wrinkly hands. "Ah, I was right! You've been Soul-Split. I can smell it."

"Congratulations," I said, turning my attention back to the Blood Queen. "I am, but not for long. Unlike you, I'm getting put back together."

"Oh, sweetheart, I've been saying that for a long time, but it's a lot harder than you think—especially when a powerful Magician is holding on to your Darkling. I knew going north made sense. Something's brewing. I can smell it."

"What are you talking about?"

Delia took another deep breath. "It's like that special crackle in the air right before a storm. Something big is coming, Gene, and I'm not about to miss it."

"Adam, get the glasses and find the Swamp Witch. Now!"

Delia ran her dumpy fingers over the piled-up stacks of plastic birds. "I had no idea that something big would include a Magickless Eugene Law. Oh my, what are the chances?"

"Terrible."

"I imagine so." Delia pointed at the thinning hairs on her balding scalp. "I've never been great at math, but I've got a memory—and it's a good one. I remember a young Magician and his wife. I remember what that young Magician did to me. That's something you don't forget." The Blood Queen's lips broke out into a hungry and crooked smile. "It makes you hungry, Gene. Very hungry."

"Adam," I said, taking a step back from the unpredictable Sangre Reina. "So help me, if you haven't found—"

"Got them!" he cried, half the backpack's contents on the floor in front of him. "Wow, that took a while. They got wedged under the cat statue thing."

Cat statue?!

"Adam, put that back in the bag right the hell now."

"Huh?"

The Blood Queen pushed up her sleeves, her tired eyes sparkling. "Perfection."

A tiny and emaciated plastic flamingo head slipped out of the stack. The bird was faded to the point of breaking, its pink skin flaking in patches.

Delia scooped up the emaciated bird and vanished.

No!

"Adam," I cried, bounding across the room toward my confused apprentice. "The statue, don't let her get the statute."

"Huh?" My apprentice pressed Jerry's Nine D glasses to his face. "Oh, right, got it."

He reached down to pick up the tiny cat woman statue, but before his hands could wrap the figure's lithe body, the tiny bronze artwork vanished.

"Shit!"

"There are trails everywhere." Adam's eyes darted behind the flimsy paper glasses. "I can't follow them."

"Just focus on the brighter one, that's got to be Kaylee. We need to find her and get out of here."

Delia popped back into view, the starving bird at her feet. One grotesque hand was wrapped around the bronze statue, while the other toyed with the cheap blindfold. "The mirror, Gene."

"I don't have it."

I lied. The stupid compact's plastic case was biting into my butt both literally and figuratively.

The Blood Queen picked at the rumpled bag that covered the statue's eyes. "Gene, I know you're lying." She pointed to the starving bird at her feet. "I've seen the forking paths. I've been doing this a long time—a very, very long time. My Darkling is in your back pocket, and you're going to give it to me. Unless, that is, you want me to take this off?" Delia's long nails scraped across the blindfold.

"No," I said, doing my best to keep my voice level. "I'm sure we can come to some agreement. You remember what happened the last time. You know it didn't end well for you."

"I'm the one holding the statue," Delia shook the tiny figurine at me, " and I have a strong feeling that's going to make all the difference."

"Wait. Let's talk about this like rational people."

The Blood Queen tucked her nail under the edge of the crumpled blinder. "No, no more talk. Time's up. You give me the mirror, or I take it from your corpse. After that, I'll eat the bearded one."

Adam froze up, the 9D glasses drooping down his nose. "Gene…"

"I got it." I placed a hand on my back pocket. "But I'm going to need assurances."

Adam's hoodie pouch bounced, its jerky movements accompanied by a muffled voice that I'd only just been introduced to, but was already getting on my nerves.

"You've just earned yourself two tickets to the gun show," the wrestling doll in my apprentice's pocket called out.

Delia hesitated. "What was that?"

"Adam?"

My apprentice removed the rubber wrestler, then looked at me. "Uh…"

"What does that mean?"

Adam hesitated. "It means—"

Boom!

Kaylee popped back into view, the Swamp Witch crashing into Delia like a linebacker at full speed.

"The blindfold!" I shouted, reaching for the falling figurine.

The tiny statue tumbled to the ground, its plastic bag slipping off in the process.

Shit!

The statue's ancient Magick seeped out, signaling for something I was not in any position to face. That power wasn't alone. It blended with a sickly blast of frigid air that rolled over the room and cut me to the bone. There was only one thing I knew of that did that.

A Thinning!

29

FRISKIES

Kaylee let go of the Blood Queen and grabbed the tiny bronze statue. "What do I do?"

"Cover the eyes." I pointed to the ring of wadded plastic on the dirty ground.

Ed's ex-wife got the blindfold back on, but the ancient Magick had already leaked out, spilling over the room like a hot desert wind and mixing it up with the unnatural cold of the Thinning.

She's coming...

Kaylee tightened the tiny covering down on the statue's eyes. "What's going on, Gene?"

"I'm not going to wait and find out." I pulled at the Wild Magick of the Thinning, its icy cold power burning in my veins.

"Gene, what did I say about pulling power from a Thinning?" Kaylee cried, getting to her feet as the unpredictable power swelled around me.

"It's bat-shit crazy." Magick swirled between my fingers. "But so is waiting around for Bastet."

"Gene—"

I lost Kaylee's words against the burgeoning tide of Wild

Magick. The Thinning pumped more power than I was ready for, but I didn't have a choice.

"Discedite!" I squeezed at the unpredictable cosmic power and willed it against the desert wind and what it was sure to bring. The Magick fought me, pushing back on my desires and flaring up like an angry wound.

Oh no, you're not...

I settled into a tug of war. The Thinning wasn't interested in listening to a Magickless Magician, and I was far too stupid to quit. Delia shouted something, so did Kaylee, but neither woman's cries made it past my concentration.

"Discedite!" I had the desert wind on the run and I wasn't about to let up.

There...

"Gene." Kaylee's voice made it past my filters. "You idiot. You just sent whatever that was directly at the burial mound."

"I... what?"

The Swamp Witch was right. The Wild Magick had helped me send away that ancient desert wind, and in doing so I had directed it straight toward an unhealthy mass of Restless Dead.

Oh, crap.

Something banged against the rusty steel roof above us.

That can't be good.

Little Ed choose this moment to join us. "Guys, we have a problem—"

"Rumble rumble in da jungle!" Muscles shouted over the junior Demon Hunter.

"Adam!"

My apprentice's face went red as he continued to fiddle with the spastic action figure. "Really sorry, guys. Let me see if I can get him turned down."

"Can you smell what The Muscles is cooking?" the tiny figure asked, making it difficult to hear Little Ed's response.

"Adam!"

"Working on it. I think if I just—" My apprentice's fiddling was interrupted by a sheet of rusted metal that broke free of the ceiling and landed on a large pile of pink plastic.

"What the hell is that?" I said, finding myself face to face with the partially decaying skin of an oversized cat.

"That's a panther," Kaylee said, pushing Delia aside. "Don't move, Gene."

"You're kidding right?" I kept a sharp eye on the rotting flesh and flexing jaws of the massive cat.

"No, I'm not. We dealt with them at the mound years ago. I don't understand why they're back now."

"I might." My eyes locked on the massive feline. "I've had cat issues in the past."

"This wouldn't have anything to do with the statue, would it?" Kaylee asked.

"We can point fingers later. Right now we need to focus on the task at hand."

The Swamp Witch reached for her staff. "Just let me get my —" Kaylee's stick vanished beneath her fingers. "Delia!"

"Looks like we got us a big one here, sir." Private Petty appeared next to me, wearing a pair of tan shorts and a loosely buttoned shirt rolled up to his armpits.

"The Crocodile Guy?"

Private Petty smiled, his boyish face beaming. "You guessed it, sir. You really are good at this."

"Either that, or we both watched *way* too much television as kids."

The decaying cat growled. The sound reverberated through its exposed tendons and rotting flesh, and gave the beast a nightmare-inducing timbre. Plastic flamingos cracked beneath its paws.

"Uh, don't suppose you plan to help the old man out here?" I asked, my hands up.

Private Petty backed up with me. "No, sir. I'm sorry, but there's nothing I can do."

"What?!"

"I'm allergic to cats."

I slapped a hand to my forehead. "You can't be serious."

"Gene!" Kaylee shouted, "Who the hell are you talking to?"

"I'm afraid so, sir."

"Oh, son of a—"

My witty retort was interrupted by hundreds of pounds of decaying flesh launching itself at me in rage-filled fury. I didn't have enough time to react, but as it turned out, I didn't have to —the pants did it for me.

Those animated capris must have picked up on the Thinning, as they kicked my legs out and sent the rest of my body crashing into Adam and The Muscles. The doll ended up somewhere in that pile of plastic, along with most of the contents of my backpack.

A bright pink flash of movement drew my attention.

Kaylee's bird!

Too late, the Swamp Witch had already made eye contact with her flamingo.

If Delia was using her bird in a Thinning, she was already more than half-crazy, but I couldn't let Kaylee go down the same path. "Stop, don't touch it."

As expected, she didn't listen to me.

"Private." I tried to untangle myself from Adam. "Get that bird."

"You got it." The environmentally fashionable young ghost scooped up the flamingo. "What a pretty bird you are, eh?"

"Damn it, Petty, be careful with—"

The flamingo's head spun around and bit down hard onto the soldier's ghostly finger. "Crikey!"

Private Petty grabbed at his wounded digit and let the plastic bird tumble into the pile.

Kaylee seized her opportunity and made a play for it, but the panther was faster. Even dead and clearly reanimated, the big cat was still plenty quick on its feet.

"Kaylee!"

The Swamp Witch ignored me, but I couldn't say I was surprised. The call of the Flock was a heady drug and not something easily shook off. Add to that the Thinning and you had a recipe for disaster. Still, I wasn't about to lose my pretend spouse after I'd only just fake married her that morning.

Show a little respect for the institution, Gene.

The cold tendrils of the supernatural Thinning snaked over my quasi-Magickal pants, bestowing a quick jolt of power to my nether regions and propelling me into action.

"It's now or never—andele' Magick pants!" The newly reinvigorated denim sucked up Wild Magick from the Thinning like a shammy and launched me free of my apprentice.

"Gene, wait," Adam cried, crawling to a seated position. "You don't have your Magick."

"Tell that to the pants!"

The rotting feline had Kaylee in its sights and was closing fast. Large paws like catchers mitts tore through the piles of pink plastic, but still the Swamp Witch didn't change course. Thankfully, the Magick pants had closing speed, and appeared to know a good bit more geometry than I did.

"Kaylee, snap the hell out of it!" Animated pants swung my butt in front of Ed's ex-wife and then out of the way of one very powerful panther paw.

"Mom!" The junior Demon Hunter broke his mom from her trance just long enough for her to watch him get leveled by a second panther from behind.

"Eddie!"

"Gotcha," I said, scooping up the flamingo before Kaylee could get her hands on it.

Across the room, the junior Demon Hunter had his own

hands full fighting off the rotting beast, but unlike the rest of us he appeared to have a decent chance of succeeding. Little Ed slipped under a swipe of claws and dug his hand into the monster's chest.

"Go for the heart!" he shouted.

"You got that, Adam?"

Much to my surprise my apprentice was already way ahead of me. He scooped up Mindy's Brain Freezer. The blender being one of the many things he'd stuffed in his backpack.

"What are you doing? You've got to plug it in."

My apprentice shook his head. "You aren't the only one who can improvise. I learned from the best of them."

"Adam!"

My apprentice ripped the top off the glass pitcher and mashed down the buttons, his Magick roaring into the machine. Inside that wide mouth tiny blades exploded to life and sliced up an icy green concoction.

"Gene!" Kaylee shouted behind me. She'd shaken off the Flock for now, but still had a rotting cat of her own to contend with. The undead beast tore through the piles of plastic slashing at the Swamp Witch's legs. Magick built up around Ed's ex-wife, but it was sporadic and uncoordinated.

She needs the staff. Well, isn't that just special?

The flamingo latched its beak down on my wrist and I almost tossed it away then and there, but that bold little bird's move gave me an idea.

Damn it, Petty. Where are you when I need you?

"I'm here," said the young ghost, his voice now solidly in my skull. "What's your plan?"

I mentally walked him through the gist of it.

"Are you sure you want to do that again?"

I shook my head. "No, I'm not, but it's the best idea I've got."

The spectral soldier vanished and his silver saber appeared in my hand. For the second time in two days, I turned over control to the young soldier, and hoped to hell and back he'd return it without a fight.

"I've learned something, sir," the Private's voice echoed in my head.

"What's that?"

"I really miss being alive."

Oh, crap.

30

MARGARITAVILLE

*P*rivate Petty went for the surprise attack—in that it surprised both me, and the cat. That cheeky spirit launched us onto the creature's back. Not being a beast of burden, the panther had no idea what to do with a Magician on its back. Instincts took over, and the monster went for the most efficient response—try to buck me off.

Petty clamped my hand down on a slimy exposed rib. "Hold on, sir."

Private!

The cat flipped. The sudden turn cost me any hold I'd had on the flamingo. That pink bird tumbled end over end through the air, only to land somewhere among its inanimate brethren.

"Gene—"

I didn't get the rest of Kaylee's words before the massive rotting cat-corpse smothered me.

This wasn't one of your best ideas.

Private Petty's voice responded me in my head. "I told you I don't have a lot of cat experience. I'm more of a dog person, honestly."

Now you tell me.

With a good chunk of my body pinned beneath the panther, the Magick pants went to work. They kicked a leg out and sent it slamming down onto what I assumed was the area where sensitive cat bits would be located.

The moldy feline hissed and flipped upright. The maneuver sent me sliding across the floor only to crash into a pile of broken flamingos.

Yahtzee.

Kaylee's hands pulled me upright. "Gene, it's coming back around."

"What?"

She was right. The monster shook off shards of broken birds and advanced on us.

Petty...

"I'm on it, sir"

Petty's silver saber returned to my hand, its grip resting comfortably between my fingers.

"I thought you had no Magick," Kaylee said, pointing at the sword.

"It's a long story. I'll explain it to you after we—"

"Eddie!" Kaylee pulled my attention away from the advancing feline.

The junior Demon Hunter lay pinned beneath the other beast's massive paw. The cat had him pressed against the dirt, its paw raised up to deliver the killing blow.

Private!

"There's nothing I can do, sir. He's too far away."

What do you mean? Throw your saber!

"And that leaves us with what? Your natural charm?"

Petty, I swear I'm—

"Bluescreen of Death!" Adam swung the pitcher of frozen margaritas like a fire bucket at the cat poised to separate Little Ed's head from his body.

Typically, never-ending margaritas had to be consumed to

get the freezing effect, but with a Thinning in play it was really anybody's guess. Bright green party booze hit the panther square in the face and icy waves of freezing crystals raced down the creature's body.

"Nice work, Adam," I said, only to have Private Petty pull my attention back to the task at hand.

"Sir, the cat…"

The crunch of broken plastic was an excellent motivator, as was the panther closing fast. We'd already backed up about as far as we could.

What's the plan, Private?

"Try not to let you get killed, sir."

Do or do not, Private. There is no try.

"Nice one." The young ghost chuckled and sent my arm into action. The saber cut a path across the feline's face, tearing at tendons and slicing away rotting flesh. Petty adjusted for a second pass, but the panther was quicker, turning the blade aside with a swipe of its rotting paw.

Go for the heart!

"Sir, the talking."

Right, sorry.

Between Private Petty's blade and my expert non-verbal commentary, we slashed and parried like a well-oiled machine. Sure, it was really the State Saber Champ, but occasionally my pants provided some fancy footwork that helped keep the two of us upright.

Petty brought the saber down again, this time catching the panther's jawline and severing a few decayed tendons in the process. The monster's counter was clumsy and gave me a few seconds to check on Little Ed—turns out I didn't need to.

The junior Demon Hunter rammed his machete home, driving it between the monster's frozen ribs and making contact with its heart. The beast disintegrated: tendons, muscles, and bones fell away like discarded wrappers, leaving nothing but an icy black heart.

Like that, see? That's how you kill them.

"Sir," Private Petty said, his voice strong between my ears. "I'm really trying to stay civil, but you aren't making that easy."

Civil? We don't need civil, kid. We need ass-kicking goodness.

"Sir, I can't do that if you don't—"

Private Petty's words were cut off by the panther's pounce. My animated denim juked us to the side, but even they weren't fast enough to avoid all of it. The beast's claws tore through my front pants pocket, rending the enchanted denim, and carving a deep gouge in the painted wooden grave marker.

Petty!

Wrenched free, the broken fragment landed among the plastic, and took with it my connection to the soldier.

Private?

I got no response, and the saber vanished from my hand, effectively leaving me defenseless. Even being an undead, the panther didn't take long to figure that out.

Kaylee's hands grabbed my shoulder. "Gene? Where's your sword?"

The grave marker slipped below the shifting plastic and disappeared like a wallet sinking into the ball pits of Chucky Cheese.

"Looks like it's just you and me." I put the Swamp Witch behind me. "Well, you, me, *and* the pants."

My animated pants must have figured out what just happened, because they suddenly tried to make a break for the door.

"Stop," I said, fighting against the panicking denim.

The cat advanced undeterred. Even with evidence of Private Petty's saber everywhere—torn tendons, split and oozing muscles—the monster still pounced. Kaylee wrapped her arms around me and I closed my eyes, digging for some Magick, any

Magick, that might help. The Thinning was full of it, but it was too strong. I couldn't control that power. To reach for it now would be like drinking from a firehose.

"Kernel Panic!" Adam shouted, and I opened my eyes just in time to avoid being splashed with the bright green margarita mix of Mindy's Brain Freezer. The panther was not so lucky.

"Adam!"

My apprentice swung the frosted pitcher on his fingers like an extra from Cocktail. "Order up!"

"You glorious bastard, don't drop the—"

Before I could finish chiding him, the pitcher handle slipped from his finger and hit the floor with a bang, shattering the glass and introducing us to a brand-new problem.

When Magickal items were unmade—even by complete accident when a Magician had done his or her best to make fools out of themselves—things typically went bad, very bad. This time, though, they went worse, because as bad as an unmaking was, doing it in a Thinning was always worse.

"Adam!"

"Whoops…"

A conga-line of ice crystals raced across the ground, freezing everything they touched, including the stacks of plastic birds, and anything they were in contact with.

"Run." I pushed Kaylee toward the door.

She pushed back and dug into the pile of quickly freezing yard art. "No, the bird. We are Flock!"

Glacier-like frost shattered plastic and fused metal legs. "Let it go, you've got to move."

"I can't! We are Flock!"

I shoved the Swamp Witch toward Adam. "Get her out of here now!"

My apprentice caught Kaylee's arm even as she struggled to get free. "Where are you going, Gene?"

"To find Private Petty!"

"Who?"

"Long story," I said, brushing at the frost building up on my pants. "Just get her out of—"

I froze, and not from the cocktail mix—the compact wasn't in my pocket.

"What is it, Gene?"

"The compact, it's gone!"

My apprentice picked up the backpack. "It's not in here either."

A cold wave of panic raced down my spine, and it wasn't from the wave of frozen booze, it was the thought of losing my Magick—permanently.

The wooden marker or the mirror? You don't have time for both. You made Petty a promise, and he's saved your life more than once... But my Magick...

I hesitated, but Adam didn't; he used his girth to wrap up the Swamp Witch and hand her off to Little Ed. "Get her out of here. I've got to help Gene!"

Ice crystals raced up my capris, stiffening the denim around my knees and making it difficult to move. From there, the freezing wave rolled undeterred, icing over Adam's feet, and pinning his sneakers to the ground.

"Uh, Gene?"

I kicked at the frost, breaking my apprentice free, but wasting valuable time in the process.

The Magick or Private Petty—it's time to decide just what kind of person you are.

More ice expanded out in all directions, submerging shattered plastic like thick frosting on a wedding cake.

"You need to go," I said, pushing my apprentice toward the entrance.

"Like hell I do." Adam threw broken birds by the handful. "I'm finding the compact!"

Time to decide, Gene. Are you like Delia? Is Gene Law the most important thing in your life? Or can you make the real sacrifices?

"Switch gears." I grabbed his arm.

"Huh?"

"There's a death marker here for a kid I made a promise to and I'm not giving up on him."

Adam tossed aside more frozen birds. "What does it look like?"

"A white sliver of wood."

Adam surveyed the frosting sea of plastic. "You're kidding."

"Less talking, more digging!"

Plastic birds fused together, their pink bodies icing up in the freezing blast of uncontrolled margarita Magick, and quickly becoming next to impossible to separate.

"Gene," Adan said, his hands broken and bleeding. "We've got to go, come on."

"No, I can't!"

"You can't save everyone!"

"That's not the point."

Adam grabbed my collar. "It *is* the point. Cathy's safe—they're all safe. She's still in Tampa, but neither of us will see her again if you don't let this go."

Ice scraped at my fingers, but still I dug deeper, snapping off broken plastic.

Come on!

"Gene, we've got to—"

My fingers brushed over the marker's white wood.

"I found it!"

"What?"

"There," I shouted, diving into the mass of frosted bird bits reaching for the broken piece of roadside cross. "I've almost got it."

Ice raced over the sleeve of Ed's old shirt and burned at my arms, but I couldn't stop, not with the marker so close.

"We've got to go," Adam cried, pulling me toward the door the instant my fingers closed around Private Petty's marker.

The last thing I remembered before hitting the dirt outside was the young soldier's faint and tired voice somewhere between my ears. "Thank you, sir."

31

CHOICES MADE

*J*n the Thinning's waning moments, the frozen concrete and steel crumbled, leaving the derelict remains of the Sturkey bird house a heap of twisted rebar, broken concrete, and small pink shards of plastic.

The mirror's gone.

I clutched at what remained of Private Petty's grave marker. The young man's spirit was still bound inside the broken cross, but something was different. The panther's claws had taken a toll on the brave kid, one that I wasn't sure he would ever recover from.

I held that marker and traced its edge with my finger.

I'm sorry, kid. I don't know if I can get you home without my Magick, or if I ever could to begin with...

I wasn't sure if I'd expected a response from the solider, but I didn't get one just the same. I placed the shard of wood back in my pocket, and as I did my fingers caught on the edge of the paper photo wheel. Very little light filtered in from the setting sun, but I held up the disc to it just the same. There was a consolation prize tucked inside those images. I'd gained a spot on my Darkling.

Huh, saving the marker won me back a little of my humanity—I'll take it.

"Gene?"

Adam's voice sounded distant and muffled.

"We have a problem," he said. His words slowly worked their way past the walls of defeated sadness I'd been building in my head.

"What now?"

Kaylee held the cat-woman figurine, its blindfold barely hanging on. She slammed the artifact against her palm like a Louisville Slugger. "Give me the staff."

Delia was back, and she looked all the worse for wear. How many times could she pick up her withered flamingo? Was the Flock taking its toll on the old woman?

She leaned against the Swamp Witch's staff, using it to keep her frail body upright.

"Not until you give me the mirror."

Little Ed had his machete out and pointed at the waning Blood Queen.

"Delia," I said, my own voice tired. "You want it? It's in there." I swung a hand to point at the shattered building. "It was lost in the fight. You'll have to dig it out."

"I don't believe you." She squeezed the oak staff in her fingers. "I know one of you has it. I can smell my Darkling."

"No, you can't." Blood rushed to my face. "You can't smell a damn thing. Don't you get it? You and I are crap now. We're nothing. We're dried-up husks of normalcy—"

"Gene…" Adam tried to stop me, but I barreled right over him in a bout of righteous pity.

"No, Adam. It's true. We are done, Delia. There is no more Magick for us. You have lost your Darkling, and with it I lost the only real way to get my Magick back. So here we are, stuck scrounging for Thinnings and hoping to survive whatever Wild

Magick we touch. Don't you get it? You don't matter anymore. *I don't matter anymore.*"

"Wait, Gene…"

"Damn it, Adam. Let me finish."

My apprentice tilted his head at Swamp Witch. "Uh, she has it."

"What?! How…"

Kaylee held the brown compact in her hand, tears glistening in the edges of her eyes. "The Flock showed me, Gene. It showed me what could happen to my son if I don't. There's no way you could understand. I had to take it. If I didn't…"

"No, that's just potentials. They might happen, and they might not. It's all probability." I tried to bite back the anger in my voice. "You can't believe them—the Flock isn't always right."

"It doesn't matter, Gene. You wouldn't understand. That staff means the world to me. I have to get it back."

A mixture of emotions rolled through me too confusing to count: anger, elation, sadness, and frustration all fought for control of my higher brain functions.

"Kaylee, do not let her have that."

Ed's ex-wife held the compact in her hand. "Give me the staff and I'll return your Darkling to you."

"Don't do it, damn it." I stepped in front of the Swamp Witch. "You don't understand how dangerous she is. Whatever you saw, it can't be as bad as what will happen if you give her back her Magick."

"You couldn't possibly understand." Tears rolled down the Swamp Witch's cheeks. "She's not keeping my staff."

"Who said anything about keeping it." Delia wedged the stick against a root ball and leaned into it. Even with her frail body, she easily possessed enough weight to snap the stick in two.

I pleaded with Kaylee to return the mirror and its bound Darkling to me. "You'll find another one. I'll help. They're doing great things with cypress these days. What about pine? It's cheap and soft—we could get someone to fashion it into all sorts of designs."

"Gene, stop trying to change my mind," Kaylee said, taking a step toward the Blood Queen. "You don't know the history."

"Did it come from your mother? No problem, we'll make another one—"

"Sear Spit."

"What? The Imp?"

Kaylee turned her red and irritated eyes to her son. "You never asked why Ed and I split up."

"You worked a deal with that Imp?" I said, my voice dropping.

"Not just any deal." Kaylee placed her hand on Little Ed's shoulder lovingly. "I can't expect you to understand, Gene. You have children."

The sudden realization hit me like a gut punch. "He's not real..."

Little Ed's machete drooped. "What's he talking about?"

Delia leaned into the staff a little more, causing it to bend dangerously close to the breaking point. "He's saying what I've known ever since you four showed up. One of these things just ain't like the other, one of these things just isn't the same, and that would be you, young man."

"Mom..."

Tears flowed down Kaylee's face. "I had to do it, don't you understand? I had to. Your father and I tried to have a child for years and we... You can't know what that's like, the sadness, the frustration, the anger—what it does to a marriage. How it makes you feel subhuman..." Ed's ex-wife dropped the bronze figurine, letting it tumble into the mud. "Everyone else is out there having children, raising families, and we couldn't..."

"Mom," Little Ed said, his voice breaking. "What did you do?"

"Exactly what I'm going to do now. What I told your father I would always do. Whatever it takes for my family."

Kaylee pushed past me and took a step toward Delia. "Don't break the staff. I'll give you the compact."

"I don't know." Delia let the staff bow against her tracksuit. "I'm old, I could fall over at any minute. Might want to hurry up."

"Stop." I reinserted myself between the women. "If she gets the mirror, there'll be no stopping her. Don't you understand? She could shatter the staff the moment her Magick is back."

"I would never." The old crone let the oak spring back. "I'm a woman of my word, Mr. Law. I promise that if my Darkling is returned to me, I will not break the only thing keeping her son animated."

Little Ed let his machete fall the rest of the way. "Animated?"

"Don't listen to her, honey. It's nothing."

"No, Mom. What does she mean by animated?"

Delia resumed her pole bending. "I've got to say, your Magick is subtle to the point of art. Using the Imp's help to craft a son out of live oak heartwood is quite a feat. Yet there he is, almost like a real boy."

"Mom?"

"She's lying," Kaylee squeezed the compact in her fingers. "You are a real boy in every sense of the word. I love you, Eddie, no matter where you came from or how you got here. I love you for who you are, and for the wonderful young man you have become."

"I'm not... real?"

Delia chuckled. "Nope, not at all. You're the most impressive golem I've ever seen though, and I've been alive quite a few years. So, that's gotta count for something."

"A golem?" the young man said, his once proud shoulders falling. "You mean like the—"

"Little rubber man the fat one carries around in his pants?

Exactly like that except, you know, actually crafted with real skill."

"And that's why Dad..."

Kaylee nodded. "Yes, that's why your father left me, that's why he treats you different. That's why—"

Realization dawned on Little Ed's face. "That's why you never let that staff out of your sight. That's why you keep me home. That's why I could never move out or get a place on my own or—"

The sound of cracking wood stopped everyone cold— everyone except for the Sangre Reina.

"Listen, sapling," Delia said, inspecting the newly formed crack in the staff. "I'd love to listen to you whine—I really would —but it doesn't look like you have much time left."

Little Ed dropped his machete and grabbed his chest. "Mom!"

"Gene, move, now!"

"Don't do it," I said, pleading with her. "We'll find a way, I promise you. I'll get my Magick back and we'll find a way."

Kaylee stepped around me, but before I could block her path a second time my feet became trapped in snaking roots—roots driven by the subtle Magick of the Green Swamp itself.

The Swamp protects its own.

"No, Gene. There's no other way, I'm sorry."

"Adam, stop her."

My apprentice lunged for her, but the twisting roots held him fast as well.

I yanked at the snaking vegetation's iron grip. "Kaylee, don't do it."

The Swamp Witch walked past me, the mirror in her hand. "I'm sorry, Gene. It has to be this way."

"You're damn straight it does." Delia stretched out her hand in quivering anticipation. "I've been waiting a long time for this. Come to Mama!"

32

SCREW DRIVEN

*K*aylee presented her palm with the simple brown compact lying gently in the center. Nothing about that bit of makeup said Magick, but I knew otherwise. Tightly carved into the narrow plastic seam was a series of complex sigils, each more elaborate that the last. It would take Delia a couple more lifetimes to unlock Quigley's Quagmire and get into that compact without her Magick.

Still, I wasn't about to risk it.

Private, can you cut me loose?

I got no response from the injured spirit. Perhaps I'd pushed him too far. It was impossible to tell without my Magick. Any chance I had of getting that power back was right about to end up in the former Skeeter's fingers.

"Give it to me," Delia said, the anticipation palpable in her voice.

Kaylee hesitated, pulling back her hand slightly. "How do I know you'll give me back my staff?"

Delia leaned on the oak and let the hairline fracture expand further. "You don't."

Little Ed fell forward, his arms holding tight to his body. "Mom!"

"Don't do it. Please." I pulled at my legs.

"Don't listen to him, sweetheart." Delia's voice regained its soft and subtle air. "He's just jealous. You see, *we* have our Magick, or at least we will very soon. Gene, on the other hand, is royally screwed."

"She's right. I am screwed, but so is my family if she gets that back. I have children too—"

"And they mean more than her son?" Delia's words trampled over mine. "Listen to him—typical magician—just give me the mirror, dear."

"Gene, I'm sorry."

"There's nothing to be sorry about, honey. You are doing what's right for you and yours. That's what the smart ones do in this world. They do what's right for them. Who else is going to look out for you? The Eugene Laws of the world? Why, he's been dragging a poor soul's Death Marker around with him like a lost puppy. You think he's going to help that kid get to the next life?" Delia snorted. "If you actually believe that, I've got a plot of land to sell you off the coast of Key West."

"Is that true?" Kaylee asked, tears in her eyes. "Have you been enslaving a lost soul?"

"Now, enslaving is a *really* strong word. I wouldn't say that. I would say I've been working very closely with a dedicated former member of our nation's armed services to—"

The old woman cut me off again. "See? Lying. All of them lie, sweetheart." Delia turned her attention to me. "Every last single solitary one of them. You don't need them, you've got your son, your swamp, and even those silly Trolls. Trust me, you'll be better off. Just give me the mirror... now."

"But how do I know you won't..."

Bridge Trolls, this place is sacred to them.

We were getting on in the day, but were we late enough yet?

When did the Bridge Trolls come to do whatever the heck it was they did in Sturkey? Could we buy more time?

"Adam," I whispered.

"Huh?"

"Keep your voice down," I said, leaning closer to my chubby apprentice. "Do you still have the can?"

"The what?"

"The Deep Magick can from earlier. The one we used to call Cathy."

"That wasn't Cathy."

It took all I had to refrain from smacking him. "Damn it, Adam. Do you have the can or not?"

"No, you kicked it in the swamp remember?"

"I did?"

"Yeah—it was kind of a dick thing to do."

Sounds like me.

"Okay. Well, let me think…"

Adam held up his hands. "Yeah, you even made me hold on to it for longer than I should have. See, look at this burn on my palm. I've got the can's damn sigil burned right into my skin."

"Right. Listen, I said I was sorry—"

"Actually you didn't…"

"Wait, it's burned into your skin?" I asked, the sight of his burned skin giving me an idea.

Adam nodded. "Yes, right here."

"Oh, we are so going to Indiana Jones this."

"Huh?"

"Cup your hands together and let's make a call."

Adam shook his head. "I'm not reaching out to the Tower of Terrible—"

"Unceasing Torment."

"That—I'm not doing that again."

I shook my head. "Who said anything about that? You're calling the Bridge Trolls."

"What?!"

I snuck a quick glance at the ladies, but they were still lost in discussion. "Keep your voice down. Okay, Stinkstone. That's who you are calling."

"Gene, I can't just reach out to a supernatural Bridge Troll without—"

I grabbed Adam's hand. "Yes, yes you can. I'll provide the visual, you make the call."

My apprentice bit his lip. "Are you sure this is going to—"

"Work? Hell no. In fact, I have no idea what's going to happen, but it beats waiting around to reacquaint ourselves with the Blood Queen, right?"

Adam cupped his hand. "Ping minus a, Stinkstone," he mumbled, and I felt the rush of Magick.

I miss that so much.

"I'm not getting any visuals."

"Right," I said, closing my eyes and bringing up a mental image of the Bridge Troll. It wasn't hard to do, ten to twelve foot tall walking slabs of granite-colored man-stucco aren't easily forgotten—plus I knew his name.

"That's him?" Adam whispered.

"Yes."

"And you want to contact *him?*"

Little Ed groaned on the ground, while the sharp sounds of cracking wood added an immediate sense of urgency.

"Yes!"

Adam's hand was a poor man's substitute for the Calling Can and Marvin's Long Line, but it did the trick—albeit with terrible reception. Faint static crackled from his cupped fingers and I leaned over to whisper into them.

"Stinkstone, it's me, Gene. You know. The Magician you don't like."

A low grumble issued from Adam's can hand.

"Right. Listen, the feeling is mutual."

My apprentice's fingers twitched. "Would you stop making him angry?"

I placed a hand over his stubby finger-receiver. "You speak Bridge Troll? I mean, if you would like to explain things in his own language…"

"Well, no."

"Then shut it."

Adam clamped his mouth closed and poured more Magick into the connection.

I removed my hand. "Well, I'm here in Sturkey and I think it's a real crap hole. In fact, I think it's so terrible I'm going to invite a bunch of my Magician friends out here to stomp on things and leave our people stink *everywhere*."

The deep rumble from Adam's fingers was loud enough to get everyone's attention.

Kaylee pulled her attention away from the old woman for just a second, but a second was all it took for Delia to rip the brown compact from her hand.

"It's mine! Oh, how I've missed you. We're going to get back together, you and I." The old woman beamed and ran her fingers over the hand mirror's seam.

The sigils carved in the crease flared to life, filling the Blood Queen's palm with a golden glow.

"Quigley's Quagmire? Really?"

I pulled away from the Adam-phone and turned my attention to Delia. "Damn straight. I've had years to prepare that. You aren't getting past them. You don't have your Magick, and those sigils will keep you from getting to it."

Delia sighed, then shook her head. She tucked Kaylee's staff under her arm, leaning into it, then held out her open palm.

"Wait, what are you doing?"

The Blood Queen dug a sharpened nail into the back of the case.

"Gah! What is she doing?" I turned my attention to Adam. "Is that a Magick nail? Where the hell is our Bridge Troll?"

My apprentice shook his head. "I don't... *Are* there Magick fingernails?"

Delia casually twisted the two tiny screws on the bottom holding the case together with her finger.

"Wait, stop!" I shouted. "You can't do that."

"And why not?"

Because... Because I didn't think of that!

"I... you..."

Pop.

Delia flicked the expertly protected case into the muck, which left only the darkened mirror in her hand.

"Gene..." Kaylee said, stepping back. "What just happened?"

"I was beaten by a fingernail."

"Give me my staff!" Kaylee cried. "You have what you want."

"Not yet I don't." Delia placed her fingers on the mirror backing.

"Wait!" I shouted, still trapped by the twisted roots. "Your Darkling is locked in that mirror, and it's going to want you gone. It's going to want to consume you. You have no Magick. How the hell are you going to stop it?"

The Blood Queen locked eyes with me, and I had my answer before she spoke.

"What makes you think I want to?"

Delia flipped the mirror over and stared into it, the vile Darkling's Magick reaching out like spilt ink.

Crap.

"Kaylee, do something!"

The Swamp Witch lunged for her staff, but the old woman was faster. She slammed the stick forward, snapping it against the roots and sending splinters flying.

Our twisted arboreal restraints vanished.

"Eddie!" Kaylee cried, ignoring the broken staff and running to her fallen son.

Black ink, like the Deserter's Tar, trickled down the Blood Queen's outstretched hand. Wrinkles smoothed out everywhere it touched, the skin losing its mottled appearance. Her thin and wiry hair gave way to thick and vibrant locks that blossomed like the unfolding of a tropical flower. The beautiful woman's color returned, a warm butternut glow that was the Delia I remembered—the Sangre Reina, the Blood Queen of South Beach.

"Gene," Adam whispered. "What do we do?"

Delia smiled, showing us the same perfect teeth she'd used to win over so many hearts through the decades, hearts she'd later bleed dry. "You die."

BELIEF

*D*elia beamed. Restored to her former glory, the South Beach Skeeter practically floated above the muck-covered ground. She looked us over like we were cattle for the slaughter, before pausing momentarily to pick at dirt that had settled along her perfectly manicured nails. "Who's first?"

"Gene..." Adam backed up.

The Blood Queen turned her attention to my apprentice. "It looks like someone is volunteering. Smart choice, the first one is always the quickest. It's the ones that come after I take my time with."

My bearded apprentice raised his hands, but whatever Magick he had sputtered beneath Delia's withering gaze. "Plan, Gene. We need a plan."

Plan?

I thought about Private Petty and his saber, but in his present state, the translucent soldier was no match for Delia. To add insult to injury, I wasn't much better. No Thinning meant no Magick, and now with the mirror exposed my Darkling would be coming, and fast. That Deep Magick would draw him out like ink from a fountain pen.

"I'm thinking," I said, backing up along with him.

"Can you think faster?"

Kaylee would be no help. She had problems of her own. Little Ed hung in her arms like limp pasta, his head painfully twisted to the side. Tears streamed down the Swamp Witch's face. "No, Eddie. Don't let go. Fight it. You are more than this. I know you are."

Her son's eyes darted around, unfocused and confused. "Mom, where are you? It's so cold..."

"I'm here, Eddie. I'm here." She pulled him close. "I won't let you go."

Kaylee's words hit me like a thunderbolt. They'd been my words so many months ago. Visions of Cathy filled my mind, and with them came the screams of her final seconds clinging to the Hellgate—it brought me to my knees.

I let her go...

"I won't let you go." Kaylee's words tore at my heart strings.

No one's letting go again.

Her shattered staff laid only a few feet away, Wild Magick ebbing out of it only to be absorbed into the ground.

The ground... Sturkey... This whole place is sacred, but why?

Kaylee's son jerked violently.

"Eddie." Tears streamed down the Swamp Witch's cheeks. "I love you. I've always loved you. From the very moment you came into my life. You're real to me—you will always be real to me."

"Mom..." Little Ed's voice was fading fast, his eyes aimless and confused.

The staff. It's all in the staff.

"Keep her busy," I said to Adam, crawling over to the broken staff.

My apprentice raised his hands, Magick sputtering between his fingers. "Uh... Format... No... Select from..."

With the Blood Queen otherwise pre-occupied, I scooped up

the staff. Its splintered wood oozed Magick, a Deep Magick from somewhere far beneath the ground. I tried to reach for it, to draw from that ebbing fountain, but it was too organic and complex. The Swamp Witch had tapped a rich vein of Old Florida, far beyond anything my brute-force skill could comprehend—this was Magick from a forgotten age.

I'd love to have studied it further, but I didn't have the time. Delia's lip rippled as if something squirmed beneath it. The Skeeter was returning to her true form. "I've had nothing but rats and possums for so long," she said, her mouth opening to reveal sharp fangs. "I wonder if I'll even remember what good blood tastes like."

Adam backed away, keeping his hands up and trying desperately to get his Magick going. "I eat really terrible…"

"What a coincidence." Delia's sharp teeth glistened in the half-light of dusk. "So do I."

I wrapped my hand around the end of the broken staff, reaching for the ebbing Magick again, clawing at it with my mental fingers.

Please, just please!

"Dad?"

I froze at the sound of my daughter's voice whispering deep inside my head.

Catherine!

"I can't see you," she said, her words fading against the sound of crashing waves. "Where are you? There's so much pain."

I tightened my grip on the broken wood.

I'm here, sweetheart. I'm right here.

"Where am I?"

How could I tell her? How could I tell her I let her go?

You are with me now.

Cathy's voice hesitated for a second before responding. "Dad, there's so much pain. I can't…"

I'm here.

"It's dark and wet. It's hard to stay above the waves. I can't see anything, but I can feel her pain. It's too much—please make it stop. She's losing her son."

I can't, Cathy. I've lost my Magick. I've lost you. I've lost everything else that's ever mattered. I'm a broken man, and a ruined father. I have nothing left.

"No, you are forgetting what you taught me."

What?

My daughter's voice broke above the mental sounds of crashing surf. "You said Magick is about belief."

I was wrong. I was wrong about so many things.

"No, you weren't."

A surge of Magick roared through the staff, erupting from the ground like a great, invisible geyser.

It's not possible.

A green shoot tore free from the end of that broken staff. Fresh growth surged where only dead wood had been before. The sapling branched and merged, twisting in on itself and becoming stronger than steel. The staff was made anew, and like the trunk of some ancient tree, its Magick swelled from the bowels of Old Florida.

Catherine?

"Magick isn't *about* belief," my daughter said, her words strong and resilient. "It *is* belief…"

How did you—

"I believe in you." Cathy's voice faded. "Find me."

Catherine!

"Eddie," Kaylee cried, breaking me from my trance. She held her son as a dying breath escaped his lips.

"Kaylee," I shouted. "For you!"

The Swamp Witch looked up in time to catch the vibrant green staff in her hands. "I don't understand."

"I don't either. Save your son and let's put an end to the Blood Queen. As far as I'm concerned, Florida only has enough room for one Magickal badass woman, and I'm putting all my chips on *green*."

The Swamp Witch smiled and her bloodshot eyes told me more than words ever could. The braided green staff pulsed in her hand, drawing with it Magick from the heart of the swamp.

That was when it dawned on me. Sturkey wasn't just some old mining town, or ruins lost deep in the heart of the state. It was something far more. Sturkey sat at the heart of Old Florida. It wasn't sacred because it had Deep Magick. It was sacred because it *was* Deep Magick.

Delia had Adam on the ground, her long fingers wrapped around his head and her tongue lapping at the blood spreading across his neck.

Adam!

"Hey!" I shouted, picking up the other half of the broken staff. "You want to settle this, bitch? Let's do it."

Okay, Cathy. Here comes that belief! Whip me up a staff.

The Skeeter wiped a sleeve over her quivering jaws. Blood dribbled down her chin and stained a swelling chest. "If you insist."

Now, Cathy!

I held the other half of Kaylee's broken staff up, waiting for my daughter to work that Old Florida Deep Magick into a Delia-ending beat-stick.

Cathy?

I got my Magickal blast all right, but it didn't come from Cathy. It came from the Blood Queen, a very much revitalized and powerful Blood Queen. Delia's Magick launched me from my feet and sent me crashing into a nearby trunk. My head slammed into the rough bark, knocking the useless stick from my hand before dropping me on the muddy ground.

"Eugene Law." Delia crossed the muck like a runway model, her perfect hips swaying gracefully. "This is going to be *so* good. I think I might savor this and keep you alive for a while.

Wouldn't you like that? We could start a new swarm, and you could be my first. How do you feel about that?" She ran a finger along my chest, absently tracing parts of a horrifyingly twisted sigil. "Being first has its privileges..."

Cathy, help me!

I listened for my daughter's voice. Anything that would tell me she was there, and that I wasn't alone, but I received no response.

Delia pulled me to my feet and pushed me against the tree, then pinned me to it with an unnatural strength. The sides of her jacket fluttered, and something moved beneath them, pressing against the fabric like expanding ribs.

"How would you like that? To be with me—forever." Delia's mouth opened wide, impossibly so, with new rows of sharp and angry teeth shining in the fading light.

"Not interested..." I said, squirming beneath the woman's mesmerizing gaze. Her eyes were like rich pools of molten chocolate, and they devoured my senses. I couldn't look away, no matter how much I wanted to. My arms went limp, along with my legs. The Blood Queen smiled, the hint of a whipping tongue sprouting from the back of her mouth.

Is this the end?

I saw myself reflected in those dark eyes—myself, and something from the stucco family.

"Delia..." I whispered, fighting to find my voice.

"Yes?"

"Duck."

Her jaws hesitated. "Wha—"

Stinkstone's fist roared past my pinned head at a speed I didn't think Bridge Trolls possessed. That five-fingered wrecking ball smashed into Delia's perfect face and sent the two of us careening into the muck.

Note to self. Bridge Trolls pack a wallop.

34

MUD BLOOD

*T*was in the muck again—how many times was this now?

I'd lost count, but at least this most recent visit had come with the righteous pleasure of knowing Delia was right there with me.

I rolled over and wiped the stinking black silt from my face. Air was in short supply, and I struggled to coax what I could back in my lungs. Sadly, the sight of my apprentice knocked all that hard-earned air right back out of again.

Adam!

The bearded one was a few yards away, his hoodie a mess of bright red blood.

No, no, no!

"Adam!" I shouted, willing myself up and dragging my bruised body toward him. "Please be okay."

"Gene?" His voice was weak, but not gone completely.

I fell to my knees at the kid's bloody neck. "Don't move. Let me get a look at you."

Adam's flesh laid like organic confetti, bright red and ground up almost beyond recognition. It took everything I had to keep my stomach's churning contents in place.

"I don't feel so good." Adam eyes slipped in and out of focus.

I tore off my mud-covered shirt and wrapped whatever clean side I could find into a ball around my hand, then pushed the entire apparatus against his neck. "Oh, no you don't. You need that life juice to stay right where it is."

Color drained from his face. "Gene, I'm sorry."

"Nope. There are no death's door speeches here, damn it." I blinked at the tears in the corner of my eyes.

"No," he said, coughing up blood. "I'm sorry."

"Not listening. You'll have plenty of time to wallow in your stupidity later. Now, you need to hold still."

"No." His coughing dislodged the bloody shirt. "Listen to me. I'm sorry I ever doubted you. I don't really know what it's like to grow up with a dad, but if I'd had one, I'd have wanted him to be just like you."

My stomach dropped and burning tears stung at my eyes. "Would you stop talking, damn it? You're just giving me ammo for later."

"Sorry…" My apprentice's arms went limp.

"Adam?!"

Crash!

Stinkstone had brought friends. I counted at least three mobile mountains, but while they were giant, they weren't prepared for the Blood Queen. Delia had a few hundred years of experience and knew exactly how to use each one of them.

Her oversized jaws left dark blue gashes on their legs and arms, and with each drop of blood that found its way to her lips she grew more powerful.

"Kaylee," I cried. "Adam's dying. Help me!"

Little Ed lay across his mother's knees, his color slowly returning. The staff's Magick was doing exactly what its wielder wanted: restoring the young golem's broken body. The Swamp

Witch was lost in the trance of Deep Magick and she didn't hear me.

Damn it!

"Gene?"

"Adam?" I turned back to find my apprentice laying still, his life's blood ebbing away beneath my hands.

"Uh, yeah?" A pleasantly round and ghostly form crouched next to me. "Wow, I *really* need to start working out."

I started to reach for the ghost's translucent hoodie, but thought better of it. "Son of a bitch. No, no, no, you need to get back in your body this instant. You are *not* dying on my watch."

Adam's ghost held up a hand in front of his face and waved it a few times like a recreational drug user from the sixties. "Whoa, I'm dead?"

"Damn it," I said, pressing down harder on the young man's bleeding neck. "No. Are you listening to me? You don't get to die, you ever-present pain in my ass."

"I don't think you have a choice, sir."

A tired and limping Private Petty stumbled into view. His hands clutched at a wound in his side.

"You know something? I've had just about enough of spirits telling me what I can and cannot do. You hear me?"

"Cool sword," ghostly Adam said, standing up to point at the young private's saber. "Is it real?"

"Yep."

"Sweet."

A Bridge Troll bashed a hole in a tree not far behind us, sending a burst of wood splinters into the air but still missing Delia by a country-mile.

"If you guys could stop the girl-talk long enough to help me figure out how to keep this one's cholesterol stream in his pudgy little body that would be really great."

Adam rolled his ghostly eyes. "I could go without the fat-shaming. I told you, I'm going to start using that YMCA membership I got from work."

"No, you won't." I let up on my pressure enough to hunt for a pulse. "If you don't get back in your body right this minute you are going to completely screwed like Private Petty."

The young spirit tilted his head. "What do you mean?"

"God damn it. I lied, okay? Nothing I told you was true. I don't have any secret tricks or amazing Magick to get you back to your family."

Petty took a hesitant step back, shaking his head. "But…"

"You're dead, Private. I destroyed your Death Spot. I've made it impossible for you to get back to your wife and daughter."

"I don't understand," the spirit shook his head.

I found Adam's pulse, it was weak, but not gone entirely. "What's to understand, Private? I used you. I'm a terrible person. I used you to save my butt too many times to count. There is *no* plan to get you to Heaven. There never was. I'm just a man, and a broken one at that. I can't help you, and I never could."

"Gene…" Adam's voice fell to a whisper. "You're not that kind of person."

"Don't you guys get it?" I placed my hands on Adam's chest and starting compressions. "I'm not the guy you thought I was. I signed the deal with the House. No one held a gun to my head— free will. I walked up those steps of my own choosing. You know why? I'll tell you why. Maybe deep down I actually enjoy it. You ever thought of that?"

"You don't mean it…" my apprentice said, but he didn't appear to actually believe the words he was saying.

"I think he does." Private Petty's face fell as he faded away.

Delia appeared behind Adam, launching herself onto the back of one of the Bridge Trolls, and latching onto its thick neck with her ever-widening jaws. The sides of her tracksuit swelled with an undulating motion. She was returning to her true form, and God help us when she did.

"You know what," I let go of Adam's chest, "if you want to die so badly, then do it. I'm done caring. Hell, I'm no match for Delia, none of us are. Even with Kaylee's new beatstick the Skeeter is too powerful. So, it's best if you just died now. It'll cut down on the traffic. Get your ride and move on. I'm pretty damn certain I'm headed the other way, so don't worry about making room for me. It's been nice knowing you."

"Wait," ghostly Adam said, realization slowly dawning on his face. "Gene, are you serious?"

"Yes."

"We can't stop her?"

I shook my head. "No, we can't. The last time we tangled it took everything I had—and more than a little luck. Look at me." I held up my blood-soaked hands. "What am I?"

"You're Eugene Law."

"No. I'm broken, that's what I am."

Delia swelled like a blooming flower from the mess of fallen Bridge Troll, her chest stained with the bright hues of blue blood.

"Gene, what about the compact?"

"What about it? She took the damn thing apart."

"But the mirror, the mirror isn't broken?"

Adam pointed to the compact mirror lying face down in the mud, black on brown, it almost vanished in the fading light.

"You think we can trick her into looking into the mirror now? Yeah, listen, that scam only works once—and it barely even worked that time."

Ghostly Adam zipped his translucent hoodie and pushed up its oversized sleeves. "I've got an idea."

"Oh yeah, what?"

"Something I saw in your book…"

"Ten Spins' Infernal Constructs?!"

My spectral apprentice nodded. "Yeah, I need a distraction."

"No! Ten Spins' Magick is dangerous."

Adam frowned. "And this isn't?"

He has a point.

"Fine—a distraction. You got anything in mind?"

"Nope, but you're Eugene Law. You'll figure something out."

"Adam!"

It was too late, my apprentice vanished.

The dead are so damn annoying.

I dug my hands into the mud and worked up a decent-sized black ball of nastiness.

"Hey, Delia!"

The Blood Queen swung around to put the full weight of her attention on me. Those warm brown eyes no longer exuded passion. They'd become a picture window to crazy—Magician and Troll blood had put her in a happy place.

That's terrifying.

I slung the mud ball and smiled as it perfectly smacked against her bloody face. If you're going to get eviscerated by a deliriously powerful Skeeter in the heart of the Green Swamp without your Magick, you might as well have a little fun doing it.

Adam, I hope you know what you're doing.

Delia hit me like a jungle cat, knocking my already exhausted body into the mud next to Adam's. Her jaw's expanded, the rows of teeth peeling back at the edges of her lips while beneath them the beginnings of a serrated tongue flickered in and out. This was sure to be my end, and I wondered briefly just how many times I could skip out on death before I got sent to the supernatural principal's office.

Any time now would be good, Adam.

35

AFTER LIFE

*T*he fleshy folds of Delia's jaws threatened to envelop me. Blood, red and blue, trickled from those swollen cheeks. The Sangre Reina lived up to every bit of my memory. She reared back to remove my throat from my neck, then stopped.

Huh?

She froze, her eyes rolling back in their sockets, before a jumbled set of words tumbled from her mouth. "It worked. I'll be damned."

"Adam?"

Delia's beautiful and bloody face twisted in frustration. "Yeah... sort of. It's like a massive ocean in here. Oh man, she is *strong*."

The Blood Queen wrestled with my apprentice for the wheel in her frontal lobe, and somehow that pudgy guy was winning.

Delia held out her hand to pull me up. "Okay, where's that mirror? I think I can hold her for—"

I hadn't gotten to my feet before Stinkstone's granite fist blasted the Blood Queen like a rogue moon-shot, knocking her off her feet and sending the woman crashing into the scrub palmetto.

"No!" I shouted, trying to get the Bridge Troll's attention. "That's not her. Well, I mean it is, but it's not. Adam's inside her trying to get her to look in the mirror."

The Bridge Troll tilted his head to one side, then shrugged, using his other stone-like arm to knock me back into the dirt on his way toward the fallen Skeeter.

"Adam!"

Delia's face appeared in the broken palmetto, but this time it wasn't my apprentice running point behind those wild eyes.

"She's back," I cried.

The Troll swung another pile-driving fist, but the Blood Queen was faster. She slipped under the clumsy punch and the sides of her jacket tore open. Something inside raked across the massive Troll's legs. Rich blue blood rained beneath the beast and Delia soaked it up like an unholy sponge before turning her attention back to me.

The mirror!

The Soul-Splitter lay in the muck a few yards away, but without Adam's help there was little chance of her looking at it willingly.

The Skeeter took a few steps toward me then stopped. "Gene, I've got like five seconds before the next wave hits. She's just too strong."

I didn't waste time responding and made a run for the mirror.

"Hurry!" the possessed Blood Queen shouted before falling to her knees, hands against her head. "She's doing something. This is Magick I don't know."

A thin white mist swelled around my dying apprentice's body.

Adam's voice vanished, only to be replaced by the Delia's alluring timbre. "Nova Mortuis!"

Hints of flame and spent embers appeared among the mist, the ashen hands of the damned reaching for Adam's body.

She's summoning New Dead!

Adam seized control back from the Blood Queen, just in time to see the peeling ashen hands of New Dead reaching for his body. "Gene!"

"Gotcha," I yelled, slapping my palm down on the tiny disc mirror. The Deep Magick trapped inside shuddered in my hand.

Magick is belief—Cathy, I hope you are right.

I turned back to Adam, only to find the Skeeter on top of me. "This ends now."

"It sure does." I held the mirror up.

"What's that supposed to be?" She said, tilting her head to one side.

"Huh?"

Muck covered the mirror's face, and with it my only way to recapture Delia's Darkling.

The Blood Queen batted the disc out of my hand effortlessly, then clamped down on my neck with her hands. "I should have killed you a long time ago, Eugene Law."

"Adam?!" I shouted, fighting the words past my rapidly closing throat.

"He's… preoccupied," Delia said, directing my attention to the ghostly apprentice surrounded by a pack of hungry New Dead. Their ashen bodies clawed for him. "Don't worry, you'll be joining him soon."

"Like hell he will." Kaylee's clarion voice shattered Delia's concentration, and new staff smashed into the Blood Queen's head. "Get the mirror!"

"Yes, Ma'am." I scrambled for the glinting light in the darkening swamp, my fingers touching it the instant a car horn echoed through the trees.

"What the?!"

A ghostly sedan, one of those old land yachts, rumbled across the sky above me. Adam's ride was coming, and that meant one thing—my apprentice was dead.

My stomach churned and took the air out of my lungs with it.

Don't focus on that. Focus on the mirror or you'll all be getting your tickets punched.

"Gene." Adam swung his arms wildly at the advancing New Dead. "Help."

"Get to your body."

"I'm trying!"

I dove into the muck, grabbing the mirror with my hand and rolling over to find a bruised Kaylee in the fight of her life with the Blood Queen. Delia had taken more than a few solid hits from the green sapling staff, but Kaylee appeared to have received the worst of the exchange—teeth marks covered her face and arms.

Adam's ghost cried out for me again. "Hurry, Gene!"

Kaylee swung her staff, but the Skeeter slipped out of its path, then yanked it away, sending the Old Magick tap root careening into the night. "I'm going to enjoy drinking you dry."

"Not if I have anything to say about it." Little Ed wrapped his strong arms around her neck from behind. She raked her hands across his face, but no blood poured out, only the faint trickle of saw dust.

The golem smiled, grabbing onto Delia's head and holding her eyes open with his strong fingers. "Do it, Gene!"

I held up the mirror, the Deep Magick inside humming in my fingers.

The Blood Queen writhed in Little Ed's hands. "I can't hold her for much longer."

'I believe in you, Dad.'

I wiped the mirror across my leg and held it up in front of Delia. "Let's do this!"

The Swamp Witch placed her hand on mine and together we unlocked the subtle Magick of the Soul-Splitter.

The Sangre Reina screamed and placed a withering hand on top of ours. "No! I won't go back to that again!"

"Gene!" Kaylee tightened .

"I see it!"

The Soul-Splitter hummed, its Deep Magick pulling apart the Blood Queen atom by atom.

"Not again!" Delia squeezed her hand and the mirror's sharp edge dug into my skin.

Boom!

The mirror exploded and sent a tidal wave of Wild Magick crashing over Delia and Little Ed.

"Eddie." Kaylee reached for her son.

The mirror had been unmade, and to stand in front of it was to take the full force of that Wild Magick. Delia's skin peeled away like curling paper, the blast furnace of chaotic energy melting organs and charring bones.

Crack!

The wooden boy's hands crushed her burned-out skull to powder before falling away himself.

Kaylee released my bloodied hand and fell on her son. "Eddie!"

"Gene!" Adam shouted, turning my attention back to the fallen apprentice, and the New Dead that had him surrounded.

"Adam, get in your body before your ride gets here!"

The silvery steel sedan coasted to a stop a few feet from his body.

"I... can't!"

I clutched at my bleeding hand and stumbled toward him. One of the New Dead caught my apprentice's ghost by the hoodie and dragged him down. "Help!"

"Get off of him." I threw myself into the mass of ashen bodies.

Clawed hands and blackened eyes filled the space in front of me, but I swung my fists anyway. I sent burned flesh packing with each blow, but still they kept coming.

New Dead released their grip on my apprentice to come after me. "Get in your body."

Adam hesitated. "What about you?"

"Get in your damn body before I change my mind."

Adam's ghostly form scrambled to climb into his fallen shell, but stopped just short of getting inside when the sedan's passenger door opened and a bright light shone down from the glowing interior. "Dad?"

"Don't take it!" I shouted before a tidal wave of New Dead pulled me under.

Burned hands, too many to count, landed blow after blow; each one pushed me further toward the ground, and sweet oblivion.

"It's not your time..." I whispered, my vision filling with the coal-black eyes of New Dead.

Is it mine?

My eulogy was cut off by the flashing silver of a perfectly balanced saber. A saber that cleanly separated the closest monster's head from its burned-out body.

Petty?

"You may be a terrible person," the spirit said, his sword a whirling dervish of righteous fury. "But that doesn't mean I am."

Thank you, Private.

The ghostly sedan's door closed, and it roared off into the night sky, disappearing among the few stars strong enough to brave the early evening.

Adam?

36

SIGHT IS FOR THE BIRDS

*P*rivate Petty swung his blade like a man possessed, the saber's edge cutting a path through tarry eyes and ashen limbs. "Go," he cried, smashing the snarling face of a fiery New Dead against his fist.

I fought through the remaining hands and dragged myself to Adam's body. My apprentice didn't move, his face quiet and grey.

"You little bastard." I pounded a fist against his chest. "If you took that ride I swear I'm going to find a way to haul your ass right back here."

Adam's still form didn't budge.

Tears returned the edges of my eyes and I slammed my hand down again. "You hear me? Get your ass up right now. I'm not doing this without you."

"Gene…" Kaylee's warm hand pressed against my bare shoulder. "He's gone."

"No, he's not. No, no, no. This kid and I go way back. You hear me, Grayson?" I grabbed his blood-smeared hoodie. "You don't get to leave yet. I'm not losing you, because I'm tired of losing. You hear me?" I shouted at the stars above. "This ends now. Put him back or so help me, you'll see the real power of Eugene Law."

Everything hurt. My hands burned and my gut heaved. A cool breeze did little to alleviate the pain in my heart. Somewhere in the pile of thawing rubble that had been the bird house a tiny baritone voice bellowed, "These Muscles are gonna..."

There was a Thinning coming. It was small, you had to reach out to feel it, but I wasn't going to let it pass without a fight.

"What are you doing?" The concern was evident in Kaylee's voice. Her hand gripped my shoulder tighter. "Don't do it, Gene. You know it's not right."

"Neither is losing him."

I fished Jerry's 9D glasses out of Adam's pocket. Marred with blood, the folded paper glasses lay heavy in my hands.

I have to try.

I wiped them on one of the remaining clean patches on my enchanted denim.

Kaylee's grip on my shoulder loosened. "Of all the stupid crazy things..." The warmth of her Magick flooded into my tired body. "If you're going to break the rules of nature, you might as well do it with some help."

I reached out to the Thinning, pulling at the Wild Magick.

"Softer, Gene," the Swamp Witch said, gingerly twisting and twirling the chaotic Magick like an artisan. "Be gentle with it..."

I unfolded Jerry's 9D glasses and pushed them on my face, then forced the barely constrained Wild Magick into action. "No time."

The swamp exploded in an infinite pattern of lines and color. The Magick of the Thinning and the deep well of old power that was Sturkey collided in mind-wrecking confusion. To see this far beyond reality was insanely dangerous. The Jerry who'd made these glasses had hung himself not long after creating them, and as I stared into the infinite I had a pretty good idea why.

"It's beautiful…"

The Swamp Witch's soft hand squeezed my shoulder, reminding me of her presence and the ticking clock. "Can you find him?"

Kaylee was right. There should have been an echo of Adam, just enough to pull him back, but like the ringing of a bell it wouldn't last long.

Lines exploded out of my fallen apprentice like spiral art. A thousand threads of life long potential: love, joy, sadness, and pain, all of them fading and snapping like spiderwebs in the storm. Something flickered in the center of the maelstrom of radiating lines—his echo.

"Gene?" Kaylee whispered. "Can you—"

"I'm losing him," I said, reaching past the threads and digging for the flickering center. "I need more power."

Kaylee's Magick hummed through me, more power than I'd expected, but still it wasn't enough. Adam's soul echo sunk beneath the swirling colors.

"I can't get to him." I pushed deeper to follow the fading beat. "I need more power."

The Thinning…

I reached back out for the Thinning, but it was already fading. It was too small and too weak—it wasn't going to save Adam's echo. The tiny light pulsed beneath my fingers then vanished, dropping deeper into the young man's chest.

Kaylee's Magick surged. It surrounded me like a warm blanket, but it wasn't enough to catch the echo. "Gene, I can't keep this up."

"Damn it, just give me a few more seconds." I pushed my fingers past the threads of Adam's life. The echo pulsed again, flooding my vision with a burst of white before falling deeper. "Damn it, come back."

A soft sadness washed over me and a familiar voice resounded in my ears.

"Sir, let me…"

Private Petty's spectral form dropped to its knees next to me. The fractured light of Jerry's glasses revealed the Private for who he was: a sad young man. Gone were the costumes, the famous actors, and movie effects. All that was left was a grief-stricken and broken youth.

"No, Private. Stay back," I said, not wanting him to get pulled into the torrent of Magick I was bleeding out to dig for the echo.

"I can help."

"No, you can't—not without risking yourself. Do you have a death wish or something?"

Those were the wrong words, and as soon as I spoke them I wanted to pull them back, but Private Petty simply nodded and placed his fading hands on top of mine.

The memory hit me like a thunderstorm. It swept up my mind and brought me to the open road. It was late, and they were flying down the dark highway far too fast to be considered safe. His wife was shouting something, but he didn't care. Her blond hair bounced in that tightly wound ponytail as she yelled at him, her words fading in and out of the stuttering memory.

"Slow down, you're drunk!"

He was. The haze of alcohol had stolen his reaction time, and his clarity. But he had to be, because it took away the pain.

What pain?

The letter on the back seat.

A flash of black and white words burned in my head.

Denied.

Private Petty was no soldier. He'd never been one, and he'd never *be* one.

A burst of headlights and the tumbling darkness as the car slid off the road. His final vision was of lifeless blue eyes beneath blood-smeared blond hair.

Private, I didn't know…

The young man smiled. "Please, call me Michael."

"I..."

"Gene." The spirit placed a second hand on mine. "It's time. I forgive you."

Michael's energy washed over me and into Adam.

"No! Stop! You do this and there's no going back. This is oblivion. Don't you understand me? The end of everything... Everything!"

"I know."

Adam's echo pulsed again, this time even more faint.

"No, I don't think you do. Kids say that all the time, 'I know,' but I've got news for you—you don't. You will never see your wife again, or your unborn child. You won't be stuck gathering lint in my pocket, you will be unmade."

"Goodbye, Gene."

Try as I might, I could no more stop the rush of Michael Petty's spirit than I could hold back the tide. He roared through my fingers and down into Adam's chest, pulling up the dead man's echo like a magnet and drawing it to me.

I latched on to that echo and yanked. "I've got him."

A kaleidoscope of white light filled the 9D glasses and I fell back, clawing at the paper lens. Somewhere the Swamp Witch screamed, but I couldn't see her. In fact, I couldn't see anything.

KAYLEE GENTLY PRESSED a paste of muck and slime against my eyes. "Is this any better?"

I blinked at the stinging goo, but my vision remained a mixture of dark and light blurs sloshed together like a child's finger-painting. "No."

"Is he... gone?" Adam's restored fingers brushed my hand. "Is the soldier gone?"

"Yes."

"Like.. Gone, gone?"

"Yes."

I didn't need sight to feel the pregnant pause in the air.

"For me..."

I ran my fingers across the broken piece of a cross. "Yes, for you."

"Gene, I..." Adam's voice was softer now. "I'm sorry."

"For what?"

"For not believing you."

I pushed away from Adam and stumbled to my feet.

"Whoa, hold on there..." Kaylee's hand slipped under my arm to keep me upright. "I still think you'll get your sight back, but in the meantime let's try not to ram into anything."

I leaned on her. "Take me to the center of town."

"Why?" There was confusion in her voice.

"Because I'm going to bury him."

"The soldier?"

"His name was Michael."

Kaylee guided me through the swirling Picasso of blacks and browns before stopping at what felt like a relatively open spot.

"Is this it?"

"Yes."

I dropped to my knees and ran my palms across the blurred earth, brushing the stray leaves aside. The wet ground squeezed through my fingers with each clawing handful of dark earth. Satisfied I'd made a shallow hole, I took out the broken cross piece and turned it over, still unable to see it.

You stupid kid. You stupid, stupid kid.

I set the wood down in its grave, then pushed the mounded earth over top with my fingers.

"Get me one of the birds."

"Huh?" Adam said, his voice closer than I expected.

"Here..." Kaylee's warm hands placed the blur of pink and brown in my fingers.

"Goodbye, Michael," I said, stabbing the tiny metal legs deep into the soft earth.

There was a shuffling noise and Adam grabbed my hand. "Hey, look what I found."

"I can't see, damn it."

"Oh, right." He placed a perfectly balanced saber hilt in my hand. "Looks like he left his sword."

37

NOT LOST

I left Sturkey and Private Michael Petty's wooden marker with a heavy heart. Seeing his sacrifice in nine dimensions had all but fried my eyeballs, but maybe it was for the best, as I wasn't sure I wanted to see what was coming for me.

Delia had torn us apart like tissue paper, and she didn't hold a candle to my Darkling. Evil Gene was coming, I could feel it in the air—the mirror's spent Magick would bring that collar-popping devil straight to me. The mirror I'd hoped to use to save my soul, and that he'd hoped to use to end me, now lay in broken pieces in the dark heart of Sturkey.

Without that mirror, and its Magick, I had little if any chance of stopping the Darkling and his Midnight Riders.

They'll mow us down like tall grass.

My foot caught on a large knot of roots and I stumbled forward, losing my grip on Adam's shoulder and falling face first into the swamp water.

"A little help here?" I said, pulling myself up and extending a hand.

Someone grabbed my wrist and dragged me to a standing

position. I blinked my eyes at the sudden flash of brilliant colors. "What the?"

"You never cease to surprise me."

It wasn't Adam, nor anyone else in our motley crew.

The House.

"What do you want?"

"First, I want you to stop trying to look at me," it said, placing a hand across my face. "The after-effects of Jerry's stupid glasses are going to boil your monkey brain in its juices if you aren't careful. Does it surprise you that I knew that nutcase?"

"I really don't care."

"He was one of the first to get a glimpse at the master plan. Fried his brain too, but then again, he was already bat-shit crazy by that time, so it's hard to know for certain…"

"Lovely," I said, closing my eyes and brushing the House's hand away. "Are you going to talk me do death, or do you want something?"

"You know, it's sad. We never talk anymore."

"Talk?"

"Remember the early days? You were a real chatterbox back then. You'd go on and on about your hopes and dreams, your love of Magick. You were insufferable, in a cute, wide-eyed puppy sort of way."

"That was a long time ago…"

"It was?"

My foot caught on another root and I pitched forward knocking my shoulder against a thick trunk. "Damn it. What do you want? Have you come to threaten Porter again? Or maybe you want to tell me the terrible things you'll do to my children?"

"Gene…"

"No, I'm at the end of my rope. I'm tired, I don't have my Magick, and I barely survived a confrontation with the Blood Queen. Now, to top it all off, I know you lied to me. I know

Cathy is still in Hell and whatever that is walking around in my daughter's skin isn't her. So whatever you're going to do to me, just do it and get it over with."

"Where's that signature Eugene Law fortitude?"

"Buried in a shallow hole." I crept forward in the dark, groping the empty air for something to hold on to.

"I know you don't get it, but I'm not the terrible person you think I am."

"You aren't a person."

"True, but I'm also not terrible. Could you not compare me to a summer's day?"

I brushed at the sawgrass running across my cheeks. "Nice try, Shakespeare, but I'm not buying it."

"Gene, you of all people should understand."

"How do you figure?"

"You are Eugene Law, hero of the masses, saver of the great unwashed. How many scary things have been banished thanks to your tireless efforts? How many Demons have you locked away? How many New Dead are back roasting uncomfortably in the pits of Hell?"

"Too many to count."

"Exactly," the House said, the excitement in its voice tangible and more than a little frightening. "You are a one-man force of nature and you know it. We aren't together by chance, you and I. We are destiny."

"No, Destiny is that dancer I met up in Micanopy a few months ago."

"True. You really do have a type."

I have a type?

"Yeah, you do."

"I saved her from the ghost of her ex-boyfriend. What's your point?" I said, feeling my way around the swelling trunk of a cypress tree that had apparently sprung up to block my path.

"That is my point entirely. *You* make the world a better place."

"I should put that on a greeting card."

The House's voice took up a hard edge. "Thankfully, though, under my tutelage you've gotten a lot smarter."

"How so? I'm stumbling around in the dark like a moron listening to you, I'd say that doesn't put me up to high on the smarts scale."

"Gene, what happened to your hand? Did you cut yourself?"

"You know damn well what happened to my hand."

"I do, but please tell me the story."

"Fine." I dragged my foot across the wide root ball. "I was using this mirror to check out my man parts, because it's important to make sure you don't have any strange growths or—"

A strong push in the back sent me crashing into the tree roots, knocking the wind from my lungs and cutting me off mid-sentence.

"I like your sense of humor, Gene—I always have—but it's poorly timed."

"Fine, you want to hear me say it? The Blood Queen is dead."

"There it is. Was that so hard?"

"I stopped her before..."

"Right, you 'stopped' her, but you didn't finish the job. Your confused primate morality got in the way. You didn't end her. Instead, you trapped her Darkling in that stupid mirror, virtually guaranteeing we'd be here years later, mourning the sober soldier back there who got his ticket punched to oblivion."

I swung my bandaged hand in the direction of the House's voice, but found nothing except empty air. "What did you want me to do?"

"Exactly what you did, Gene."

"And what was that?"

"You're coming around to it. It all started with that Old Dead in the movie theatre last year, then the monsters I've sent you after since, and now Delia. You've finally figured it out. Screw banishing and trapping—it's time to get real and start ending things."

"At least I'm good for something."

"That's the way to look at it, because you've got some real problems headed your way."

"Well, they won't be testicular cancer, because I check for that every day."

"So do monkeys."

Strong hands wrapped my skull in a vise-like grip. I tried to fight them off, but the visions that followed overpowered me: Evil Gene and the Midnight Riders, their convoy of destruction roaring up the interstate, Porter's grave, and my son standing shoulder to shoulder with the Darkling.

The hands let go, and I fought to get air back in my lungs. "Has that happened?"

"Like I said, Gene, time and I aren't on speaking terms, but I believe this is just one of a myriad of outcomes, most of which are really terrible for you."

"And for you..." I said, pushing my back up against the trunk.

"Of course for me. We are linked. You've tried too hard to deny it for so many years, but you can't. We're meant to be together."

"Like ebony and ivory?"

"I prefer to think of it like Smith & Wesson."

"What if I do nothing? What if I just sit here in this swamp until the mosquitos and Alligator Men carry me away?"

I had the distinct feeling of someone sitting down next to me.

"Nice try, Magick man, but not tonight."

Even though I knew it wasn't my wife, the sound of Porter's voice hit me like a gut punch.

"Please, not her..."

"But why, Dad?" It was Catherine's voice now, the carefree lilt of youth ringing in my ears.

"Stop! Damn it, stop!"

"We love you, Daddy." The giddy sound of Kris's voice reduced me to tears.

"I love you too..." I said, my own voice cracking with each word.

"Good. Now that we have that out of the way," the House said in a matter-of-fact tone. "Let's get down to business."

"Fine."

"You've done a great job recruiting members of the 'A-Team.'"

"Whatever."

"You've got the little wooden boy and his machete. Very 'Wizard of Oz,' if you ask me—not to mention the Swamp Witch. Nice work getting her to join the Flock without letting on exactly what that entails."

"She didn't ask—"

"You're right," the House said. "Sometimes it's best if they don't know the full extent of what they're signing on for, eh?"

Bastard.

"Guilty as charged. Still, you've amassed a decent crew, but even I don't think it's enough to restore your Magick and get us back on track."

"Oh yeah?"

"You need Magick, Gene. A lot of it," the House said, dropping a large duffle bag into my lap.

"What's this?"

"*This* is how you're going to get it."

I unzipped the bag and carefully slipped my hand inside. My fingers traced the outline of a smooth plastic flamingo and something else. Something smaller, muscular, and all together rubbery.

"The doll?"

"It's crude, but effective. You are going to need a Thinning, and not just any Thinning. You are going to need to hit the motherlode, and that little rubber man is going to help you find it."

I wrapped my fingers around the rubber doll. "I don't get it."

A strong hand pressed against my eyes. "You're about to; just don't say I didn't warn you."

"Wait, what the—"

An explosion of light and color consumed my distorted vision. My hands no longer grasped the little rubber man; instead, they felt the cold bite of hard iron.

The cemetery.

I pulled the gate open only to be greeted by rows of graves, a seemingly infinite monument to the tragedy of war.

"The Florida National Cemetery?"

The hand fell away, and when it did I found my distorted vision slowly returning.

"Wait, what happens then?"

"You pull yourself back together, honey," my wife's soft voice said.

"Porter?"

"Hey, I found him." Adam's words were supplemented by the sound of feet sloshing through the swamp. "Gene, were you lost?"

I zipped the duffle bag closed and pulled myself up. "I was, but not anymore."

PART III
WON'T BACK DOWN

38

OF BOOKS, BOWLS, AND BUTTONS

Flickering orange light bathed the tiny house in its warm glow. The Swamp Witch didn't have much of a dining table—in fact, she didn't have much in the way of seating at all—but what she did have we'd pushed together around the tiny lamp.

"The House gave you that?" Kaylee said, pointing at the scuffed-up rubber wrestler standing in a fierce pose on her table.

"Yes."

She shook her head. "Then we should unmake it."

"Hey," Adam said, standing up from his stool. "I made that."

"Exactly."

"I don't see you letting anyone unmake Little Ed."

Kaylee's face hardened. "That's completely different."

"Not to me it isn't."

The junior Demon Hunter shook his head and pushed back from the small table. "Stop, you two. We aren't unmaking a damn thing. Listen to us. We're squabbling about what few things we have when we know damn well Gene's Darkling along with Donnie and my father are headed here as we speak."

"He's right," I said, rolling up the sleeves of Ed Senior's last leftover shirt. This one wasn't quite as poor fitting at the ones before, but it also had twice the peanut oil stains. "Adam, what do we have?"

"We only have the book, and what I was able to salvage from the storage facility after I got your email." My apprentice pointed to the mismatch of Magickal items laid out on the table.

"That's it?" Little Ed said, leaning over to inspect the yard sale rejects strewn across the table.

I frowned. "You're talking about my life's work here…"

"Sorry, I meant, *that's it!*"

"Much better."

Kaylee shook her head. "Very funny, but some of these things are dangerous as hell. Is that the Five Star Toaster?"

"Yes."

"Holy crap, Gene. You are certifiable."

Little Ed picked up the silvery two-slot toaster. "I don't get it, it's a toaster."

Adam jumped to attention and grabbed the appliance out of the young man's hands. "Unless you're ready to burn down the Green Swamp, that needs to stay exactly where it was."

"I wasn't going to turn it on."

Kaylee yanked her son's hands away from the toaster. "You wouldn't have had to. Have you ever wondered why things like the Prussian Wedding Bowls worked for you?"

"I just assumed it was because I'm your son…" Little Ed's words hung uncomfortably in the air.

A tear welled up in the corner of Kaylee's eye. "You are like me, more than any other child could ever be. But no, sweetheart, you aren't a Magician."

"I'm not?"

I shook my head. "A golem as expertly crafted as you exudes Magick. It's in your body and it sets off other Magickal items without you knowing it."

"Is that how I saw Private Petty?"

I nodded.

"Damn..." the junior Demon Hunter slumped back in his chair.

I turned my attention to Kaylee. "Wait, did you say Prussian Wedding Bowls, plural?"

"Yes."

"You're worried about the Five Star Toaster, yet you have more than one of those curse buckets?"

"I have a son made of wood."

"Oh, right—that."

Kaylee sighed and pushed back from the table.

I directed Adam to place the toaster back down. "We'll keep it away from Little Ed."

Kaylee knelt down in front of a tiny plaid couch. Its green and orange cushions had done their damndest to hide stains over the years, but at this point they'd all but given up, which was likely why no one was sitting on that couch right now.

She flipped up the furniture skirt and slid out a large brown box that had been stored underneath.

"Is that..."

Kaylee placed the box on top of the couch and pulled off the lid. "It is."

The Swamp Witch gently removed tissue-paper packing material to reveal an exquisitely crafted bowl. Like something Porter's mother would have used to serve the world's largest salad, the Blue-tinged porcelain shined in the hurricane lamp's light. Detailed patterns resplendent with woodland animals danced in relief along the scalloped edge: foxes chased rabbits, wolves howled, and bears roared.

"Where did you get that?" I said, stunned to see in person something I'd only ever read about.

"It was a wedding present."

"You're kidding?"

Kaylee wiped her eyes and stepped back from the open box. "No."

"I don't get it." Adam joined me next to the couch. "I mean, it's fancy and all, but I'm not getting any Magick from it."

"That's because it doesn't want you to," I said in hushed tones.

"Whoa…"

Kaylee ran a finger along the edge of the bowl. "Prussian Wedding Bowls are fickle things, and this one isn't happy at having been tucked under my couch for the last decade."

"I wouldn't be either," I said, pointing at the couch. "When was the last time you replaced your furniture?"

The Swamp Witch bit her lip. "Eighty-five, I think?"

"It shows."

Kaylee closed the box before Adam could get a closer look at the bowl. "I don't get it, what does it do?"

"We don't know."

"What do you mean you don't know?" my apprentice said with more than a little surprise in his voice.

"She doesn't know," I said, "Because this is the last one."

"The last one?"

"I mean this is the last Prussian Wedding Bowl ever made. No one knows what happened to the Magician who made them, and since Prussia doesn't actually exist any more it's not like we can go find his or her family. We aren't going to know until it's activated."

Adam raised an eyebrow. "So this could…"

I pantomimed an explosion with my fingers.

"Right," the Swamp Witch said, placing the bowl box on the tiny table with the rest of my artifacts. "So now you can see why I've kept it in a box under the couch."

My apprentice nodded vigorously.

Kaylee gently pushed the bowl into a prominent location on the table. "Good. What's left, Gene?"

I pointed at the odds and ends. "I've got Betty's Glasses. They're a little scratched, but they do a great job of providing a quick view of the Gloom."

Little Ed reached for the bright red horn-rimmed glasses, but his mom cut him off. "I wouldn't."

"Why?"

"Do you really want to see what the Green Swamp looks like from the Gloom?"

Little Ed pulled his hand back. "No."

"What else have you got?"

I pointed at a small thimble, which was more of a decorative game piece than an actual sewing tool. "That's my portable threshold generator. Great for creating a home away from home to keep the dark things out."

"And what about these?" Kaylee asked, pointing at the small bag of buttons.

"Lost Buttons."

Kaylee snapped her fingers back like she'd seen a rattlesnake. "You carry around Lost Buttons?!"

"I don't carry any of this around. I had Adam get it all out of storage. If anything he's been the one carrying it around in the trunk of his mom's car."

"I have. Wait, what have I been carrying around in the trunk of my mom's car?"

Kaylee gave the buttons a wide berth. "You're responsible for those." The Swamp Witch turned to her son. "Eddie, stay far away from the buttons."

Little Ed did as his mother instructed. "What do they do?"

"They lose people." I picked up the small bag and setting it aside.

"What do you mean?"

"Have you ever lost a sock in the dryer?"

Little Ed shook his head. "We have a clothesline."

Of course you do.

"Well, if you *had* a dryer, you'd know that socks go missing from time to time."

"Where do they go?" the junior Demon Hunter said, leaning in.

"Most of the time they end up behind the dryer and against the wall. It's like a no-man's land of lint and fabric softener sheets back there."

"Huh?"

"Eddie." Kaylee pointed at the buttons. "To hold a Lost Button in your palm loses you in space and time."

"Damn."

His mother nodded. "You understand?"

Little Ed held up his hands. "Got it. Don't touch the buttons."

"Well, just don't hold them in the palm of your hand," I said, gently setting the bag aside.

The Swamp Witch turned her attention back to me. "While it's really great to have a stack of terrible and insanely dangerous Magick on my dining room table, it's not going to be enough. You can't wield even half of this stuff in your current state, and what items you can handle aren't going to be nearly enough to stop your Darkling, let alone save Donnie and Ed."

"Mom, he's trying—"

I cut Little Ed off. "No, your mom is right. We can't just scrape together a bunch of stuff and hope for the best. We need a plan, but we need something else."

"What's that?"

"An army."

39

SEAT OF MY PANTS

*A*dam rolled down the Cadillac's window. "I don't know, Gene. Are you sure this is going to work?"

Nope.

"Absolutely positive."

My apprentice played with the zipper of his hoodie. "I'm not sure. You think I can convince him to help?"

"If you can't I'm pretty sure your mom can."

My apprentice scrunched up his face. "What's that supposed to mean?"

"Nothing," I replied, innocently holding up my hands. "You'll understand when you get older."

"Very funny." Adam checked the rear-view mirror and with it the bowl box sitting in the back seat. "Is there anything I should know about having *that* in my car?"

"Try not to put anything in it, okay?"

Adam sighed, visibly distressed. "Are they as dangerous as you say they are?"

Sweet mother-of-pearl, yes.

I shook my head. "She kept it in a box under her couch. How bad could it be, right?"

Adam put the car in drive, then stopped and threw the shifter back into park. "You're going to do it, aren't you?"

"What do you mean?" I said, backing away from the car door with my hands behind my back.

"God damn it, Gene. I'm not going to go through that again. I told you she's not there. She's in Tampa. She's safe. Whatever it is I connected to at the Tower of Terrible—"

"Unceasing Torment."

"Whatever." Adam brushed me off. "It wasn't her. I know it."

"She came to me, Adam."

"What do you mean?"

"The staff, Kaylee's staff, that was Cathy. Her Magick is stronger now. It's more powerful than mine at her age—far more powerful."

My apprentice shook his head. "That's what I mean. Your daughter is what, sixteen, seventeen?"

She's... why can't I remember?

"I bet you can't even remember," Adam said, shaking his head. "You're losing touch, Gene. You're seeing things that aren't there. Something on the other side is taking advantage of that. You've said it yourself, you've screwed over a lot of monsters over the years. Could it be that at least one is using this opportunity to get to you?"

He may have been making valid points, but I had no interest in listening to them. It was Cathy, I knew that like I knew the sun would rise tomorrow. "You have children, Adam?"

"No, but that's not the poi—"

I placed a hand on the hood of the car. "That's *exactly* the point. You don't understand."

My apprentice slammed his hand on the steering wheel. "Oh really? You think I don't understand what love is? You think because I live in an apartment above my mom's garage I'm some sort of emotionally stunted loser?"

"No, that's not what I'm saying—"

"You gave up everything, you idiot! Porter, Cathy, Kris, you gave them all up—willingly! You didn't even try to find another way. You didn't come to me. You just woke up one day and said 'screw you' to the rest of us and signed on with the other team. I had to find out after the fact. Is that how much I meant to you?"

"It wasn't like that…"

Adam threw the car back into drive. "Like hell it wasn't. I'm going to find my mom and that Leprechaun, and then I'm going to tell him exactly what you said. You know something? I hope he tells you to go pound sand."

"Adam, wait, I didn't mean it that way."

"Damn it, Gene. I'm not going to stand around and watch you destroy yourself again. I was there the first time and it damn near killed me. You took the most amazing life, a life some of us would have done damn near anything for, and burned it to the ground. I'm not going to watch you do it again."

"Adam!"

My apprentice hit the accelerator and tore out of that small clearing, kicking up white sand and pine needles in the process.

I waited until those bright red taillights faded from view before I pulled out the picture wheel. I knew I'd screwed up, and the photos confirmed it. I was down to my last image. The single still frame of Cathy's bike laying on the street. I stared at that scene and tried to understand the significance but came up blank.

This is all I have left…

The Darkling's power had grown, and with it went any chance I had of coming out ahead in the face of the reconciliation wheel.

I shoved the disc back in my pocket and took a deep breath.

It was a decent plan, but in the end would it be enough?

∾

"THIS IS INSANITY, GENE," the Swamp Witch said, clutching a newly remade staff under her arm. Together we crouched in the thick palmetto fronds not far from the Alligator Men village.

"You bet it is, but do you have a better idea?"

Kaylee squinted at the thatch roof huts. "What about the Bridge Trolls?"

I nodded. "That's where you're headed next."

"Gene, Alligator Men *and* Bridge Trolls? What the hell are you thinking?"

I scratched at the second pair of loaner jeans I'd had to wear since I got here. Unlike the Magickal capris I'd been sporting, these weren't broken in yet. "I'm thinking this is actually a pretty smart idea, truth be told."

"You would think that. I'm starting to wonder just how much planning goes into your thought process?"

I removed the folded-up pair of muddy capris from under my arm. "According to my wife, basically none. I prefer to think of them as improv."

"And she married you of her own free will?"

I unfolded the Magickal denim and laid it across the ground. "Yep, sure did. I wonder myself sometimes exactly why."

The Swamp Witch kept one eye on the distant reptile-men and the other on my pants. "So, you're going to do what, exactly?"

"Me? I'm going to get Little Ed and his dad's pickup and head to the Florida Cemetery."

"Then what are we doing here?"

Satisfied the pants were exactly where I wanted them, I pulled Kaylee's attention back to the denim. "*You* are going to wake up these pants."

"Wait a second, you want me to rouse your trousers?"

I pursed my lips. "When you say it that way it sounds so—"

"Horribly wrong?"

"Pretty much."

The Swamp Witch sighed. "What's in the bag?"

"You'll see. Just do me a favor and light up the 501s."

Kaylee's Magick bubbled up like fine champagne. She really was a gifted woman with a subtle talent for Magick I'd never seen before. Most of us bent reality to our will, and sometimes reality wasn't keen on that and it bent back. But for Kaylee, Magick was like convincing the universe that what she wanted was its idea all along. Pretty much the same thing Porter had been doing to me for more than a decade.

Sneaky powerful.

The Magick pants filled out like you'd shoved an air hose in the cuffs. In seconds they were up and ready for action, if a little muddy.

"There," she said, opening her eyes. "They really stink, Gene."

The pants shook like a wet spaniel.

"I think they like it," I said, carefully unzipping the small bag while keeping the Swamp Witch from seeing the flamingo inside. I retrieved Adam's golem and placed him in the driver's seat of the strangest-looking pair of self-directed denim I'd ever seen.

"What's that doing?"

The tiny wrestler gripped the waist band like a bull rider. "Yippee ki yay, mother—"

"That's enough," I said. "Alright, you two, here's the plan. You run in there like a mad fool—"

I wasn't sure, but it looked like the pants nodded.

"Good. Next, Muscles, I need you to shout obscenities and taunt the living hell out of those Alligator Men."

This time I was certain the little rubber wrestler winked.

"Great, on the count of three. Ready? One, two—"

I didn't get to three. My animated pants exploded off the mark like a world-class sprinter with Muscles bouncing along in the driver seat.

Kaylee frowned. "Is that it? Just taunt the Alligator Men?"

Damn it!

"Get their attention, then run like hell for the Florida National Cemetery!" I shouted, watching the pants break the tree line and blast their way past a group of Alligator Men guards.

"You think this'll work?" the Swamp Witch asked, getting to her feet to join me and watch the animated duo swerve and dance their way through the confused reptile men.

"These boots were made for walking, and I'm-a-gonna make em outta you!" the boisterous golem yelled, his baritone voice carrying on the night air.

I cringed and shrugged my shoulders. "Well, we can't make it worse, can we?"

"Is that the last of it?" I asked as Little Ed threw another bag on the truck bed.

"You said get all the salt Dad has, right? Well, that's all he keeps in the staging area."

Little Ed had been able to scrounge up enough gas to get the red pickup rolling again, and together we'd driven out to his father's home base. It wasn't much, just an old concrete-walled shed I'd spent a very uncomfortable hour in what seemed like a lifetime ago.

"How many bags?"

"Four."

I pursed my lips. "It'll have to do."

Little Ed slammed the truck bed shut and tossed his machete on the passenger seat. "Listen, Gene. Is there still a chance for either of them?"

"Donnie and your dad?"

"Yeah."

I put a hand on the wooden man's shoulder. "Sure."

Little Ed didn't move; he just stared deep into my eyes. "Don't lie to me, Gene."

"Okay, you're right. It's not fair to you. I'm going to level with you, kid. Each day that goes by they lose a little more of themselves to the Eternal Shame. If it goes on too long, then there's no coming back."

The junior Demon Hunter's shoulders fell. "I knew it."

"But," I said, getting his attention. "I know your dad. I may not have been around him the last few years, but Ed Lovely has about as much give as granite, and is twice as hard-headed. If anybody can withstand the tar, it's your dad."

"And Donnie?"

"He strikes me as a tough nut."

"He is."

I smiled and gave Little Ed's shoulder a squeeze. "Then it's settled. Let's go save those two knuckleheads before they give the Eternal Shame a bad name, eh?"

The wooden man returned my smile. "Yeah, let's do that."

Little Ed climbed into the driver's seat and revved the rumbling engine. "Florida National Cemetery here we come."

I pressed my fingers against the House's bag. Private Petty's saber and the flamingo remained safely in its folds, both of which I'd need, along with a lot of luck, and more Magick than I could shake a stick at.

We pulled out on the highway, and Little Ed coaxed the engine up to speed. Before long we were cruising along at a good clip. A burst of lightning shot across the night sky, filling the space between the clouds and lighting up the treetops like a flash bulb. The first hints of an unsettling cold chilled my tired bones.

"Gene?"

"Yeah, I feel it. Can you step on it?"

Little Ed punched the accelerator and the rusty red pickup roared in response.

"Is this plan going to work?" the wooden man asked, unwilling to take his eyes off the boiling sky.

"I sure hope so."

The pickup kicked up gravel along the dark road. "That's not really inspiring."

Another crack of lighting split the sky.

"You're right. Drive faster."

40

ENLISTED MEN

The wind had picked up by the time we passed the first sign. Little Ed gripped the wheel tighter and fought to keep the rusty truck from sliding across the road. The night sky clearly wasn't happy with the Thinning preparing to spill out across the cemetery and it made sure we knew that. Irritated clouds twisted and folded in on themselves above that sacred place, making me painfully aware just how unpleasant it was about to get.

"Pull over outside the gate," I said, directing Little Ed to an open patch of grass not far from the entrance.

"Isn't that where you…"

"Shattered Private Petty's death spot?

The wooden man nodded.

"Yeah, not one of my finer moments. Try not to run over it at least."

The pickup cut a path through the soft grass and Little Ed avoided what we both assumed had been the grave marker's prior location.

"Now what?"

A gust of wind shook the ancient oaks that lined the road.

"Now, we work like hell." The Thinning's Magick trickled into my bones like a low-voltage battery. "I don't know how long we have before they get here."

As if in answer to my words a thunderclap rattled the truck and made the young Demon Hunter jump. "Right, let's get the salt."

"Good idea."

The junior Demon Hunter and I had the pickup emptied in minutes.

Nothing quite like terror to get the blood going.

"Okay, where are we putting these?" Little Ed asked, wiping the sweat from his forehead.

I removed a piece of paper from my pocket and unfolded it in the whipping wind. "Can you follow this?"

Little Ed tilted his head and turned the paper sideways. "Is this the cemetery?"

"Well, it's part of it. That thing there is the gate," I pointed at a broken squiggle, "and this over here is the first line of markers."

The kid pursed his lips. "I guess I see it. Drawing isn't really your thing, huh?"

"No, I'm more a saving-your-dad sort of guy."

"Oh, right."

I sighed. "Can you see where I want the salt?"

"Yeah."

"Then get to it, Picasso."

"Wait, where are you going?" Little Ed folded the directions up and put them in his pocket.

I opened the passenger door and grabbed the duffel, satisfied Michael's saber and bird were still safe inside.

"I've got a few people I need to talk to." Cold tendrils of supernatural Thinning snaked their way between my legs. "And it looks like I'm going to have just enough juice to make the call."

～

THE IRON GATE pulled against its chains in the wind. It was locked, but I found the dug-out spot we'd slipped under a few days ago pretty quickly. I shimmied beneath the black metal rail and thought about just how far I'd come without my Magick: I'd survived a run-in with Alligator Men, Grundel, a pissed-off Delia, and a couple of undead panthers. That wasn't bad for a guy who didn't have enough Magickal reserves to light his own farts on fire.

The temperature dropped on the other side of the gate. Not everything that prowled those grounds were happy to see me, and the Thinning wasn't helping.

For a moment, I wondered if my Darkling and the Blood Queen were right. Was there really something big going down? Was I making plans at seven minutes to midnight with no idea of the bigger picture?

I brushed those thoughts away and unzipped the bag. My hands found the flamingo out of habit, but I pulled them back quickly. The lure of the Flock was strong, and even though this bird and I weren't the bosom buds I'd been with Gertrude, it didn't stop the attraction.

Not now, Gene. Stay focused.

I paused for a moment and considered removing the saber, but then thought better of it. Michael hadn't been allowed in this cemetery, and I wasn't about to make a show of bringing his sword in here—not when I had spirits to enlist.

I followed the main path, turning back periodically to check on Little Ed. The kid could follow directions and had already used some bolt cutters to get the gate open. I just hoped Evil Gene was as lousy as I was with geometry.

Sorry, Mrs. Wilson. If it makes you feel any better, you were right. I did wind up needing Geometry 202 one day.

The wind kicked up again and sent broad maple leaves

rolling across the paved path. A snapping branch froze me where I stood. The rows of grave markers spread out beyond the asphalt in perfect rows, and I felt my stomach tighten.

Since when do the dead bother you?

Sickly Wild Magick oozed around me, rolling between my legs and brushing against my rolled-up sleeves.

Oh that's right, since you're depending on Wild Magick to save your bacon—no pressure!

I set the duffel down on the path and bent down to untie my shoes. I wasn't sure what the decorum was for what I was about to do, but tracking mud in anyone's house would most likely be considered bad form. Satisfied my shoes and mud-caked socks were a sufficient distance away, I stepped out into the cool, damp grass.

I didn't need my Magick to feel the pride that swelled in that deep earth. I was treading on the ground of heroes and I knew it.

Deep breath, Gene.

I knelt down and placed my palms on the short grass, digging my fingers into the rich earth. I pushed past the blades, and through the roots, until the cold loam sifted between my fingers.

The Thinning rolled over my hands and slid between my legs. It was like that time as a kid I'd tried to sit at the end of a waterslide. Like the water had back then, the wild power pushed against me now, and with each second it gained strength. At some point the swelling force would knock me over.

It's now or never.

I reached out to the untamable Magick and tried to coax it like the Swamp Witch. I gently directed it where I wanted it to go. I gave it subtle directions, and mental words of encouragement, but I wasn't Kaylee. The Wild Magick pushed back, hard, and instead of going where I wanted it to go, it caught in the grass roots and pulled my hands deeper into the soft earth.

Oh no you don't. Looks like we're going to have to do this my way.

I squeezed my fingers harder, grabbing hold of the Wild Magick and telling it exactly where to go. The Thinning's power got tangled up between my hands and I seized the opportunity. I pushed the chaotic power out across that sacred ground. Like the roots of a massive oak, it split and splintered, seeking the hallowed souls still waiting deep within the quiet earth.

"Surge Sursus…" I whispered, letting my words ride the Wild Magick and hoping against hope I hadn't just made a bad situation a lot worse.

More lightning split the sky and a few stray raindrops stung my face, but still I wrangled with the Wild Magick.

"Surge Sursus," I cried as the first tugs against my lines appeared, trying to mask the fear in my voice. "Rise up, damn it!"

The wind picked up again and threw large clumps of Spanish moss from the trees like old netting. I dug my hands in further, giving into the Thinning and letting the Wild Magick pull me along.

"Surge Sursus!"

"We heard you, damn it. You don't need to shout."

A single spectral soldier appeared among the grave markers. He was tall and well muscled, with a wide mustache and more than a few tattoos. He walked toward me with a military precision, then stopped as if catching the scent of something on the air.

"What do you want, Magician?"

Boney digits wrapped mine from below and like a terrifying child's game of finger wrestling those hands dragged me down —in an instant I was up to my wrists in the rich earth.

"I need your help."

"And why should we help you?"

I had had a feeling this was coming. The dead do not suffer the living, and it appeared they certainly weren't very happy to see me either.

"You smell it in the air." I pulled back against the bones beneath the ground. "You know what's coming."

"It doesn't concern us. Those things cannot enter this sacred field."

Here it goes—no going back now. I'm coming Cathy, one way or another, I'm coming.

"Actually," I said, squeezing the boney hands that held mine. "I think you'll find I just undid your protections..."

The wind shifted, and the spirit was on me in an instant. His spectral eyes were only inches from mine and channeling a well of anger I knew would be coming.

"In no time two Midnight Riders are going to come down that road and drive right past your desecrated gate. When they do, they're not going to stop with me and the kid. They're going to destroy everything you hold dear: your loved ones, the spouses buried here alongside you, and those that came after you."

The boney fingers dug into mine and I knew my blood was mixing with the sacred ground. I wasn't a full soul—my very nature was unwinding the protections of this consecrated space.

"Give me one good reason why I shouldn't drag you to your death right here," the soldier said, anger evident in his ghostly eyes.

"Because," I said, swallowing hard. "If you do this, the land will never recover. I am cursed. You know that. You want a cursed Magician with a tarnished half-soul bleeding out on your ground?"

The soldier froze and I could almost see the ghostly gears grinding to a halt. "No."

Whew.

"Right, so you're going to help me stop these guys, and in turn you have my promise I'll never set foot here again."

Please take it, please take it...

The ghost turned away, his translucent form conferring with the multitude of solemn markers behind him. "We accept your terms—"

"Hot damn. All right, first thing we need—"

The ghost didn't let me finish. "With one caveat."

"Yes?"

Images flashed in my mind, too many to count, but the general theme was easy enough to pick up on. "I'll do what I can..."

The boney fingers squeezed and my eyes stung as the sharp nails dug into the flesh of my hands. "You'll do it, or you will never find rest the remainder of your days."

I squeezed back, not breaking my gaze with the old jarhead. "Get in line. My life has been an almost nonstop suck-fest punctuated by brief periods of joy, and since all those are gone now there's really nothing left to threaten me with. But I promise you now I'll do my best to do what you ask. Do we have a deal?"

"Oorah."

41

GET DOWN

collected the last empty bag from Little Ed. "You got it all down?"

"Yeah, I think so," the world's most impressive golem said without looking even the tiniest bit worse for wear. "Do you think we'll have to wait long?"

Lightning chased clouds across the sky, followed by the distant rumble of heavy bikes.

"Nope." I pointed to the first beams of light breaking the horizon. "That's my car."

"How do you know?"

The right bulb flickered a few times before returning to full power. "I just know. Is everything in place?"

"I think so." The clearly nervous junior Demon Hunter's hands found their way to the machete at his waist. "How am I going to separate my dad from the tar?"

"You let me worry about that. You know what your job is, right?"

Little Ed nodded and turned toward the tree line. "I think so..."

The Dad Wagon cleared the horizon, with two devilish choppers running alongside it.

"Just wait for my signal."

"Which is?"

"Trust me, you'll know."

The golem nodded and disappeared into the dense palmetto scrub that crowded the edge of the road.

Here goes nothing...

I stepped into the middle of the highway and placed the duffel bag at my feet, unzipped and open. The plastic flamingo's coal-black eyes shined up at me in the streetlight's muted orange glow.

Don't look at me like that. It's not my fault the last one of you I carried shattered against a patrol car. I was kinda busy at the time. Yes, too busy to see a four door squad car with its lights on.

In seconds, I found myself bathed in the bright light of the Dad Wagon's head lamps.

Hold your ground, Gene.

The old Mazda slowed its approach, but even as it did the two, glistening tar-covered motorcycles shot past. Those choppers circled me and provided no indication of my old friend or his dedicated partner in Demon Hunting.

Come on, Ed. You can fight this...

The Dad Wagon rolled to a stop a few yards away from me.

Damn it, you couldn't have rolled forward a few more feet? Make it work, Magick man...

The driver-side door opened and creaked in the damp air. It was somewhat heartening to know my evil half hadn't figured out how to keep the door from making noises in the time he'd had the car either.

A sharp-looking jet-black oxford shoe hit the pavement, followed by tailored black slacks and a dress shirt. I shifted uncomfortably in my borrowed denim and peanut-oil-stained plaid shirt. I could say a lot of bad things about my evil half, but I had to give it to him: he knew how to make an entrance.

"Gene," he said, rolling up the sleeves of a well-cut dress shirt. "Great to see you. Wow. Looks like you've been rolling in the mud."

I used my foot to push open the duffle just a little more, and I swear if such a thing were possible, the little bird smiled.

"It's all part of the excursion I've been on over here. Something about getting back to my roots—and twigs, and mud, and sand. You get it."

My evil half nodded. "I knew there was a nature-streak somewhere inside us, I just didn't know it extended to swamp rats."

Sharp-dressed Evil Gene pointed to the tree line and whispered a few words of Magick under his breath.

Little Ed made a run for the street, pushing a wheelbarrow as fast as he could. He didn't make it to the pavement before he collapsed forward, sprawling into the tall grass and losing the thirty or so pounds of salt that had been meant to close the trap.

No, Little Ed!

"He'll be fine." Evil Gene held his wrist and clicked the button on an expertly crafted gold watch. "Well, no. That's a lie. He'll be fine *if* he can survive having his heart stopped."

The young demon hunter lay motionless in the tall grass.

"Son of a—"

"This is so pointless. We're the same person, Gene. You think you can outsmart me? You *are* me. Let's wrap this up right now."

"The mirror is gone."

Evil Gene slammed the Dad Wagon's door shut. "Damn it. Now, I'll admit I didn't see that coming. Kind of crazy to destroy the best option for you getting your Magick back."

"I didn't. Delia took care of that."

That caught the Darkling off-guard. "The Blood Queen was here?"

"Was being the operative word, yes."

My Darkling smiled. "Gene, look at you. You're finally figuring it out. I leave you for just a couple days and look at how much you've grown."

"I'm a quick learner."

Thunder rumbled.

"Is that a Thinning?" Evil Gene asked, watching the lightning cut across the sky.

The pink flamingo's neck twisted in the duffel at the sound of my Darkling's voice. I did my best to use my hand to call it off.

Not yet...

"Yeah, it's a Thinning."

The Darkling took a deep breath. "Wow, yeah, that's one hell of a Thinning. Nice timing. I assume you've gotten a handle on how to pull Wild Magick from a Thinning."

"It's a work in progress."

"I'd say you're doing pretty good—all of your organs are still on the *inside*. That's not half bad."

More lightning erupted and its flash bulb reflection in the windshield revealed creeping Midnight Riders with swords drawn.

Just a little closer...

"So is this it?" I asked, keeping one eye on the approaching Riders. "Are we going to stand around and talk?"

"Well I'd love to catch up with you more, but I'm ready to get put back together. I've got a plan for the House and I'd like to see it through."

I had been prepared for a lot of responses from Evil Gene, but that one caught me completely offguard. "What plan for the House?"

"I'm sure it's been visiting you. I find those visits *so damn annoying*, don't you? Of course you do. I'm going to guess by the look on your face that I'm right. I'm also going to guess it's been pushing you like crazy to get your Magick back."

The flamingo twisted in the bag, again trying to get a look at the Darkling.

"Maybe..."

"Ha! You really do suck at lying. Don't worry, when we're back together I'll run point."

"Like hell you will," I said, crouching down to scoop up the bird. The tiny, plastic yard art, however, had other ideas. She shot out of the bag and away from my grasping hand.

Evil Gene whistled, and the bird dashed across the damp pavement to him on sharp metal legs.

"Hey!"

My Darkling placed a hand on tiny bird's head as it nestled its beak against his stupid dress slacks.

"The Flock likes winners, Gene—take him, boys!"

The Midnight Riders approached, their hands outstretched.

"Wait, you can't get the tar on me!"

My Darkling sighed. "Did you think I forgot?"

"Well, I just wasn't going to risk it."

Evil Gene chuckled. "Sure, I get that."

The Eternal Shame peeled back from the closest Rider's hands like the receding tide, revealing the rough fingers of my old friend.

You do this and there's no going back...

The Thinning's Magick swam around us, and I fished a small button from my shirt pocket.

"I'm sorry, Ed!" I shouted, grabbing his hand and exposing his palm. "I'll find you, I promise."

Before I could get the Lost Button to him, a pair of muddy capris broke the tree line with a rubber wrestler in the driver's seat. "Rumble, rumble in the jungle!" the angry little action figure shouted.

Ed yanked back his hand, the tar covering it once again and

taking away my best chance to separate my old roommate from the Eternal Shame. Animated pants raced across the swale and out onto the road, the little rubber golem bouncing along atop them.

"What in the hell?" My Darkling said with more than a little confusion in his voice.

"What, you've never seen animated pants?"

The Darkling snapped his fingers and a lunging Midnight Rider's blade separated the golem's top half from his bottom, the former bouncing across the pavement, and the latter falling somewhere into the nether reaches of the mud-covered denim. "No, I haven't."

The muddy pants stopped and turned around to face the tree line.

"Nice work, pants."

Evil Gene shook his head. "Well, that was nothing if not entertaining, but I—"

My animated denim broke into a dance, an epically cringe-worthy display of hip-thrusting and butt-shaking that was, at the same time, nearly impossible to look at or turn away from.

I didn't think you had it in you.

"What are they going to do, Gene? Dance me to death?"

I pointed to the opposite side of the road, where a dull rumble echoed in the dense cypress. "Nope, that dance isn't for you."

"Lovely. Then who is it for?"

Alligator Men by the dozens crashed through the tree line, spears raised, their hissing cries bone-chilling in the humid dark.

"Them."

42

SCALY BALANCE

"*P*ants, that way!" I shouted, directing the disembodied denim toward the open gate and the grave markers behind it.

The animated denim unleashed another barrage of cringe-worthy gyrations, but pulled up short when the first spear whistled past an outstretched leg.

My dancing isn't that bad... is it?

Alligator Men by the dozens poured onto the slick pavement like a spilled box of rubber toys. There was some initial confusion, but it didn't take long for those oversized reptile brains to put pants and people together.

A second spear shot past my head and embedded itself in the dirt not far from the road.

Time to go.

The Midnight Riders had their sabers out and were on the defensive. Spears and black tar blades clashed on that narrow ribbon of asphalt. Not to be outdone, my pants did another little jig, waving its butt to the crowd of assembled fighters before making a break for the epicenter of the powerful Thinning.

"Hey, quit hamming it up."

I avoided another stone-tipped spear and scooped up Private Petty's saber. The Riders had their hands full, which gave me an opening to scramble past and follow that glorious denim.

"Wait for me!"

Spears skidded across the wet street, sending the pants and I into an improvised slalom routine.

"We've got to get to the gate." I pointed to the cemetery.

My animated capris nodded.

"I'm so glad you agree."

The pants shrugged their waistband, high-stepping to avoid a spear to the man-bits.

"Nice work. Wow, that one was close—"

A surge of Magick hit me like a fifty-pound cement sack to the midsection.

Damn it, I miss being able to do that.

I pitched forward and lost my balance on the suddenly shifting road.

He's conjuring something, crap!

My Darkling was summoning without a circle, meaning whatever was about to come through that industrial-grade Thinning would be practically uncontrollable.

The pants turned back, no doubt feeling the same oily darkness building around us like high tide.

"Go! Get on the other side of the damn gate. That's an order, you stupidly awesome high-waters!"

Like a trusted canine, the enchanted denim hesitated.

"Go! Now!"

Another near miss from a wicked-looking spear provided the pants with their missing motivation. The mud-covered 501s saluted me, raising a cuff in a comical sign of unity.

"What are you—lookout!"

It was too late, the pants spun around only to find themselves at the mouth of a waiting Sobek Demon—my evil half had been busy.

This was the full-size version of the demonic alligator that had come after Maurice. This beast made Grundel look like a pool toy. Silent and deadly, it rose out of the swirling mist and spilled over the pavement. The gator was as large as a school bus and easily twice as wide. Eyes like blood-shot beach balls stared down at us like my son looked at chocolate cake. "Pants, run!"

My animated denim didn't stand a chance.

The Sobek's jaws snapped closed, effortlessly snatching the clothes right off the pavement and out of my life. With a flash of teeth and a whip-crack of monstrous jaws, the enchanted high-waters tore in two. The Sobek Demon swallowed the left leg like I'd slurp up a stray noodle, and the right landed somewhere in the tall grass.

I suddenly couldn't remember which pocket I'd stuffed the photo wheel in.

Please be the right.

The monstrous Demon blocked my path to the cemetery, its colossal tail cutting a deep groove through the dark pavement.

I turned to make a play for the remaining leg, but the Sobek's claws cut off my route and threw sparks on the dark pavement. I jumped backward and into the waiting arms of a dozen or so very confused Alligator Men.

"Listen, guys, I know it looks like your great grandmother, but don't let that—"

Barred teeth and soul-shivering hisses told me they weren't really interested in what I had to say.

Crap!

I shimmied out of the way of an errant spear thrust, then danced around another swipe of the Sobek's claws. My plan appeared to be going off the rails at a rather spectacular pace, which had me wondering exactly how I'd believed it would work in the first place.

I was neck deep in that complex introspection when a

booming voice cut through the rolling thunder above me. "Suck it, mega-gator!"

What the?!

A brilliant golden chariot roared over us. Heavily armored war horses dragged the shining spectacle across the sky, and in the driver seat was one remarkably well-muscled ex-Demon Hunter.

"Maurice?"

Resplendent in ancient Roman armor and swinging an impressive spear, the peanut vending powerhouse waved. "Hell yeah it's me," he shouted, pulling the reins and coming about. "What is it with you and alligators?"

"Wasn't it you that brought the last one?"

The Centurion pushed up his helmet. "Oh, right."

The chariot hit the pavement and kicked up sparks, knocking aside two Alligator Men in the process.

I swung Private Petty's saber and deflected another spear, again pretty darn impressed with my nascent skill even with the former spirit long gone—the kid must have rubbed off on me.

"What are you doing here?" I shouted, blocking the next thrust and slicing off its stone tip with the edge of Petty's blade.

Kid'd be proud.

"I get one 'thank you,'" the deceased peanut vendor cried, his war horse's hooves clattering on the pavement. "You sort of saved my eternal bacon back there."

"Damn right I did."

"Yeah, so I get to come back long enough to even the scale."

Hot damn—it's about time the dead did me a favor.

I slashed back at another thrusting spear. "Go for the eyes!"

The Centurion nodded. "Geez, man, everybody knows that."

How am I the last person to get this information?

Encroaching Alligator Men pulled me back to the present. I had to let Maurice and his golden chariot worry about my

Sobek problem—there was an enchanted pant leg that needed saving.

Deep breath, Gene.

"I'm coming, pants!" I cut a path to the downed denim with expertly timed fury. Whether the pants could hear me or not, I didn't care—it was the thought that mattered.

Clang!

Narrowly bouncing off the saber's hilt, that last stone-tipped jab was too close for comfort and forced me to break into a run in the general direction of the lost denim.

Centurion Maurice cracked his whip and sent the powerful horses surging forward like an out-of-control theme park ride. The chariot's wheels left glowing grooves in the dark pavement, and the Alligator Men, not sure what to make of another inter-loper, did what Alligator Men did best: they attacked. One of them caught the edge of Maurice's chariot, but the newly deceased Demon Hunter peeled it off with a muscled leg kick to the snout. In doing so, however, he took his eyes off the monstrous Sobek Demon—bad move.

"Maurice!"

The Demon opened its jaws wide enough to consume the golden man whole.

Maurice turned around just in time to pull the reins hard to the right—the horses obliged, but the chariot didn't. Maurice and his golden spear sprawled out across the pavement directly in front of the beast.

"Maurice," I cried, changing my trajectory away from the lone pant leg. "I'm coming."

Undeterred, the golden Centurion pushed himself up and brushed off his armor. "I see it. You do you, Magician. Let me handle the kickass hero shit—"

The Sobek's claw blasted into the Demon Hunter, flinging his ghostly body into the tall grass while at the same time sepa-rating him from his spear.

Damn it. The pants are going to have to wait.

I switched the saber's hand and dove for the spear, scooping it up while skidding across the pavement.

"Spear me!" Maurice cried, running out of the tall grass with his helmet askew.

"What?!"

"Give me the spear, damn it. I can take the shot."

"I've got it—"

Maurice shook his head. "Somebody's got your pants, bro."

The lost leg!

I turned around to find Evil Gene with the flamingo now at his side as he dug his hand into the pocket of the what remained of my tattered denim. "Stop!"

The Sobek roared and crashed down in front of me, scoring the pavement and blocking any path I had to the Darkling, its jaws wide and ready to consume me whole.

There was only one option left.

I tossed Maurice the spear as he raced past.

"Thanks, bro. Go save your pants. I got this!" The deceased Demon Hunter launched himself, along with the golden spear, into the air and on a collision course with the monster's mouth.

43

SMALL HOLES AND BIG PROBLEMS

"*Maurice, wait don't—*"

Too late.

"Eat spear, Gatorzilla!" The golden Centurion disappeared inside the toothy folds of the beast's oversized mouth.

The Sobek Demon's jaws clamped down hard, and I could have sworn I heard the clink of metal on bone.

Damn it, you glorious bastard.

Lost in the visual of the peanut cavalry's demise, I wasn't paying attention as the Midnight Riders seized their opportunity to surround me. The Sobek moved to enjoy its Maurice feast, and when it did I found my Darkling, photo wheel in hand.

He still needs to get to me...

The Eternal Shame dripped from the Riders' blades. Black as pitch, it speckled the ground where they circled. They'd cut their way through scores of Alligator Men who were laid out like stacked cordwood around them.

"Okay, now... Let's remember, guys, the fashionable Gene wants me alive..." I said, using Private Petty's blade to keep them at bay.

One of the Riders lunged, slashing with his black tar saber. I caught the blade with mine just in time and cast it aside with a flick of the wrist. Private Petty's saber cut back quickly, turning a defensive move into a strike all of its own. The silver sword left a clean line through the tar.

"Ha!" I shouted, almost in spite of myself. Michael would have been proud. My excitement was short lived, though, as the wound sealed itself almost instantly.

Son of a...

The Riders attacked in unison, their blades moving almost too fast to follow. The saber and I fought back with everything we had. Silver and black metal clashed in the night air, and each parried slash sent flecks of shameful tar sailing toward me, only to evaporate against the gleam of the silver blade. All around us, Alligator Men pressed in and filled the space with their scaly bodies.

"Who's next?" I shouted, continuing my wild slashes.

Something rumbled behind me. The Sobek gurgled and puckered up its massive jaws like a toddler at vegetable time.

Come on, Maurice. Stop messing around!

The golden spear burst through the Sobek's neck, along with a flood of noxious bodily fluids and one bile-coated Demon Hunter. "Ah yeah! Now that was worth leaving the third quarter for!"

The Sobek pitched its body forward, slamming against the pavement and sending a wave of Alligator Men running. Apparently witnessing the large Demon being brought down had shaken their morale more than a little, and the remaining reptile men ran for the tree line.

"Great work, Maurice," I said as I went back to parrying slashes from the Midnight Riders. "How about you get down here and help me with these guys?"

The golden man pulled himself out of the rapidly disintegrating monstrous remains. "No can do. I've got to get back to eternity. The fourth quarter is about to start."

"Fourth quarter?"

"Oh yeah. It's a tight game, but I like your odds—call it a hunch," he said, uprighting his chariot and climbing back on. "Don't let me down, Magician."

Black blades slashed like a windmill of deadly precision and it was all I could do to just keep up.

The Centurion started to yank the reins, then stopped. "Oh, before I forget. I might have torn a 'tiny' hole in the Thinning just now…"

"What?!"

"Quit your bellyaching. It's like," Maurice held up his fingers, "this big."

The Centurion snapped at the reins and his horses were off, roaring across the pavement and then up into the boiling sky. "On, Snacker! On, Mixins!"

I backed up toward the black cemetery gate, carefully stepping over the Demon's fading remains, all while keeping a sharp eye on the Riders' blades.

Just a little further…

Once again, I was too focused on the Midnight Riders in front of me to notice Evil Gene sneaking up behind me. The flamingo-carrying Darkling caught me completely by surprise and trapped me with his arms. He dropped the plastic bird in the process.

"It's over, Gene. The band is getting back together."

"Right, but I'm lead vocals—you can be the bass player. Do it now, Eddie!"

Little Ed's face reappeared at the edge of the road behind the Riders. He waved, then dug in with his wheelbarrow and made a break for the street.

"I stopped his heart!" Evil Gene shouted, squeezing my arms.

"What? The Little Wooden Boy? You're way behind on

current events." I slammed an elbow into my Darkling's ribs. "Little Ed's reveal was earlier. He shops in the garden section now."

Salt poured from an expertly placed hole in the wheelbarrow and streamed out to finish the now perfectly unbroken line that surrounded the entire cemetery. Little Ed had locked us in, just like we'd planned, and now it was my turn. I reached out to the Thinning, probing the edges of that untamable tide of Wild Magick, and gathering up the power I'd need to end it all.

There was no mirror, but we had the photo wheel.

Can I do it?

"Nice try, Gene," the Darkling said, his words hot against my head. "It just means we're all trapped in here together."

Magick. I needed a lot of it and fast.

I found the hole in the Thinning Maurice had left. It was a good bit larger than Maurice's two fingers had led me to believe, and to make matters worse something was gathering around it from the other side.

Guy comes here to save my butt and ends up leaving cigarette burns on the couch.

I could fret about the hole all I wanted, but without that Magick I was a sitting duck. I knew this was going to be a long shot, but it was a shot, and that was more than most people got.

Especially people like me.

I sucked up the Wild Magick, siphoning it from the Thinning like I was pulling gas through a cheap plastic hose. Just like gasoline, it burned my chest and turned my stomach in on itself. This was fiery Magick beyond rational thought, and it was downright terrifying, but even with Mother Nature by the short hairs I was still locked in a death match with the Darkling. His Magick was stronger, alien, and more powerful—it was the House, all but unstoppable and deadly. To stand on the other side of it made me question everything I'd ever known.

The Darkling spun me around and pulled me toward him,

putting his eerily similar face directly across from mine. "You can't win, Gene."

The photo wheel spun in my evil twin's hand.

"Who said anything about winning?" I dug into the Thinning for all it was worth. Wild Magick surged through me like a live wire—it was now or never.

The paper disc in his hand shined, but only a single image remained for me. It wasn't enough to win.

It's been a good run. Now, see it through to the end.

I grabbed the edge of the wheel and pulled.

Rip!

Something tore, but it wasn't what I thought it would be. Lost in the scorched disc, I'd forgotten about the hole Maurice had left in my Thinning, but that didn't stop the crashing wave of Wild Magick. The tear gave way like tissue paper, and when it did the resulting surge of Magick threw Evil Gene and I to the ground.

Yeah, it's just a small hole—not anymore.

Wild Magick roared over us like badly planned fireworks, singeing my eyes and forcing me to look away. My Darkling wasn't doing much better—Evil Gene had covered his own eyes and was searching the ground for something.

He's lost it!

I scrambled to my knees and forced my eyes open against the swirling lights—I had to find the photos before he did. The paper wheel with its burnt edges blew past me in the wind. I reached for it, but found my hands being pulled back by something else, something that wasn't my evil half.

Ashen-white fingers gripped mine, coated in the burning flakes of fiery embers. Those fingers lead to hands and arms that looked like spent logs from a long-forgotten campfire.

New Dead.

Fire and ash poured through the hole in the Thinning and brought with it scores of New Dead. The burning fingers of the damned pulled me away from the picture disc and I could only watch as the wind blew reconciliation from my reach and directly into the waiting arms of Evil Gene.

Thanks to me, we'd just opened a hole in the Thinning and filled this salt-locked space with the fiery evil of Hell itself.

Isn't that just special.

44

EVERYTHING BURNS

"*L*ittle Ed." I pushed back against the clawing hands of angry New Dead. "He's got the wheel."

The wooden man stepped into the massive salt circle, his machete in hand. "What do I do?"

"Get it back!"

The Alligator Men might have all but cleared out, but there were still two Midnight Riders, and they'd never back down again—the tar would see to that.

I swung my fist and connected with the sunken coal-black eyes of a New Dead, only to find the body immediately replaced by another. There were too many of them. The hole in the Thinning must have been roughly the size of the Dad Wagon by now, and the fiery damned poured through it like lemmings.

Evil Gene held up the photo wheel to the bright light of the Magickal tear and turned the pictures until he found what he wanted. "Bring him to me," he snapped, and the New Dead surrounding me obliged. Burning hands and scorched fingers pulled me to my feet and dragged me toward the Darkling.

"It's over, Gene. I'll give it to you, you sure made quite a show of it, but it's still over. Now, I'm going to do you a favor.

The first thing I'll do after this is finished is end the House, and after that I'll be paying a visit to Porter."

Little Ed charged at my Darkling, machete in hand, only to be blocked by Donnie and his tar-coated father. The Riders' blades glistened in the light of the Thinning's hole. "I don't want to hurt you, Dad."

"You can't." Evil Gene grabbed my shirt and pulling me in. "He isn't your old man anymore."

New Dead and the Riders circled the wooden boy. Inky eyes and clawing hands reached for the junior Demon Hunter. Little Ed kept his machete out in front and swung it wildly to keep the monsters at bay, but he wasn't going to last long.

Magick swelled in my Darkling, the Deep Magick of the House, and he held up the photo wheel. "It's time to go home."

"Now, Sergeant!"

My Darkling tilted his head. "Huh?"

Bam! Bam! Bam!

Translucent rounds erupted from the cemetery, their brilliant white light leaving stunning arcs in the evening air. Ghost soldiers in perfect formation fired with deadly accuracy, mowing down New Dead by the dozens.

A spectral shot tore the paper wheel from Evil Gene's fingers. "Argh!"

I had my opening and threw an elbow into the Darkling's gut. That quick jab sent the air rocketing out of his lungs and gave me the escape route I needed. The photo wheel flipped end over end and I chased after it—only to hesitate when I found Little Ed locked in a losing battle with the Riders.

"Fire!"

Another volley of spectral bullets sliced through the ashen damned, getting their attention and drawing the horde toward the cemetery gates.

"Don't stop shooting!" I shouted, scooping up Private Petty's blade.

More New Dead streamed through the hole in the Thinning. They crashed over the pavement and tore a path toward the cemetery.

Bam! Bam! Bam!

Ghostly bullets by the hundreds ripped through their bodies, but the damned were too many—they outnumbered the right-eous ten to one, and they knew it.

Come on, Kaylee!

My Darkling lunged for the paper wheel, but a perfectly timed slash with Private Petty's saber forced him to pull back his hand lest he lose it.

"Fine, if this is how you want it." A brilliant black sword—a twin to Petty's—appeared in his hand. "Nigh-infinite power and we're going to swing swords around? Whatever, it ends tonight."

"You got that right," I cried, spinning Private Petty's saber around to separate my Darkling's head from its body, but Evil Gene was faster. He parried my strike with practically zero effort and launched a counter assault of his own.

"Gene!" Little Ed shouted. "A little help here."

The Midnight Riders had him surrounded, and it was taking all the wooden boy had to keep from being cut to splinters.

Another slash from my Darkling forced me into full-on defensive mode, his strikes coming faster than I could defend. "I'm a little busy right now."

"I was afraid you'd say that—" Little Ed said, his words cut off by the ringing of steel on steel.

Honk! Honk! Honk!

Bright headlights cut across the dark pavement like a beacon —the Grayson Cadillac had arrived, and not a moment too soon. My pudgy apprentice kicked the driver door open and broke into what had to be the most labored run I'd seen in years.

"Adam!"

"I'm coming," he shouted, his backpack bouncing comically behind him.

My Darkling turned his blade and pinned my saber to the ground before pointing a hand at my apprentice. Magick surged in the evil thing's fingers.

"Hell no." I swung for the Darkling's head. "Adam, get down,"

My apprentice jumped the salt line, then took a glancing blow of concentrated Magick to the shoulder. The inky blackness tore through his hoodie like acid, chewing at the soft cotton and peeling off the skin underneath in wet globs. My apprentice screamed, as did his mother, who still stood at the passenger door well outside the salt line.

Adam hit the pavement hard. His impact sent the backpack's contents skittering across the blacktop. The Five Star Toaster toppled end over end and landed next to Little Ed.

"Eddie, don't do it!"

My Darkling was back on the offensive and it was all I could do to keep the black blade from separating my saber from my arm. Locked in his own battle, Little Ed parried another pair of slashes, but in doing had accumulated tar on his arms, along with dozens of cuts. The wooden boy might not have been bleeding blood, but the sawdust that dropped from his wounds told me all I needed to know. "Eddie!"

"Tar burns, right?" the junior Demon Hunter asked.

"Don't—"

Little Ed wedged his toe into the toaster slot and kicked it into the air.

"Eddie, you can't survive the Five Star Toaster."

"Good. I won't want to live with myself after I do this."

The Demon Hunter tossed his machete aside and clutched the evil machine to his chest. "Tell my mom I love her."

"Don't do it," I cried, frustration boiling in my blood. "Your mom is coming. The cavalry is coming, damn it. You don't need to—"

Little Ed pulled the handles down.

Click.

No!

Flames erupted from the Five Star Toaster like a malfunctioning firework display. Bright red and hungry, they consumed everything in their path. The white-hot bonfire raced up Little Ed's arms, and he screamed, throwing the hot box to the ground, but once the Toaster's arms had been triggered, there was no stopping it. The inferno blazed across the pavement and set fire to the Eternal Shame.

I shielded my eyes, but that did nothing to stop the wooden boy's cries.

"Eddie!"

Fire covered his face, licking at his eyes and cracking his features like dry kindling.

In the confusion, Evil Gene's slashing blade came at me fast —almost too fast—but somehow my saber was ready. It parried the strike and slashed back with a fury of its own. Little Ed burned but still the Darkling didn't relent, and neither did Petty's blade.

"I got this," said a familiar voice deep inside my head, a voice that seemed to resonate from the blade itself.

Private?

"Yeah."

But how did you—

The saber pulled my arm down, parrying a cunning attack and responding with one of its own.

"It's really hard to talk and do this. Go, save him before it's too late."

How—

I didn't get a chance to finish my thought before the ghostly private stepped out of my body. That little bastard had been hiding in the back seat all along. No wonder my saber work had been so damn impressive.

"Go!" he shouted, taking the fight to the Darkling.

Evil Gene's surprise was palpable, but short-lived. Private Michael Petty pressed the advantage, while just beyond us the inferno roared. By now the Magickal flames had consumed the space occupied by Little Ed and the Midnight Riders and was expanding further. Solid pavement buckled like magma in the overwhelming power of the Five Star Toaster.

I held a hand to my eyes to block the heat. "Eddie!"

I found the young Demon Hunter burned like spent firewood deep in the white-hot center. His body was blackened and charred, and his arms barely moved in the shimmering waves of heat.

"I can't get to you!"

He tried to wave me off, but his broken movements only drove me on.

No, damn it. Think, Gene...

I dug into my pocket, fumbling around with the drawstring top of a small pouch.

This is madness.

The flames rose higher, and I dug out a small white circle. I had no idea where this Lost Button would end up, but anywhere was better than ground zero with the Five Star Toaster.

"Catch!"

The button tumbled end over end in the burning night air, a spinning drop of hope in the darkness. The wooden boy's burning hand closed around it, and for a brief moment I thought I saw a smile.

"Eddie!" Kaylee screamed, appearing at the tree line with a host of Bridge Trolls just long enough to watch her only son vanish in the hazy smoke.

45

IN YOUR EYES

*B**am! Bam! Bam!*
Ghostly bullets ripped past and pulled me from my mental haze. The fight was on and in full gear. New Dead continued to pour out of the hole in the Thinning at an unstoppable rate, and while they dropped by the dozens against the hailstorm of bullets from a well-positioned firing squad at the cemetery gates, for every one that went down two more took its place.

"Eddie!" Kaylee screamed. Her voice sounded raw and aching, and it cut me to the core.

The Five Star Toaster's blaze expanded outward in all directions, turning the pavement and painted highway lines into a technicolor slurry. The Midnight Riders writhed within the column of flame—nothing, supernatural or otherwise, could survive the Toaster forever.

"Ed and Donnie are in there!" I shouted, getting the Swamp Witch's attention. "We've got to get them out before they burn to death.

Kaylee's shape rippled beyond the waves of heat.

"Adam." Angela climbed out of the Cadillac and made a run

for her fallen son. The Swamp Witch's bowl bounced in her arms. "I'm coming, sweetheart."

"Stop! Don't break the—" I shouted, but it was too late. The senior Mrs. Grayson ignored me and ran straight through the salt line, snapping it, and taking away just about any chance we had of keeping the situation contained.

The binding popped with an audible crack and the New Dead sensed it. Like a pack of hungry wolves, they changed tactics. No longer interested in the cemetery, the fiery damned streamed for the exit.

I found the Swamp Witch barely visible through the flames and heat. "Kaylee, do something."

"But Ed and Donnie…"

"They'll be better off as Riders if we fill the world with New Dead."

The Swamp Witch said something to Stinkstone and the other Bridge Trolls, but I was too far away to hear it, and the Toaster's expanding inferno was getting too close to the paper wheel for comfort.

"I've got the bowl." Angela set the Prussian Wedding bowl next to her son. "Oh my God, are you okay?"

My apprentice tugged at his hoodie, pulling the melted fabric away from an oozing wound.

"Stop, honey." She tried to pour the contents of the bowl on his shoulder.

Adam shook his head and pushed the bowl away. "I'll make it, Mom. They won't." He pointed to the Midnight Riders caught in the inferno.

Mrs. Grayson was clearly confused. "What do we do?"

"There's nothing you can do."

Evil Gene!

I spun around to find Private Petty pinned to the ground like a mounted butterfly. "I'm sorry, sir." The young soldier's ghost pulled at the black sword driven through his chest, but it didn't budge.

The Darkling admired the Five Star flames. "Ah well, they've served their usefulness. Besides, they get that damn tar on everything." Evil Gene got the paper wheel and was on me in an instant. I didn't have time to react before we were face to face again. "Now, let's get this over with."

With my back to the inferno, all I could see were its fires reflected in my Darkling's eyes. Slowly those fires shifted, and what had been the tips of flame became me—me at my worst. Moments I wasn't proud of rolled by in excruciating detail. I reached for the disc, but my hands were too tired, I couldn't unmake it.

More images flowed past, too many to count, and each one was a reflection of a lifetime of disappointment.

"Gene!"

Someone called my name, but I couldn't hear their words; they were lost in the eyes of my darker half.

A deep and rolling timbre washed over us. It wasn't the roaring flames, or the cries of the New Dead. This was different. This was singing.

The Bridge Trolls were singing.

The Thinning and its hole shifted and twisted in their haunting melody. I didn't know the words, but I could feel the Magick. They were opening a Hellgate. They were going to send the New Dead packing.

What does it matter? I'm done. I don't deserve to live.

"Dad…"

Cathy's voice washed over me like a cool breeze. Even in the bullets and screams of the New Dead I knew that voice.

Her beautiful face appeared in his flaming eyes. "Dad, don't do this."

"Do what? It's over, Cathy. I've failed. I'm a terrible father."

"No, you aren't." Her sly smile billowed wind into my sails.

"You just aren't seeing yourself how I see you. Let me show you who you *really* are."

The flames shifted, and I found myself in the photo wheel's final still frame, a young Cathy's bike at my feet. "You did great," I said, my words somehow distant. "You'll get it."

A young Cathy unhooked her helmet and angrily tossed it on the sidewalk. "No I won't. I'm terrible."

"Hardly. You just fell down. Everyone falls down, Catherine. Everyone."

My daughter crossed her adorable little arms.

"It's true," I said, as if hearing myself for the first time. "We all fall down, but the real trick, is getting back up." I picked up the bike and pointed to her helmet. "Now, how about we try again?"

Cathy vanished and the image changed. The Brighton Hellgate exploded across my mind in withering detail, my daughter clinging to the fiery edge. Once again, my words echoed back to me. "I will find you!"

Cathy!

The Hellgate vanished, and the vision of my only daughter returned, filling me with hope. "The real trick, Dad, is getting back up. Everybody falls down—even you."

"But…"

Catherine shook her head. "Even you. Now, how about we try again?"

"I will."

With a twist of flame my daughter vanished, but she'd given me what I needed, and it was more than any Darkling could withstand.

Magick may be belief, but in this moment it doesn't hold a damn candle to hope.

I could sense the shift in the Darkling's power. The reconciliation was a battle of wills, and he'd just lost his upper hand.

"What are you doing, Gene?"

Magick, vibrant and glorious, rolled through me. It was a Magick born of something far deeper, something I didn't understand. Images popped into life on the photo wheel, pictures of my life, a life worth living, a life worth getting back to.

"Going home," I said, pushing back against the Darkling.

I flooded his fractured mind with visions of that life. The love and joy I'd known and would know again. In that moment, I understood Delia. The Blood Queen had had nothing to remember, no hope, and because of that she'd surrendered to her Darkling.

I was not Delia, and never would be, no matter what the House did.

"Stop, Gene. You need me," Evil Gene said, his face slowly fading. "Don't you understand? The House fears me. I know things it doesn't want you to know. I know what it's planning. Without me things are going to get a lot worse. I know—"

"You know nothing."

The Magick surged and my Darkling screamed, his body tearing apart in the moment of reconciliation.

My soul was mine again, and damn did it feel good.

The Bridge Troll's song approached its climax, and as it did the tear in the Thinning began to pull the New Dead like a high-powered vacuum.

"They're dying!" Kaylee's cries pulled me away from the gate and back to the roaring inferno. Even covered in the Eternal Shame, Donnie and Ed weren't going to survive much longer inside the flames of the Five Star Toaster, but now there was something I could do about it—Magick crackled between my fingers.

I'm back, baby.

"Give me the bowl," I said, crouching down next to my apprentice

Adam's mother placed the Prussian Wedding Bowl in my

hands. Its Magick hummed in the night air and I knew what I had to do.

"Gene?" Adam squeezed a hand against his shoulder. "Is that... you?"

"Who else? How about you and me go save some peanut vendors?"

My apprentice extended his hand. "Hell yeah."

I pulled the young man to his feet. "You know how this works now?"

"I sure do, but it needs pure water."

"You don't say."

I reached out with my Magick into the cool pre-dawn air. The boiling clouds above me felt my presence and could no longer resist my calls.

"Pluviam!"

The first drops of rain pelted my smiling face and soon the drizzle had become a down-pour, filling the Prussian Wedding Bowl and unlocking the Magick tied up in the enchanted porcelain.

"Are you ready?"

Adam nodded.

"Then let's do it." I stepped into the Five Star inferno with Adam and the bowl.

Flames roared around us, but thanks to my Magick we remained unharmed. I couldn't say the same for Ed or Donnie. The Midnight Riders' tar had all but boiled away, leaving them like spent matches on the melted earth.

I placed the beautiful bowl between the two of them.

"Redemption and forgiveness, right?"

My apprentice nodded. "How did you know?"

"The last gift of the bowl maker—I had a hunch."

Adam tilted his head. "I don't understand."

"After a lifetime of screw-ups you have a new found appreci-ation for redemption... and forgiveness." I lifted Ed Senior's lifeless hand and placed it in the cool water as my apprentice did the same to Donnie.

"On three. Ready?"

Adam nodded. "Yes."

Ding!

The appliance's malevolent arms reached the top and the Five Star Toaster went cold.

"Now, Adam."

Together with my apprentice, we unlocked the Magick of the bowl and with it extinguished the inferno. The bowl's water washed away their inequities, and with them, the last vestiges of tar.

Ed opened his eyes, and I saw my friend again, something I hadn't been sure I would ever do.

"Gene?"

"Yeah, buddy. You gave us all quite a scare."

My old roommate sat up and rubbed his bald head. "I'm... what happened?"

"It's a long—"

I didn't get to finish my answer before the Swamp Witch tackled him back to the ground. "Oh, Ed. He's gone! He's gone!"

"What? Who's gone?" the confused Demon Hunter said.

My eyes drifted to the shinning silver saber, and the broken young spirit pinned beneath it. Behind him, twin headlights appeared in the swirling mist, Private Petty's ride was finally coming.

46

COMPLETE

The New Dead wanted a piece of Private Michael Petty, and ride or not, they weren't going home empty-handed.

"Behind you!" I shouted, but my young friend was too far gone to react—his soul flickered in the dark like a motel TV. The ashen limbs tore him free of the black saber, his spirit barely recognizable. The young soldier had saved my bacon too many times to count over the last few days, and now I was more than happy to return the favor.

"Extinctus!" Magick rolled through me like an ocean wave. Resurgent and powerful, it crashed into the fiery damned, scattering them like dust in the wind. "Petty!"

The young man didn't respond. He only had eyes for one thing: a meticulously detailed ghostly Volkswagen bus that had pulled up next to him.

The remaining New Dead surged. Like sharks they smelled blood, and a ride to the hereafter was more than enough to put them in a frenzy.

"Michael!"

The bus's door opened and brought with it a beautiful white

light. The warm glow surrounded the young man. He was lost in that aura, his flickering fingers reaching for it, and oblivious to the New Dead claws pulling him back.

Damn it, kid. You're going to miss your ride.

A long and slender arm stretched out of that warm glow. The arm traced back to a stunning and ethereal beauty. Long blond hair fell gently on narrow shoulders and framed eyes of the purest blue. There was no sadness in those eyes, no pain, only love: pure, simple, and forgiving.

She reached for him, but the New Dead had other ideas.

Fiery claws and ashen hands pulled the lovers apart. The screaming cries of hungry damned filled my ears. They had their prize.

Not on my watch.

I reached deep into my Magick, past the House's corruptive sheen, and into the core of my being. The words of power came to my lips, but I hesitated. Could I do anything that wouldn't risk Petty in the process?

Bam! Bam! Bam!

A swarm of ghostly rounds erupted from the cemetery. Deadly accurate, they tore through the damned like tissue paper, sending ashes scattering in the swirling air and lost to the Hellgate. Through those spent embers and drifting Hell Fleas I found the young man's saviors. Soldiers, tall and small, old and young alike, saluted him. In that moment, Private Michael Petty had earned his rank, every last ounce of it.

The beautiful young woman stepped out of the bus, her face soft and her eyes full of joy. "Michael..." she said. Her voice was like a summer's day, a soft breath of fresh air in the ash-choked cloud of death.

"Jolie..."

Petty's young wife placed a hand on his cheek, her smile lighting up night. "I've been waiting for you."

"I…" Tears streamed down his ghostly face. "Jolie, I'm… I'm sorry, can you forgive me?"

"Oh, sweetheart," she said, cupping his face in her hands. "There's nothing to forgive."

"But…" His saber drooped, its edge scraping across the broken pavement. "It was my fault."

"Ssh." She smiled and let her hands slide down his arms. "There's someone I want you to meet."

"But I—"

"Daddy!" a young girl's voice cried from the back of the bus. "It's me, Daddy!"

Private Petty fell to his knees as a toddler bounded out and into her father's arms. "How?"

"I love you, Daddy. Are you coming home?"

Private Petty looked at me with tear-filled eyes and I nodded. *You've earned it.*

"Yes," he said, scooping up his dead daughter. "I'm coming home."

The private carried her to the bus and helped the young girl into the back seat, then opened the door for his wife.

She started to join him, then stopped in front of me. "Thank you."

"It's nothing," I said. "Your husband did all the work. I just—"

"Don't sell yourself short, Magician. You gave him purpose, but more than that, you taught him how to find forgiveness."

"I…"

The young spirit winked at me. "I just hope you learn how to find it yourself, Eugene Law."

Before I could respond she climbed into the bus and shut the door.

Private Petty hesitated. "This is the end of the line for me I think, sir."

In the distance, New Dead wailed as the Hellgate pulled

them in by the dozens, burping up a halo of Hell Fleas in the process.

"Damn straight it is, Private. Get on that bus and go. You've got a family—don't lose it. Take it from me, you can never appreciate them enough."

The ghost smiled and placed a spectral hand on my shoulder. "It's been a lot of fun, sir. I don't know if I'd ever have made it here without you."

"Nope, you'd still be moping about in the tall weeds over there."

"True, but I think you'd have joined me no less than three times if I hadn't saved your bacon."

I chuckled. "Damn straight, kid. I know how to pick a winner."

The soldier started to climb into the driver's seat then stopped. He turned back to me and held out the saber.

"Where I'm going, I won't need this anymore."

"Private, I couldn't—"

The young man shook his head, his face serious. "I've seen what lives in your head. You need this more than me."

I accepted the saber, the blood and ash on my fingers marring the brilliant silver.

"I'll try to live up to it."

"Come on, Dad, let's go!" the private's young daughter shouted from the back seat.

Petty smiled and climbed into the bus. "Seatbelts everybody."

He closed the door and rolled down the window. "I don't want to see you anytime soon, you hear me?"

I nodded. "The feeling is mutual, Michael."

Private Petty banged his hand on the side of the van and revved the engine.

"Go on, get out of here. Hit the road." I pointed to the stars.

The spirit smiled, his eyes twinkling in the Hellgate's flickering light. "Roads? Where we're going we don't need *roads!*"

The bus roared to life and drove off into the starry sky, leaving me staring up at infinity far longer than I should have. A shift in the Thinning pulled me away from Private Petty's departure. The song of the Bridge Trolls must have been coming to an end as the Hellgate was shrinking.

Cathy!

Private Petty had just given me an idea.

The Dad Wagon.

I turned around to find Kaylee in tears. "Where did you send him?" She clutched at my shirt, and even with her diminutive stature, pulled me down to stare into red-ringed eyes. "Where?"

"The Lost Button—"

"I want to know where he is."

"I… I don't know."

"We need to get a dog, and I'm betting we'll find one on the other side," my old roommate said, limping up to his ex-wife and pointing at the Hellgate.

"How—"

"Because," he said, placing his worn hands on her shoulder. "I've been there before."

That was enough to shock both of us to our core. "What?"

"You two aren't the only ones with sins to atone for, believe me; the tar reminded me as much."

"What's on the other side? Take me with you," the Swamp Witch demanded, pulling her shoulder away from him.

Ed shook his head. "It's different for everyone. You don't know what you're asking. Being on the other side… it changes you."

The Bridge Trolls song softened and their strong rumble faded.

"Look, if you're coming with me we need to go now."

I opened the Dad Wagon's doors and let Ed and Kaylee pile in.

"Donnie?"

The large man shook his head. "Oh, hell no. I'm going to take some horse aspirin and call it a week."

"That's the smartest thing I've heard today."

I climbed into the driver seat and slammed the door. It was good to be back in my car, even if I was about to drive it into Hell.

Adam ran up to the passenger door. "Gene, wait!"

"Don't try to talk me out of this."

My apprentice shook his head. "I'm not. I'm coming with you."

The Hellgate flickered, swallowing the last of the New Dead, and burping up yet another swarm of Hell Fleas.

"No, this isn't your fight. You've got a mom to take care of. She may have charmed the pants off a Leprechaun, so that's going to be a problem…"

"He's too needy," said a new voice from the backseat. Angela had squeezed in alongside Kaylee and Ed. She had the Prussian Wedding Bowl in her lap. "Besides, this sounds like a lot more fun."

"No, you need to get out of my—"

Adam climbed into the passenger seat. "Good luck telling my mom no."

I put the car back in park. "It's easy. If you don't get out, I'm going to Magick your butt to—"

"Your swirly fire thingie is closing, sweetheart."

"What?!"

My apprentice's mother was right. The Hellgate was a fraction of its prior size.

Cathy!

"So you can either argue with me, or you can drive."

"Adam?"

"Yeah, boss?"

I threw the car into drive. "Do not make me regret this. Hold on, everybody."

The Dad Wagon exploded off the mark, racing past a waving Donnie and the chorus line of Bridge Trolls. I traded a salute with the cemetery's speaker the instant before we hit the swirling Gate.

I'm coming, Cathy. Hell isn't going to know what hit it.

47

SOUTH GEORGIA

"This is Hell?" Adam leaned against the passenger window. "It looks like South Georgia."

Sigh.

"Hell, South Georgia... is there a difference?"

My apprentice ran a finger over the hazy glass. "I guess not. I just expected more... fire and stuff. You know?"

Ed's head popped up between the seats. "I keep telling you guys, it looks different for everyone, but it's still uniformly terrible."

Large oaks streamed by at a rapid pace, but nothing said, 'Here lies eternal torment.' In fact, I had to agree with Adam—it really *did* look like South Georgia, or at best Jacksonville.

Is there really a difference?

"Do you think the gate closed before we made it through?" the Swamp Witch asked, her voice strained from crying.

"No..."

Maybe.

Adam's mom ripped out a loud snore, and I gave my apprentice's mother a hard look in the rear-view mirror. "She can really sleep anywhere, eh?"

"Yeah…"

"Is she normally that loud?"

"This is quiet."

Ed's face re-appeared in between the seats. "Have either of you guys seen another car, or anything?"

"No," we both said in unison.

"Hell, I haven't seen the sun." Adam stared out at the unending gray. "Is there a sun in Hell?"

"Like I said, it's different—"

"For everyone," I said, cutting off my old friend. I'd heard this no less than a dozen times today.

"Look!" Kaylee poked her red-rimmed eyes through the gap in the seats next to her ex-husband. "You see that up there, in the mist? It's a light."

The Swamp Witch was right. There were lights, lots of them in the distant mist. I squinted in the hazy gray half-light. "What do you think they are?"

"Will-o-wisps?" Adam fingered his seat belt nervously.

Ed shook his head. "Doubtful, do you hear any intoxicating melody leading you on to your doom?"

Angela Grayson choose that moment to rip out yet another car-rattling snore.

This time I turned my attention to my apprentice. "No."

"What about a boatman? Perhaps the River Styx is coming up?" Kaylee said, some sadness ebbing from her voice.

It was possible. We'd know in a minute—the lights were coming up fast.

"Hey, that's a sign." Adam pointed out a bright green sign in the rapidly approaching mist.

I flipped the wipers on. "What does it say?"

My apprentice pushed his face up against the glass. "Rest stop."

"Rest stop?" Ed leaned forward to get a better look at the letters.

Adam hadn't been kidding, the bright white letters reflected in the Dad Wagon's headlights perfectly.

REST STOP. NEXT STOP UNKNOWN.

There was something else scribbled underneath those bright letters and it shot past almost too fast to see, but my apprentice was good enough to read it to me as we rocketed by.

"It says… Abandon Hope All Ye Who Enter Here."

Ah, Hell.

MARTIN SHANNON'S WEIRD FLORIDA

Short Stories

0 - Danderous Delivery (Newsletter Subscribers Only)

1 - Hook, Line, and Slinker

2 - Ballroom and Chain

3 - Bahama Blues

4 - Plasma Pistols

5 - Lights Out

6 - Mourning Paper

7 - Ignorance and Unleaded

8 - Black Valentine

9 - Soulless

10 - Ten Turns (Coming Soon)

Novels

1 - Dead Set

2 - Gathering Gloom

3 - Beaten Path

4 - Bloody Deed

5 - No Fury (Coming Soon)

BLOODY DEED

NOW AVAILABLE

Married life wasn't supposed to be this way, but haywire Magick, crushing debt, and a chronic lack of employment has a way of leaving even the best of relationships in the tall grass.

For Eugene Law, guilt packs a heavy bag. Haunted by ghosts of doubt, Tampa's newest Magician must reconcile his past if he is to have any hope of seeing his future intact.

Bad luck and poor decisions land Gene up to his neck in blood-thirsty Skeeters, eye-to-eye with the Five Star Toaster, and at the wrong end of more than one Lost Button. Through it all, he'll be forced to learn membership in The Flock has its privileges, but it always comes at a price.

Because with Magick, sometimes you have to be the hero, or die trying... Get it now.

AFTERWORD

Beaten Path takes place down the spine of the state, an interesting backwater of hidden places and mysterious locales.

A long and lazy drive down US 301 with my trusty golden provided ample imagery, most of which made its way into this latest installment in some form or another.

The Green Swamp a unique part of Florida and one that certainly shouldn't be missed, but don't take it from me, come down and see for yourself—just stay on the Beaten Path.

Martin
Under the Cypress
March 2020

ACKNOWLEDGMENTS

This book and all of its Magick could not have happened without the help of the following people:

Amber Townsend, my alpha reader—thank you for being you, and for your love of all things Weird Florida.

Jacob Faust, my beta reader—thank you for pulling me out of those dark places.

The Flock—thank all of you for keeping me sane, and believing in the story.

Last but not least, thank you, reader. To know you've made it this far warms my heart more than you can imagine.

ABOUT THE AUTHOR

Martin Shannon's been using his imagination to avoid weeding since he was in short pants. His first series, *Tales of Weird Florida*, is an homage to the Sunshine State he knows and loves, and spent countless hours riding his bike through as a kid. It's got mystery, mayhem, and more than a little Magick. He hopes you enjoy the supernatural side of the upside down state, but if not, he's got a banjo, and he knows how to use it. You can find out more at www.martin-shannon.com.

ON NEWSLETTERS, WRITING, AND REVIEWS

Thank you for making it this far. It is my sincere hope you enjoyed the story, and the opportunity to slip into the sometimes too tight shoes of Eugene Law and company. If you did, please take a few seconds to help me spread the word, and in exchange I promise to send out free short stories as well as keep you up to date with each new novel in the Tales of Weird Florida world.

Writers live on reviews, newsletter sign-ups, and tiny scraps of praise. The writing life can get rather lonely, as evidenced by my social-media presence. So, drop by, say hello, sign up for the newsletter, and if you feel strongly enough, write a review or tell your friends. Remember, every time you write a review, an angel gets its wings.